Playing In Shadow

What Reviewers Say About Lesley Davis's Work

"*Playing Passion's Game* is a delightful read with lots of twists, turns, and good laughs. Davis has provided a varied and interesting supportive cast. Those who enjoy computer games will recognize some familiar scenes, and those new to the topic get to learn about a whole new world."—*Just About Write*

"*Pale Wings Protecting* is a provocative paranormal mystery; it's an otherworldly thriller couched inside a tale of budding romance. The novel contains an absorbing narrative, full of thrilling revelations, that skillfully leads the reader into the uncanny dimensions of the supernatural."—*Lambda Literary*

"[*Dark Wings Descending*] is an intriguing story that presents a vision of life after death many will find challenging. It also gives the reader some wonderful sex scenes, humor, and a great read!"—Reviewer RLynne

"[*Pale Wings Protecting*] was just a delicious delight with so many levels of intrigue on the case level and the personal level. Plus, the celestial and diabolical beings were incredibly intriguing. …I was riveted from beginning to end and I certainly will look forward to additional books by Lesley Davis. By all means, give this story a total once-over!"—*Rainbow Book Reviews*

Visit us at www.boldstrokesbooks.com

By the Author

Truth Behind The Mask

Playing Passion's Game

Dark Wings Descending

Pale Wings Protecting

Playing In Shadow

Playing In Shadow

by

Lesley Davis

2015

PLAYING IN SHADOW

ISBN 13: 978-1-62639-337-0

This Trade Paperback Original Is Published By
Bold Strokes Books, Inc.
P.O. Box 249
Valley Falls, NY 12185

First Edition: April 2015

Credits
Editor: Cindy Cresap
Production Design: Susan Ramundo
Cover Design By Sheri (graphicartist2020@hotmail.com)

Acknowledgments

Thank you Radclyffe for making Bold Strokes the best publisher for me to unleash my characters from.

Thank you always Cindy Cresap for having the patience of four saints when editing my work. I appreciate everything you do to help bring out the best in my writing. Quite simply, you are awesome! Or bostin', to use the Black Country term that's equally as appreciative of all you do for me!

To Sandy Lowe and all the marvelous folk at Bold Strokes, thanks for all that you do to get these stories out there.

For Sheri, your covers are such fantastic works of art. Thank you for sharing that talent and giving me covers that shine.

To my friends Jane Morrison and Jacky Morrison Hart, Pam Goodwin and Gina Paroline, Annie Ellis and Julia Lowndes. Ladies, your unceasing support of my work and your friendships with me are the blessings I truly treasure every single day.

Toni Whitaker, as promised, now the nursery will be filled!! Thank you for all your kindness and your techie wizardry.

To all my readers who champion each and every one of my characters and write to me about them, you keep me writing so thank you all!

And thank you Cindy Pfannenstiel for always being my most excellent friend xx.

Acknowledgments

Dedication

To those who battle with shadows every day of their lives.

Chapter One

Bryce Donovan watched anxiously as the doctor scribbled something on her chart. Her patience stretched to the breaking point, Bryce finally bit. "*Well*?"

Dr. Hudson laughed at her. She was more than used to Bryce's gruff demeanor when it came to her health. "I've never had a patient so intent on getting back to work as quickly as you. Most of them want me to add another week to their time off." She signed off her notes and looked up at Bryce. "You've had cracked ribs. You need to let them heal."

Bryce bristled. "I'll be careful not to bang them on anything. Believe me, I'm more than aware of my limitations." She sat stiffly, knowing when each and every breath hurt.

"You also sustained a dislocated shoulder. I know that you're a plasterer. Are you going to tell me that you can do that one-handed so as not to cause damage to the shoulder joint?"

The doctor's imperial tone only served to rile Bryce more. Gritting her teeth until her molars hurt, Bryce tried to rein in her exasperation. "I'll be even more careful where that's concerned. The physical therapist said I needed to keep it moving so it didn't seize up on me. We've discussed at length all my limitations."

"I'm sure you did. I have his notes here in front of me. Neither of us expects you to be carrying your mortarboard and slapping plaster on a wall for more than a few hours a day. Not yet. It's too soon." The look she leveled at Bryce brooked no argument.

Bryce cautiously lifted her hand to her face and traced the injury there. "And what about this?" She brushed her fingers over the livid wound that ran from her hairline down to slash through her eyebrow in a jagged scar. The stitches were long gone, but nothing could mask its cruel marking of Bryce's skin.

"It's healing nicely, but the scar won't be fading any time soon. You were lucky it never went lower. You could have lost that eye."

Bryce shuddered at the starkness of Dr. Hudson's words. Every time she had heard the words "you were lucky," she felt a cold and unsettling dread lodge deep in her chest.

"How are your headaches?"

"Manageable enough with the painkillers you prescribed."

"And the nightmares?"

Bryce stiffened at the subtle way Dr. Hudson slipped the question in like it was just another innocent query to tick off her list. They both knew it wasn't. She wouldn't meet the doctor's eyes. "Not as frequent," she lied.

"You don't look like you're getting much rest. Are you even sleeping, Bryce?"

Bryce shrugged, grimacing at the pain that ran through her body at such a simple gesture. She felt nauseous and had to close her eyes against the bright white flashes of light that made her head ache and her stomach roll more. Gasping for breath, teeth clenched against the pain, Bryce managed to answer. "I'm sleeping more than I was after the accident."

"How about I up your dosage of sleeping pills to help you with that?"

"Sure. Whatever," Bryce said. She knew full well that no matter what the dosage, she wouldn't be taking the medication any time soon. All for fear of what their inducing slumber might cause her to dream. She would rather be awake and facing the demons than fighting them off under the influence of drugs. She had spent days in the hospital while they had ascertained that her head injury and the nightmares she'd experienced under medication had left her terrified to sleep.

No more drugs and no closing my eyes to the dark.

"I can't see why you can't go back to work," Dr. Hudson said.

Bryce slipped off the bed and began buttoning up her shirt from her examination.

Dr. Hudson forestalled her with a hand. "But light work only until you get your full strength back. You went through hell, Bryce. You need to recover."

"I will," Bryce told her, tucking her shirt into her jeans and carefully easing into her jacket. "Will you sign me off now so I can go see my boss to make sure I still have a job to return to?"

Dr. Hudson made a tutting noise at her. "I hope your boss appreciates how eager you are to get back to work against *my* recommendation."

"I appreciate the fact that he's kept my job open for me and hasn't replaced me while I've been laid up in here or at home twiddling my thumbs."

The doctor signed off on the recovery forms, then hesitated in handing them over to Bryce. "You'd better not stop seeing your physical therapist."

"I won't. He's helping me, so I'm not going to quit until my shoulder is back to full mobility."

"If your headaches get any worse, you come back and see me immediately, okay?"

Bryce nodded. "I will."

She had no intention of stepping a foot back in the hospital. She'd spent more than enough time there and had hated every minute of being poked, prodded, and sympathized with. A hand on her arm stopped Bryce in her tracks and brought her out of her reverie.

"Bryce, I don't need to tell you that you were incredibly lucky to survive. But you're not one hundred percent yet, and you have to heal mentally as well as physically. You need to be careful not to undo the healing you've already done."

"I'll take it steady," Bryce said, wincing as her ribs pulled and ached. "I don't have much choice in the matter." She accepted the paperwork and tried not to be too obvious in making a hasty exit.

"Feel better," Dr. Hudson said. "And take it easy."

"I just want my life to get back to normal, and these frequent hospital trips aren't helping me do that. It's nothing personal, Dr. Hudson. I've had great treatment here, but I'd rather get back to my life and put this all behind me." Bryce shook the doctor's hand. "Thanks for everything." She ducked her head at the doctor's compassionate stare and slipped out of the room as quickly as her injuries would allow.

She closed the door behind her and paused to find her bearings. A woman rushing down the corridor brushed past Bryce a little too closely and caught her side. Pain lanced through her, and she sagged against the wall for support. Bryce breathed in harshly as she tried to control the pain. Sweat beaded on her forehead, and her rebellious stomach pitched. Bryce spotted a sign for the restroom and made her way toward it as quickly as possible, barely making it inside before she threw up in the sink. Every heave of her stomach pulled at her damaged ribs and made her head pound. Finally, with nothing left in her stomach to throw up, Bryce clung to the sink and willed the shudders to cease. Her legs felt like rubber as she ran water into the sink to clean it and then took a handful to swill out her mouth.

She looked at herself in the mirror. Her eyes were drawn instantly to the scar cutting through her brow. Her hair was missing a patch at the front where the hair had been shaved off to remove the glass and debris that had sliced into her forehead. The rest of her hair wasn't much longer, but the bare patch made her feel exposed. Her eyes looked bloodshot. Bryce was no longer surprised by the pale face she saw, marred by shadows under her eyes. She tried to conjure up a smile, but it didn't look convincing. She looked older than her thirty-one years.

"Still as handsome as ever," she muttered and roughly took a cap out of her pocket and pulled it on. She slanted it to cover the left side of her face. She'd been told the damage there would fade in time to leave a white ragged scar, but Bryce didn't like the looks it generated from well-meaning people. She needed nobody's sympathy.

Her legs finally steady, Bryce left the bathroom to carefully walk out of the hospital without anyone else knocking her down. Once outside, she breathed in the fresh air and squinted up at the sky.

Back to normality, she thought despairingly.

Like I'll ever know normal again.

❖

"Dad, you really didn't have to drive me to the job today. I could have driven myself there." Scarlet Tweedy regarded her father fondly. Victor Tweedy just grinned at her then returned his eyes to the road.

"I was in the neighborhood," he replied.

Scarlet laughed. "No, you weren't. You've just driven miles out of your way to come pick me up."

"I just wanted to see you, to spend some quality time with my daughter before you start working for that slave driver boss of yours." His eyes held a twinkle that just made Scarlet chuckle even more.

"Really? I've heard tell that my boss is a real teddy bear at heart."

"Don't you believe it. State your source."

Scarlet smirked. "Grandma."

Laughing, he shook his head. "You can't believe a word that comes out of that crazy old lady's mouth."

"That old lady gave you a perfect landscaping duo that you have been raving about since you joined forces, so she can't be all that crazy."

He pondered this a moment then nodded. "True, she always says that things happen for a reason, and look what happened. Her neighbor finally gets that wreck of a yard cleared up, and I get my own team of professional landscapers from it. Then you came from Illinois, finally back home to Columbia, and got to move straight in with one of them."

Scarlet settled back in her seat and enjoyed the heat from the sun bathing her through the windshield. "I can't believe my luck on that. Monica is a great roommate, and she hadn't shared with anyone for ages after Juliet moved out. It was fated."

"And you're perfectly suited. You both...*dress* alike."

Scarlet shook her head at her dad's hesitancy. "Dad, I'll never understand how you can find my being gay so easy to live with but you're frightened to use the *Goth* word."

Her father shifted in the driver's seat. "I just don't want you getting hurt because of how you dress. It's bad enough worrying about someone hurting you because you're gay." He let out a big sigh. "I'll never understand why someone would chase you down because you just happen to wear black. I've read about it happening."

"It's a crazy world, Dad." Scarlet looked down at herself and tugged at a loose thread on her T-shirt. "I do, however, dress down for work so you should be able to worry less. I haven't been chased for years. At least"—she shot her father a cheeky grin—"not in the way you worry about!"

He rolled his eyes. "That's my girl." He glanced over at her T-shirt. "What's Epica?"

"One of the bands I listen to."

"Would your mother have liked them, do you think?"

Scarlet hesitated and thought back to the woman she'd known for so few years. She and her father still mourned her loss keenly. "I think she'd have found the lead singer striking. She has Mom's vibrant shade of red hair."

He reached over and stroked her red locks. "You follow your mother for her beauty, my girl."

Scarlet smiled at the compliment. "That's just as well, Dad, because you're starting to go bald, and I really don't need to inherit that trait from you."

His laughter made Scarlet smile. She was so glad she could make her father happy when they both still felt the sorrow at her mother's death. Scarlet had barely been ten years old, the time when a girl needs her mother to walk her through the pitfalls of puberty. Scarlet eyed her father fondly. They hadn't done too badly just the two of them. She decided to lighten the mood.

"So, have you got all my paint ready? Picked up the rollers and brushes I asked for? Got me my own stepladder so I can reach the ceilings just right?"

"I got everything like you requested. I know all too well how an artist likes her own tools."

"I'm a painter and decorator. The only artistry I perform there is to wipe up the spills off the ceiling molding."

"And yet your grandma was adamant you'd turn your talents to watercolors and not drip dry gloss and emulsions. Maybe she's not so crazy after all. She keeps telling me she wants to invest in your oil paintings. She's certain that's where your future lies."

Scarlet remembered telling her grandma what she wanted to be when she grew up. The arguments of "but you're a girl" had fallen on deaf ears. Her dedication to decorating had soon brought her grandma around to see her commitment and drive. Scarlet's need to please her father had been a major deciding factor in her choice. As she'd grown up she'd developed her own skills and dreams that took her away from her father's side. The fact that Scarlet had found a talent for using her painting to do portraits seemed to appease her grandma's sensibilities. "If painting and decorating was a good enough start for my father, then it's a good enough profession for me to fall back on," Scarlet told him as she scrutinized the houses she was going to be working on as her father pulled into the large driveway.

"It's what I get for taking you with me on jobs when you were a child." He stopped the car. "I swear you had a paintbrush in your hand before you'd finished learning how to spell your name."

"I learned at the knees of the master." Scarlet unfastened her seat belt and leaned over to kiss her father on his cheek.

"God, it seems like only yesterday you were that small and look at you now. Twenty-eight years old. Where did all those years go?" He cupped her cheek in his hand. "You make me so very proud."

"I love you too, Dad. Now, I need to get started before the boss catches me outside chatting."

"He'd be lenient on you. It's your first day after all."

"Maybe I can catch him later, ask him about the possibilities of a raise." She flashed her father a smile. She got a wagging finger back.

"Your first day on the job and already you're pushing your luck. Go paint. I'll come by later and bring you some lunch."

"Daaaad!" Scarlet whined.

"What? I didn't say I'd be paying for it, did I? You can treat your old man. He'll appreciate it after you being away from home for so long."

"I had to be sure I could make my own way in the world before I could come back home." Scarlet caught sight of her father's work crew as they all filtered in. "Gregor is still here, I see. He's as old as you are. Hasn't he retired yet?"

He made a rude noise in her direction. "He's the best plumber in the business. And he's known you since you were a child so you won't get away with anything with him either."

Scarlet got out of the car, waiting for her father to do the same. "When do I get to see your landscaping start? Monica said she wouldn't see me today."

"Should be tomorrow. I'm getting the skips removed so they'll have no trouble getting in and out in the yard. Bryce might be back soon too, all being well."

Scarlet caught the hopeful tone in her father's voice. "Is she well enough to come back to work? You said the crash she was in was a bad one."

"It was a miracle she got out alive." He ran a hand through his thinning gray hair and grimaced at her. "That first time I saw her in the hospital, I thought she'd never recover. But she's a fighter and her survival was no mistake. She's at the hospital this morning for her last checkup to get the all clear. Said she'd pop in later to see me so we can start her back on the job as soon as she's able."

"What's she like, Dad?" Scarlet was curious about the only woman who worked for her father's business.

"She's hard working, excellent at what she does, a true craftsman." He winked at her. "Or crafts-*woman* if you prefer."

"Dad, I don't mean work-wise. I meant *her*. I'm well aware how good her work is since you've been praising her skills since day one. And you haven't stopped grumbling about the work the temporary plasterer has been doing while she's been off."

"You know I'm no good at describing folk. You'll just have to form an opinion of her yourself when you see her."

Scarlet saw Gregor spot her and start heading in her direction with astonishing speed for such a big man. "I think my welcoming committee is here." She just managed to squeak out her comment as she was gathered up in a big hug and swung around like she weighed nothing. "Gregor! I'm not a little girl anymore. You can't swing me around like this and not put your back out!"

"Little Scarlet Tweedy. Your dad said you were finally taking your rightful place in his business. It's so good to have you home." Gregor Reeves finally put her down and looked her up and down. "You look gorgeous, lass. Just like your mother. God rest her soul."

"Thank you, Gregor." Scarlet brushed a kiss over his bristly cheek. "It's good to be home. I missed you all."

"You done working for everyone else now? Are you going to settle down and start learning your father's business?" Gregor asked, familiarity allowing him his brusqueness.

"I just might be staying a while to help out," she said. "However, I'm still doing my photography apprenticeship on the weekends. I enjoy taking photos too much to ditch that job. And thankfully, the studio I work with had a part-time opening for me that fits around me being here."

"Well, I'm glad you're back from Chicago finally. You need to plant those roots of yours, girl. This business is a Tweedy business. Your dad needs to know it can be passed down to his lass."

Scarlet tried not to roll her eyes at the all too familiar comments she had heard time and time again. She was well aware that the Tweedy business was going to be all hers one day. Her father had grudgingly made sure though that Scarlet had the opportunities to try her hand at anything else she wanted to explore. From that loosening of the reins, she'd found a surprising aptitude in portrait photography. When her father had lost a painter, the position opened up for Scarlet to come back into the fold. She'd been glad of the chance to take a place in her father's trade. Her job in Chicago had been long and happy, but the studio there had to close, and Scarlet had been left jobless. In her father's business, she was happily starting at the bottom. She knew she was going to be expected to learn all she could in preparation for when she took over the whole business.

Scarlet prayed that was a long time coming. Her photography had to be curtailed, but Scarlet was determined to keep it as something more than just a hobby. She knew she'd need a creative outlet aside from painting house interiors. And truth be told, she didn't have a head for the business her father expected of her. She just hoped he would take that confession well when she had to deliver it.

Lecture over, Gregor cocked his head at her. "You've grown into a real beauty. Got yourself a fellow yet?" He brushed back his wild mane of hair as if readying himself for consideration.

Scarlet laughed at him, knowing full well he knew she was a lesbian. "Gregor, should I ever switch teams, you'll be the first man on my list for an eligible suitor." The grin he gave her warmed her heart, and Scarlet gave him a swift hug. "I need to go find where all my gear has been stored so I can get started. I'll see both of you later, no doubt." She walked away, leaving the men to talk business.

Chapter Two

Scarlet looked over the large row of houses and their surrounding yards with a critical eye. "Someone sure let these places go," she muttered, taking in the decayed brickwork along the side of the buildings and the wild yards that needed serious work to get them back to some semblance of order. She knew Monica Hughes and Juliet Sullivan would have no problem restoring them to their full potential.

Living with Monica in her apartment had opened Scarlet up to the world of landscaping, and she'd been fascinated by what Monica could conjure up after garnering a few measurements and drawing out a plan. As for Juliet, Scarlet had adored the talented businesswoman on sight. Monica's dark hair and Gothic style of dress was what Scarlet favored, but Juliet was a true ray of light. Her long blond hair framed a pretty face, and Juliet was such a lovely woman at heart that Scarlet couldn't help but be drawn to her.

Juliet's partner, Trent Williams, had lived next door to Scarlet's grandmother for many years. Scarlet had been fascinated from afar with Trent's handsome good looks as she'd grown up. She'd always known that women would be a source of delight for her, but her heart was always searching for a different kind of woman, someone like Trent. Strong, handsome, yet gentle to the core. She'd watched Trent with Juliet and envied their closeness.

Their love for each other was a force that was almost tangible. Scarlet wanted that. She wanted a true love with someone who would let her be strong yet hold her close so she didn't always have to be.

"All the best girls are taken." Scarlet sighed as she put her musing aside. She entered the house and jogged up the stairs to the back bedroom where she was set to start work. She whipped out a bandana from her back pocket, gathered up her hair, and tied it back. At her feet were the cans of paint for that room along with her tool bag. She gathered up her equipment and pried open the first can, smiling at the all too familiar smell of fresh paint. First day on the job working for my dad, she thought. *I've come home at last.*

❖

The bus ride was long and tedious for Bryce. Every jolt and shudder of the ride made her grimace at the ache in her ribs. Public transportation was going to be her only way of getting around until she could sit in another car without hyperventilating. Her Dodge Neon sat unused outside her apartment building. Since her accident, she'd been physically unable to get behind the wheel. She'd spent three days going out to her car and only once had gotten as far as sitting in the driver's seat and turning on the engine.

The unmitigated fear that washed over her had left her shaking and scrambling to get out. The enclosed space inside the car, the sound of the engine, all had propelled her out of her seat. She'd been left clutching at her ribs in agony while hanging off the car door fighting for breath. Her sight had diminished to a black fog, and her heart had pounded so loud she was deaf to everything else around her. That included a neighbor who had rushed to her aid and had just stood beside her until Bryce was able to stand again. She hadn't touched her car since.

Public transportation had taken her to every appointment she had to make and now was taking her back to work. She was grateful the new job was handily situated on a bus route. Using the excuse that her ribs hurt too much for her to be cramped in a car seat wouldn't stop people from wanting to offer her a well-meaning lift. Bryce hoped that before long she'd be able to get back behind the wheel of her own car. The psychiatrist she'd seen once after the accident had said that it was all perfectly natural and she'd soon let her fears go as she settled back to a routine. Bryce wondered how long *soon* had to take. She was thankful her tools were already at the site.

She got off the bus at her stop and checked the street for the houses Tweedy Contractors were working on. She recognized Gregor's big white van emblazoned with the Tweedy logo, and some of her anxiety dissipated. The houses were old enough to let her do something other than the standard drywall she usually worked with. The owners wanted to keep some of the original features so Bryce was looking forward to doing some old-school plastering.

If I can just get back to work, everything will go back to normal again. I can lose myself in it and maybe, just maybe, forget everything else.

Bryce could hear music playing from one of the windows upstairs so she followed the sound to see who was in there. She slipped off her cap. All the guys had been to visit her in the hospital so they were used to her scar. They hadn't made a big deal over it. The general consensus had been that the women would flock to her side for the dangerous air she now sported. She had appreciated them not fussing over her. They all just wanted her well so she could return to work.

Bryce could hear the sound of drilling on the lower floor, hammering just beyond that, and the heavy pound of a guitar coming from a bedroom down the hall. She followed the music, intrigued by the sound because usually her work mates listened to a radio station filled with golden oldies. She'd lost count of the times she'd had to listen to their off-key accompaniment to one song or another. She'd honestly missed it, however cringe-worthy it had been. This music was heavy guitars mixed with a choir. *Who the hell is listening to that?*

She poked her head round the door and froze on the spot to stare at the sight before her. High on a scaffold was a woman in worn black jeans that hugged a neat rear end that Bryce couldn't fail to admire. A black T-shirt was riding up to reveal a slender toned stomach as the woman stretched to paint along the ceiling. Leering skulls were dotted about on a loud red bandana that covered up most of her head. Bryce could see tendrils of red hair, a rich red color like the hottest flame. She watched mesmerized as the woman worked.

Bryce never heard the woman speak to her over the sound of the music and her own distraction. She was jarred out of her reverie by the abrupt ceasing of the music.

"I said, can I help you?"

Bryce saw when the woman noticed her scar. She jammed her cap back on, but it was too late to hide what had already been seen.

"You've got to be Bryce, right?" She started down the scaffold toward her and put out a hand. "I'm Scarlet."

"You're the boss's daughter."

Scarlet rolled her eyes. "I am so much more than that. But yes, I'm currently working for my dad, and no, I don't get special treatment because of it."

"I wouldn't think you would. Your dad is extremely fair." She shook the proffered hand, enjoying the long, tapered fingers in her own more work-roughened grasp. She had to look up a little to see Scarlet. She guessed she was at least two inches taller than Bryce's own five foot six. Scarlet had the most fascinating shade of hazel eyes that sparkled at Bryce as she did her own perusing. She was makeup free, and Bryce could make out a faint smattering of freckles across her softy rounded cheeks. She was prettier than anyone Bryce had ever seen before, and her eyes fell to watch Scarlet's smiling mouth as she talked to her.

"Please tell me you've been released from the doctor's care and can come back to work to plaster the walls I need to paint? The guy who did this one did an okay job, but I'm told you are a master."

Bryce ran her fingertips over the bare wall. "Let's hope I can recapture that mastery. My shoulder is still a bit bothersome, but I can't sit around at home any longer."

"Going stir crazy?"

"Kind of," Bryce said. Most of her time spent recuperating had been sitting shell-shocked after coming home from the hospital alone to find her newly moved in girlfriend moved out. The note left on the kitchen table had told Bryce that Gerri just couldn't cope with an invalid and that the scar Bryce now bore was too much for her to take. Gerri had couched the words in pity, but Bryce knew her all too well. Now that Bryce was no longer the handsome young buck that had driven Gerri to all the right places, she was to be tossed aside so that Gerri could find another meal ticket. One with fewer scars. Bryce hadn't been heartbroken to see her go, but her timing could have been better.

She pulled at her cap, feeling the need to hide.

"I need to go find Victor. I can come back to work tomorrow." She looked around the room. "Take your time with this room today, and I'll try to get the rest done for you as quickly as I'm able."

Scarlet rested her hands on her hips and regarded Bryce closely. "Well," she said, drawling the word out purposely, "I'll try not to rush, but I'm telling you, there's nothing more boring than watching paint dry."

Bryce shook her head at Scarlet's humor. "I can see you're going to be a riot."

"I'm here all week. Be sure to come see the show," Scarlet said, bowing theatrically and favoring Bryce with a beautiful smile.

Bryce backed out of the room and went to find her boss. Returning to work might be the welcome distraction she needed after all. She heard the steady beat of the music as it was turned back on. Its rhythm was strangely soothing to Bryce's frayed nerves.

Chapter Three

Juliet Sullivan was puttering around the kitchen preparing the evening meal when she heard the front door opening.

"Hey, babe," she called over her shoulder as she swiftly dried off her hands so she could welcome her partner home.

Trent Williams walked straight into her arms and gave her a long, lingering kiss. She groaned when they finally pulled apart, and she nuzzled her face into Juliet's hair. "God, you smell good. I missed you so much today."

"I missed you too." Trent slipped from her hold and stepped back a little to run her hand over Juliet's belly.

"Hello, baby." Trent squatted and pressed a kiss to Juliet's seven-month-pregnant bump. "Hope you've been good for Mommy today."

"The baby has been fine. I'm the one who kept you up all night."

Trent grinned. "Ah, I remember the days when that had a totally different connotation. It meant us tangling up the sheets to all hours engaged in some hot and sweaty lovemaking."

"Whereas now it refers to me keeping you awake all last night while I suffered the agonies of damned heartburn." Juliet feathered her fingers through Trent's short black hair. "I'm sorry I kept you awake too."

Trent got up off the floor and cuddled Juliet to her as best she could, given the bump between them. "Hey, I said I'd be with you every step of the way with this pregnancy, and I have been. Good or bad."

"Sure, but you got the fun things like the cravings," Juliet teased her, loving the fact that when her pregnancy had started Trent had been the one who had developed a hankering for some very unusual foods. Her yearning for doughnuts had escalated to the more elaborate the better. Juliet had lost count of how many times Trent's best friend, Elton Simons, had told her he'd had to do a doughnut run while they were at work together at Gamerz Paradise. She knew he'd gotten adept at recognizing Trent's sympathetic morning sickness and had hastily gotten goodies for her to combat the nausea. In a show of solidarity, he had joined Trent in every treat and was still complaining about how many extra pounds he had gained.

"Well, frosted doughnuts aside"—Juliet led Trent into their living room and sat her down on the sofa—"you needed to sleep last night, and I didn't let you. If it happens again I'll come down here and just camp out on the sofa."

Trent shook her head. "No, you won't. I don't want you sleeping elsewhere. I can cope with a sleepless night or two. I'm going to need to get used to it once the baby comes anyway." She laid her head back against the sofa's cushions and closed her eyes. "Though it's a good thing I had a busy day at work, otherwise Elton would have found me asleep in the stock room. There's a nice little nap nook between the World of Warcraft and Zumba titles."

Juliet eased herself down on the sofa next to her and gestured for Trent to swivel around and give Juliet her feet. Juliet had just enough room on her lap to accommodate Trent's long legs. Trent was six feet tall, much taller than Juliet, so laying her down was really the best way for Juliet to reach all she desired. She began massaging the soles of Trent's feet through her thin socks. She loved how Trent moaned with the pleasure. Juliet took her time rubbing over every inch. "Are these the socks Kayleigh got you?" The pair in question were black with brightly colored bats on them.

"Yes, they're my Halloween socks."

"Trent, we're nowhere near Halloween yet."

"I know, but they were the first pair I came to this morning and I like them."

"My little sister loves you to pieces." Juliet smiled as she acknowledged that, without Kayleigh's interference, she and Trent might never have met. Trent's rescuing her eleven-year-old sister from a gang of boys and then bringing her home had been just the start of their story. Kayleigh was thirteen now and still idolized Trent. It made Juliet smile to see how Trent treated Kayleigh like the adult she was becoming. She had no doubts Trent would be a wonderful mother to their own child.

"I love her too. She's a good kid, and she has great taste in socks." Trent spoke lazily, her voice soft and low as Juliet worked her magic.

Juliet rubbed at a particular spot on Trent's foot and was amused to see Trent relax even more under her ministrations. She felt terrible about keeping them both up the previous night. Her heartburn had been courtesy of a spicy rice dish they'd had at a restaurant that the baby had obviously wanted at the time but then regretted later. Juliet had rolled about the bed in agony until the pain had finally eased at around four a.m. She hadn't had to go in to work today, but Trent had. Juliet was joining the landscaping crew tomorrow on site of their new project. She'd been able to catch up on her sleep throughout the day by taking naps. The shadows still visible under Trent's eyes showed Juliet that she still needed to rest.

She continued to caress Trent's feet, loving how long they were to match her height.

"So, did you have a good day today despite you having no sleep?"

When there was no reply, Juliet glanced up. Trent was fast asleep. Her hands were resting on her stomach, her mouth was slightly open, and soft breaths were escaping.

"I've got to remember this trick and hope it works as good on our baby." Juliet smiled as she checked the clock. Trent had plenty of time for a nap before their meal would be ready. Juliet relaxed and lost herself in the simple pleasure of looking after her beloved who usually did all the looking after her.

❖

Bryce was mixing up a batch of plaster when she heard the familiar *thump thump thump* coming from the room next door. Scarlet's here, she thought as the familiar music played just loud enough for her to hear. She carefully loaded up her hawk, a flat square surface with a thick handle, with wet plaster and prepared her trowel. The background noise of the music faded as Bryce concentrated on smoothing out a perfect layer of the mixture onto the wall she'd readied. She felt the pain in her shoulder ease as she lessened the weight off the hawk. The ache in her ribs was a constant, but she ignored it as best she could. In swift, practiced strokes, she plastered the top half of the wall in very little time and was soon climbing back down her stepladder to mix up some more plaster.

She was so lost in her work she never heard when the music stopped playing or when someone stepped in the room behind her.

"Hey, Bryce, it's lunchtime. Would you care to join me outside to catch some sun?"

Bryce looked up from where she was squatting on the floor finishing off the last layer. "Are you insinuating I'm too pale, Ms. Tweedy?"

Scarlet made a show of looking her over. "Well, a little color other than the brown shades of plaster wouldn't go amiss in your cheeks."

Bryce wiped at her face with her sleeve. She noticed Scarlet bore a smudge of paint on her wrist. "You appear to be wearing more than you've probably put on the wall yourself." She pointed and watched as Scarlet checked her skin for any more paint she'd missed.

"Oh, I'm used to having my skin resemble a canvas." She waved her lunch bag at Bryce. "Are you ready to eat? I'm starving. I skipped breakfast today, and my stomach feels like I haven't eaten in weeks."

Bryce rose after finishing up one last swipe to the wall. "Sure, let me just put this aside and I'll join you. What's so important about the outside world today? Usually you just eat where you're working." She hadn't seen a lot of Scarlet since they'd started on the house a week ago. Bryce had had her work cut out for her preparing the walls for re-plastering, and Scarlet had been cooling her heels until a room was finished so she could paint it. Today though, she looked excitable. Bryce was curious as to why.

"You can come meet the landscaping crew who work with Dad. They're all here today."

Bryce couldn't quite see the reason for the excitement in that but decided to humor her anyway. She tried not to be too obvious as she turned her back on Scarlet to fish out her cap from her back pocket to put it on. She grabbed up her messenger bag and swung it over her shoulder without thinking. The grimace of pain brought Scarlet over to her in an instant.

"Are you okay?" Scarlet hesitated to touch Bryce, and her hand fell away. For a moment, Bryce wondered what it would have felt like to be touched by her. She hastily rearranged the bag's strap and just nodded briskly. She hoped that the nausea that had just shot through her wouldn't stop her from eating her sandwiches. She needed to keep her strength up to heal.

"I'm okay. I just caught my shoulder in the wrong spot. I must have too much mayo on my sandwich."

Scarlet didn't look all too convinced but she didn't pursue it and just led them out of the house. Bryce dutifully followed until Scarlet pointed her toward a small wall where they could sit and watch the yard being worked on. Bryce had never met the landscapers she knew Victor Tweedy had on his staff. Her job had never coincided with theirs, and Bryce usually kept to herself even in work. Sitting out with Scarlet was a change to her usual routine. Bryce wondered if anyone ever said no to Scarlet Tweedy.

Scarlet dug into her bag and pulled out a large tub full to the brim with salad. Bryce thought her own sandwich of cold cuts and mayo looked decidedly pitiful alongside Scarlet's feast. She took a healthy bite anyway and chewed without really tasting anything while she watched the landscapers doing their thing.

"See the one in black?" Scarlet said around a mouthful of lettuce.

"The one with the demon heads on her shirt?" Bryce was intrigued by the dark haired woman's choice of landscaping attire.

"That's Monica. I share an apartment with her. She makes all her own clothes. She's major talented."

Bryce took a closer look. The woman didn't seem like a typical landscaper. Her long jet-black hair was tied back by a bandana decorated with barbed wire. Looking at her, Bryce had to admit the woman was beautiful, too beautiful to be working in dirt.

"She's Goth, like me," Scarlet continued. "You should see her in her dresses. Oh God, she looks so gorgeous. I can only dream to be half as striking as she is."

Bryce gave Scarlet a look. "You're as pretty as she is, prettier even, especially with your red hair." Realizing what she had inadvertently blurted out, Bryce stuffed her sandwich in her mouth before she said anything else. Scarlet was the boss's daughter after all, and Bryce didn't want to lose her job over admitting she found her very attractive.

Scarlet was grinning at her. "Why thank you, kind sir." She bumped Bryce gently with her shoulder.

Bryce felt the warmth of that touch linger long after Scarlet pulled away. She focused back on the landscapers. "Hey, should she be lifting that?" Bryce had noticed a heavily pregnant woman bending to pick up a pot. She was relieved to see Monica descend on her swiftly and slap her hands away briskly.

"I'm guessing not," Scarlet said. "That's Juliet. Isn't she beautiful?"

Not really one for people watching, Bryce tried not to be overly obvious as she stared at the woman Scarlet had sounded so dreamy over. Juliet was the complete opposite of Monica. She had a mass of blond hair that shone brightly in the sunlight. She currently sported a scowl that soon turned into a smile as she tried to shoo Monica away from her, obviously exasperated at being hovered over. "Yes, she is, and she's very pregnant."

She noticed that both Monica's and Juliet's attentions were suddenly diverted away from their playful bickering. She looked over in that same direction. Two newcomers were walking around the side of the building. The first thing she noted was they were both incredibly tall. The male had a very long beard captured into a single braid like a Viking. He looked like a pirate with his long dark hair and sharp features. The other person Bryce wasn't too sure about at first until she caught sight of a hint of breasts beneath the crisp white shirt she wore. She was tall, austere looking, and very masculine. The man greeted Juliet with a kiss on her cheek and a hand on her belly but then scooped Monica up in his arms for a more enthusiastic welcome. Bryce watched in amazement as it was the tall woman who wrapped herself around Juliet protectively. Even to Bryce's eyes, it was clear they were undeniably a couple. They kissed and then the woman dropped to her knee and seemed to be speaking to Juliet's belly.

"The guy swinging Monica around is her boyfriend Elton. He's the most awesome man on the planet," Scarlet said while eating her lunch.

"And the obvious butch?" Bryce found it sweet how the woman stood back up and tucked Juliet into her side. She kept a proprietary hand resting on Juliet's protruding belly.

Scarlet sighed dramatically. "That hunk of gorgeousness is Trent Williams. I've had the biggest crush on her since I was a teenager." She gave Bryce a goofy grin. "I think it's because of her that I finally figured out I was gay."

Bryce's eyes widened as that piece of information was casually tossed out in the air.

"Your Trent is seriously butch. She looks more masculine than the Captain Jack Sparrow she rolled in with." Bryce had to smile at Elton. He really did resemble the pirate with his long hair and gangly body.

"She's seriously butch and seriously gorgeous with it," Scarlet enthused. "But alas, she's not mine. She's all Juliet's." She let out another sigh. "But they're so happy together. It's wonderful to see."

Bryce eyed the couples surreptitiously. She hadn't had much experience in the serious relationship department so she wasn't sure whether to regard their obvious happiness with amusement or a touch of envy.

"Does this Juliet know you harbored a crush on her woman?"

Scarlet laughed. "Oh, yes. I informed her the first time we were introduced. I shocked the hell out of Trent when she found out. She went incredibly shy. It was so damn cute."

Bryce eyed Trent again and didn't think "cute" was something applied to her very often.

"They are so excited about the baby. I'm scheduled to paint the nursery for them. Trent will probably want a gaming theme, but Juliet might lean a little more to a traditional layout." She rubbed her hands together gleefully. "I'll be interested to see who wins that debate."

"Do they know what they're having yet?"

Scarlet shook her head. "They want it to be a surprise. How cool is that?"

Bryce had never had any inclination toward children one way or another so she just nodded. She'd only just had a girlfriend take the big step to partially move in with her, but all that had changed once the accident had happened. Finding Gerri's stuff cleared out and a Dear Bryce letter left on the kitchen table had been a shock. She rubbed at her forehead. So much for the whole in sickness and in health thing.

"Trent will be a fantastic mother," Scarlet said. "She's such a sweetheart."

Bryce could see Trent smiling at her friends, and it totally changed her appearance. She didn't look half as brooding when she stood with her arms wrapped around Juliet. Bryce wondered what that felt like, to love someone that much to commit to having a child with them. That spoke of forever. Trent was giving Juliet such a look of adoration, and Bryce could see it shining back just as brightly from Juliet's eyes. She felt like she was intruding into their privacy watching them together.

"You've gone very quiet." Scarlet touched Bryce's thigh gently.

"I'm watching your friends. They're quite the bunch."

"Two Goths, two gays, and a baby," Scarlet rattled off with a laugh. "Sounds like the perfect synopsis for a rom-com."

"I take it by the identical clothing that Trent and Elton work at the same place?"

"They work at a gaming store together." Scarlet checked the time on her watch. "It must be their lunch break. The mall isn't very far from here so they obviously came by to say hello."

"I think Trent's checking that Juliet isn't doing too much. She seems…" Bryce saw the way Trent held Juliet. "…very solicitous."

Scarlet chuckled. "Juliet's been calling her Mama Bear because she won't let her do hardly anything. I think it's wonderful she wants to keep Juliet safe."

"It's a good thing she didn't see her trying to lift that pot then."

"You'd better believe it. When everyone was helping me move in with Monica, Juliet went to do something and Trent nearly had a cow. Juliet was banished to the kitchen and was only allowed to refill drinks after that."

"A protective mama bear." Bryce smiled. She liked that Trent was obviously sensitive around her partner. Bryce had hung out with a crowd of butches when she'd first come out. It had been tiring watching them all try to outdo each other in who was the biggest badass. Trent didn't seem to act like they had, for all her masculine looks.

"You'll have to come out with us all one evening," Scarlet said, drawing Bryce's attention away from the laughing group.

"You hang out with those guys?"

"Hell yes, and there's more besides. Trent's work colleagues come too, and we take over Pizza Hut. It makes for an entertaining evening."

"Thanks, but I…" Bryce wasn't sure how to explain she wasn't the social type anymore. She fingered her scar again as she wondered how to explain her reticence. She saw Scarlet's face lose some of its animation at her rebuff, and Bryce felt awful.

"That's okay, I understand. You're only just back after…" Her words trailed off. "When you're more ready to socialize maybe then you can join us. You'd be very welcome."

"Maybe," Bryce said and went back to her lunch, effectively closing the conversation. She only looked up when she noticed that Trent and Elton were getting ready to leave. Monica kissed Elton like they were the only two people in the yard. They pulled apart for breath, and she tugged on his beard, pulling him back for one last lip lock. Bryce was more interested in Trent and Juliet. She could tell Juliet didn't want Trent to go. She had a hand behind Trent's neck and had pulled her down for such a gentle kiss that Bryce felt her own body tighten in response. Trent rested her forehead on Juliet's and said something to her that made Juliet smile sweetly and hug her close. Trent laid a kiss on the top of Juliet's baby bump and ran her hand over Juliet's face in farewell. Juliet wiped at her eyes briskly. Hormones, Bryce figured, but swallowed against the lump of emotion that had risen in her throat. *What's my excuse?* She couldn't help smiling when Juliet's raised voice suddenly rang out loud and clear across the yard.

"Grab a pizza on your way home. I'm craving pineapple again tonight."

Trent's face took on a resigned look as she nodded her acceptance. Bryce could hear Elton teasing her as they left.

"Yo, Mario! You're-a gonna look-a like-a da pizza!"

Trent cuffed at his head while Elton danced out of her reach, chortling. Trent ignored him to wave at Scarlet, favoring her with a smile. Bryce wondered if that toothy grin had made Scarlet's day.

"Bye, Trent. I'll see you later," Scarlet tossed back.

Bryce really wanted to know what later entailed but couldn't bring herself to ask. Scarlet told her anyway.

"I'm taking over some of my nursery sketches I've done for them tonight. I have a feeling, if Trent gets the vote, I'll be painting Epona riding into a Hyrule sunset."

Bryce had no idea what Scarlet was referring to. "*Epona*?"

"Link's horse. You know, from the Legend of Zelda?" Scarlet said, giving Bryce a considering look. "You don't game much, do you?"

"Game, like in a poker game?"

"Game like in console games and a controller in your hands."

"Not so much, no." *Or closer to the truth, never.*

"That won't last long once you meet my friends."

Bryce wondered why Scarlet felt it necessary to include her. She stayed silent. She didn't do groups, not now. Parties and get-togethers only led to trouble, and Bryce had had enough trouble for one year. She concentrated on what was left of her meal and hoped Scarlet wouldn't press any further on them hanging out. Bryce needed to be left alone; it was safer that way.

CHAPTER FOUR

Scarlet had visited Trent and Juliet's home before, but this time she came prepared for a more professional meeting. She waved over the fence at her grandmother who had followed Scarlet out of her home and seemed determined to watch her safely to the house next door.

"You'll come see me before you leave?" her grandmother asked for about the fifth time.

"Yes, Grandma. I've already told you I will." *Ad nauseam.* Scarlet sighed.

"I'm just checking, dear. You know how forgetful I am."

Scarlet shook her head at her blatantly pulling the "old lady" trick. "Grandma, you're as sharp as a tack and you know it." She grinned at the sparkle that lit up her grandma's eyes.

"Go show them how talented you are, my girl." Her grandmother peered over the fence and smiled at Trent who had come to the front door to invite Scarlet inside.

"Hello, Mrs. Tweedy," Trent called, opening the door wider for Scarlet to enter.

"Hello, my dear. How's that wife of yours doing?"

"Getting more beautiful every day," Trent replied with a smile.

Scarlet enjoyed being around Trent and watching how she always treated Juliet with respect. Scarlet wanted that kind of relationship and that kind of love. She'd seen it in her grandparents and how her father had worshipped her mother. She wanted nothing less for herself.

Trent led Scarlet through to the living room. Juliet was sitting on the sofa and beamed when she saw Scarlet.

"Oh, you have no idea how excited we are about what you have to show us," she said.

Scarlet laid her portfolio case on the coffee table and knelt beside it, waiting for Trent to settle in beside Juliet. "I just hope what I've come up with is what you were thinking of."

"I'm sure whatever you've designed will be amazing. We've seen your photographs, Scarlet. You have an amazing eye for detail. You're an artist with a camera in your hands. But that portrait you painted of Monica in her full Gothic regalia was just breathtaking."

"Elton is still refusing to let Monica share it. He says she'll have it when she finally decides to move in with him," Trent said.

"He did commission it, but I know Monica was disappointed to have it leave the apartment when it was done." Scarlet was pleased by the reaction her painting had received. To have people fighting over it was very satisfying. But Elton had paid for it so, even though Monica was her landlady, Scarlet had handed the painting over to its rightful owner. Considering how much time Monica spent at Elton's house, it would only be a matter of time before they both had ownership of it. The subject had been Monica in a floor-length black spider webbed gown. Her long, straight hair fell over her bare shoulders, and her eyes were dramatically made up. The portrait was striking. Even Scarlet had been proud of her own artistry. Usually her portraits were done with her camera, but she'd started branching out.

She looked up at the framed photograph hanging above the fireplace in the living room. She'd managed to capture a private moment between Trent and Juliet at a party Elton had thrown. The scene caught through Scarlet's lens showed Juliet leaning back in Trent's arms while Trent's hands were wrapped protectively around both Juliet and their growing child inside her. Their love was all too clear on their faces, and Scarlet had almost deleted the shot because it looked so intimate. She had decided instead to get the picture blown up and framed for them as a gift. Their reactions had been worth it. The photo had caught a moment in time for them and had captured the couple perfectly.

"I'm hoping what I've designed here will be what you'd choose for such a special room." Scarlet opened her case and slipped out the first design. She heard a soft chuckle from Juliet and a stifled groan from Trent. "Now, I went the traditional route first," she explained as she pointed out the more familiar nursery patterns of teddy bears and building blocks. Then she pulled out another sheet. "Then I went to the other extreme."

This artwork showed a room painted to resemble the landscape of Hyrule, home to Link and his Princess Zelda.

Trent pulled the paper closer to examine it. "Forget the baby's room. That would be perfect in my gaming room."

Juliet leaned in to look. "Sweetheart, you don't have any wall left in there this could go on because of all the games you have lining them." She brushed a finger over the sketch of a heroic young man in his green uniform. "I think this would be more suited to an older child, but, Scarlet, just this sketch alone is amazing."

Scarlet pulled out a few more sheets, each with its own specific design for either a boy or a girl or a more neutral room for a baby of unknown gender.

"The flower border in this one is lovely," Trent said. "And appropriate because of Juliet's job." She ran her hand over Juliet's arm. "It would be nice to have something that meant something to you on the walls."

Juliet leaned into Trent. "You just don't want bunnies and bears lining the walls."

Trent bumped her good-naturedly. "You know I want something unusual for our kid. They're going to be awesome. They don't need something ordinary to look at every day like all the other kids out there do."

Scarlet had left what she considered her best piece until last. She slid the paper in front of Trent and Juliet and waited for their comments. Trent didn't disappoint.

"That's the one!" she said emphatically, looking to Juliet for agreement.

Juliet nodded. "Scarlet, that is so perfect for Trent's child."

The nursery art was a simple plain wall in a pale mint green. In a border that ran around the room was a procession of highly colored Yoshis, the little dinosaurs that inhabited the Super Mario games. They were running, jumping, flying, sleeping, or eating brightly colored apples, each one a different color until the pattern repeated.

"I know from the Yoshi's Island game that there were all these colored Yoshis so you could have almost a rainbow flag symbolized here." She scrutinized her own drawing. The little characters all looked happy and playful. She'd been pleased with how effective a design it was for something so simple.

"Do you think this will suit your baby, Trent?" Juliet held the artwork up for them both to consider.

"I love it and it's perfect for our child. Who wouldn't love Yoshi?"

Juliet laughed as Trent mimicked the voice of the little green dinosaur perfectly. Scarlet was astonished by Trent's surprise talent and joined in the laughter.

Juliet's eyes never left the paper. "It's got to be this one, Scarlet. It's perfect for us."

Scarlet was relieved. She'd been unduly worried they wouldn't like any of her work. "To be honest, that's the one I thought you'd go for."

"Lots of happy little Yoshis." Trent pulled out her phone and began working on a message.

"Who are you texting?" Juliet asked then rolled her eyes. "As if I didn't know."

"I'm telling Elton he's got to order in every color of the plush Yoshi toys we can get in the shop. If they're going to be painted on the walls we're going to need a cuddly version on shelves in there too."

"I can get shelves made up to resemble Mario blocks," Scarlet said and loved the joy that lit up Trent's face. She noticed Trent deferred to Juliet again though.

"What do you think?"

"A Mario theme. I like it. It's a relief quite honestly. Considering how many graphic and violent games you play, I'm all for the happy Yoshis playing instead of soldiers fighting or zombies on the rampage."

"I wouldn't want anything like that in the baby's room. Although…" Trent flashed Juliet a sly look. "Our bedroom could do with a makeover, maybe?" Trent moved quickly to escape Juliet's swift playful slap at her arm.

Scarlet laughed at them. "Can I go measure the room? Then I can work out the dimensions of how big the border should be and how many Yoshis it's going to take to circle the walls."

"Sounds like a Professor Layton puzzle," Trent said as she slipped the artwork off Juliet's lap to look it over again. "Scarlet, I can't thank you enough for this. It's fantastic."

"You're welcome. Now let's get the technical stuff out of the way." She pulled out her tape measure. "Let's get this nursery ready for the arrival of Baby Sullivan-Williams."

Scarlet followed Juliet upstairs. The proposed nursery was bare except for a rocking chair sitting in the middle of the room. Quickly and efficiently, Scarlet worked her way around the room. She judged what she'd need and wrote herself notes as to how she could make the border work.

"Thank you for making this exactly what Trent would have wished for," Juliet said once Scarlet had finished jotting all her measurements down.

"I didn't think she'd be one for a regular nursery setup. But how about you? Is it what you want?"

Juliet nodded enthusiastically. "It's exactly what I want. Games are such a huge part of Trent, and I've been introduced to so many of the worlds she plays in. Having some of the cuter characters from one is just perfect. I like Yoshi. He's one of the good guys."

Scarlet tucked away her stuff in her jeans pockets. "I'll gather up the supplies and then I'll set a date with you to get this room transformed."

"You let us know when you need the money and we'll get it for you."

"Oh no, this is my gift to you both. You won't pay me a dime."

"You can't do this for nothing, not with all the paint you've got to buy and your time."

"I know a man who can get me the paint cheap," Scarlet said with a grin. "What's the point of being in the business if you can't use it to your own advantage? The rest will be a labor of love. You and Trent have been such wonderful friends to me since I've returned home. This room is my gift to you for the little one I can't wait to meet."

Tears trickled down Juliet's face and she brushed them away briskly. "Damn hormones," she complained as she pulled Scarlet in for a hug. "Thank you. That is more than we could have wished for."

"I can't wait to start. It will make a change from my painting neutral colors in the houses Dad has lined up for me." She looked about the room. "I think I might ask Bryce to come point up the walls a little so everything is smooth and clean for me to work on."

"How is Bryce doing? I've seen her coming and going but haven't had a chance to actually speak to her other than to say hello in passing."

"She's…" Scarlet didn't know how to explain what she felt around Bryce. "She's quiet. I can't help wondering if that's her personality or a result of the accident. And she's very self-conscious of her scar. I've only seen it briefly before she covers it up again. "

"It hasn't been long since she was released from the hospital," Juliet said sympathetically. "She went through a lot too from what I understand."

"So Dad says. Something tells me Bryce will never mention it though."

"You think she's the strong and silent type?"

Scarlet hesitated. "More the 'never admit there's something wrong' kind. I see her sometimes and she seems to be hurting, but she brushes it off. I don't want to overstep with her. I don't want to alienate the only other woman on Dad's team."

"It's strange being with you guys on this job. Usually we come in after you've all packed up and left." Juliet sat in the rocking chair and rested her hands on her belly. "It's been nice meeting all the people your dad has working for him." She made a face. "They all seem very concerned when I waddle past them. I think they're just worried I'll go into labor while they're working!"

Scarlet laughed at Juliet's exasperated expression. "I think it's more of a case that they're worried you're going to attempt to lift something that you shouldn't be touching."

"Don't you start," Juliet grumbled. "I've got Monica watching over me like a hawk as it is."

Scarlet decided not to needle Juliet any further on her apparent habit of trying to do too much. "You know Monica is so excited she's going to be an aunt. The second that child enters the world it will be measured from head to toe for exclusive clothing."

"I know Elton is equally as excited. He'd been collecting the Disney Infinity figures so that the baby has its own set to play with on Mama's Xbox when they're old enough. Seemingly, gone are the days of baby showers with diapers and extra bibs as the standard."

"Your baby is going to be so loved."

Trent walked in at that moment. "No argument from me there." She cast a critical eye around the room. "I can't wait to see this all done and painted."

Juliet reached out to clasp Trent's hand. "It will make it more real, won't it?"

"It was real the minute you and I sat waiting for the blue lines to appear on the pregnancy tester."

Juliet chuckled. "I'll never forget Monica's scream when we told her."

Trent smiled at her memory. "Elton outdid her though. He was such a girl when he was informed. My ears are still ringing from his squeals."

Scarlet laughed at the mental image of that particular scenario. "Let me get Bryce on board and we'll get this room started."

"A Yoshi nursery," Trent said as she bounced on her feet with barely restrained excitement. "Thank you, Scarlet."

Scarlet waved away the praise. "Hey, my part of all this is easy. It's Juliet who has the hardest job to do."

Juliet tugged on Trent's hand. "Speaking of hard, Trent, help me get up out of this rocker. I think I'm stuck!"

As Trent solicitously aided Juliet, Scarlet couldn't help but wonder if she'd ever get the chance at family like these two were embarking on. She hoped to, one day. She just needed to find someone to share it all with.

CHAPTER FIVE

Bryce sat alone in her apartment. The TV was on, but whatever show was playing held none of her attention. She was tired, physically and mentally, but was fighting the urge to sleep. She looked at the clock on the wall. It was three o'clock in the morning. She groaned and contemplated reaching for another energy drink, but instead she picked up her beer can and drank what remained in two gulps. She hadn't slept properly since the accident. At first, it was the excruciating pain, then it was the nightmares, and then it was the guilt.

Bryce threw her can in the already full waste paper basket and changed the channel. She was searching for something, anything, to take her mind off the million things running around in it. Endless reruns of police shows flashed on the screen before her. If it wasn't those it was hospital dramas, shows filled with death and dying. She turned to the Food Channel and breathed a sigh of relief. She watched as a man set to making a meal she would never think of eating, but the mindlessness of the subject matter calmed her brain. She dozed intermittently to the sound of his voice droning on about cuts of meat. All the lights were on in her home, there was noise from the TV, and someone talking at her.

Not for the first time she wondered how Scarlet's nursery ideas had gone over. She was curious as to what Scarlet could do. She was curious about Scarlet period. Scarlet's hair was the most amazing red she had ever seen. A vibrant red shot through with flecks of gold.

She recalled her mentioning she was a Goth. She didn't appear to be pierced or tattooed to excess, but Bryce was sometimes a little put off by the clothing she knew some Goths wore. Black was all very well, but Bryce had been too close to death to find its symbolism comforting. She wondered what drew someone as pretty as Scarlet to something Bryce saw as dark and macabre. Her eyes drifted closed on a memory of Scarlet sitting beside her in the sunshine, her eyes bright, and her smile captivating. Bryce knew she shouldn't be drawn to her, but there was something very appealing about Scarlet Tweedy.

Bryce's shoulder cramped, and the violent pain wrenched her out of the light sleep she had fallen into. She scrambled for her painkillers and rammed them in her mouth, chasing them down with a mouthful of yet another energy drink that didn't live up to its promises. All the while she berated herself that no one would ever be interested in her now. Not when she bore the scars of what had happened to her both inside and out.

The pain receded to a dull roar, leaving her nauseous and shaking. Bryce resigned herself to the fact that sleep would have to elude her for yet another night. She found no peace in it anyway, no matter how much she craved it.

❖

Scarlet's camera was never far from her side. She'd taken to bringing one of her less professional rigs with her to work just in case she saw something she wanted to record. Like yesterday, Gregor had taken a break from his own work to go sit and flirt with Juliet. He had been helping her un-pot flowers to be planted in the garden Monica was preparing. He looked like a gruff old grizzly bear sitting beside the more fragile Juliet, but Scarlet had caught them in a moment where Juliet had held up a flower for him to get the scent of. Every time Scarlet looked at it, it made her smile. The look on his face was tender for such a gruff old man. She aimed on putting it in a frame for him as a Christmas present; she knew his wife would love it. She'd considered doing the same for all the guys she worked with. She lowered her camera for a moment and watched Bryce cut across the driveway to get something out of the work van. Now there's someone I can't take enough shots of, Scarlet thought ruefully, but I just can't seem to capture her completely. Scarlet had asked if Bryce would mind helping her do the nursery and Bryce had easily agreed. She had been surprised by how dark the shadows were beneath Bryce's eyes that morning. She had started to ask if Bryce was okay, but she'd been brushed off with a brusque "I'm fine" and the conversation had been abruptly over. Scarlet couldn't help but wonder what was keeping Bryce up at night…or *who*? The flare of jealously that pierced through her chest startled her and left her feeling flustered.

"You look thoughtful, girlfriend," Monica said as she walked past pushing a wheelbarrow.

Scarlet quickly moved out of her way. "Sorry, I was in a world of my own."

"Are you still coming with us tonight?" Monica began unloading her flower trays, shooing Juliet away and instead laying the trays within reach for Juliet to handle without bending down. Scarlet bit her lip to stop her amusement from escaping at the sight of Juliet rolling her eyes at Monica's solicitude.

"Yes, I've brought my change of clothes with me so I can leave straight from here. The guys have gotten the bathroom reasonably habitable in the house we're working in so I'll skip in there to get dressed up."

"It should be a good night," Monica said. "A live band on stage and the club is even laying out a spread."

"It's a good thing there will be food. I'll be starving by the time I leave here tonight."

"You wearing the dress I made you?" Monica pushed the wheelbarrow aside and began helping Juliet sort through the plants. Scarlet nodded.

"Yes, the one with the ornate stitching. It gets its debut tonight."

"You look beautiful in that," Juliet said, having seen Scarlet being fitted for the dress. "And the stitching is the exact same color as your hair. Monica, you outdid yourself with it."

"I had a good form to fit. I mean, look at her..." She waved a hand at Scarlet. "She's drop-dead gorgeous with a body perfect to design for."

Scarlet just grinned. "Well, as much as I'd love to stay here and have you boost my ego, I'd better go back to work."

"Have you taken any more candid shots we should know about?" Monica asked. "Elton loved the one you e-mailed him of me looking all imperious, directing my workers."

Scarlet pretended to hide her camera behind her back. "You looked delightfully bossy. I know for a fact Elton loves that about you."

"You have no idea," she drawled.

Juliet chuckled. "At least you're dressed in your photo. Trent adores the studio picture you did of us though."

Scarlet was immensely proud of the professional photograph she'd done privately for Trent and Juliet. She'd set up the living room in the apartment with a simple white backdrop. Trent and Juliet had disrobed enough so that Juliet's prominent belly had been visible and Trent's naked body had been shielding both Juliet and their unborn child. Scarlet had positioned them so that nothing was really revealed while the nakedness of their pose was still easily apparent. Trent's vibrant rose tattoo incorporating Juliet's name was a blaze of color against their pale skin and the stark white of the background. Scarlet had captured a very sensual picture, Trent's obvious dark strength in contrast to Juliet's pale softness. The look in Trent's eyes alone had revealed just how much she was in love with the woman in her arms. Juliet had gasped when she'd seen the finished photograph and had hugged Trent to her. Trent had been quiet for a long moment.

"Thank you. It's beautiful," she'd said. "It's going in our bedroom though because I don't share Juliet's naked beauty with anyone else." That had earned her another hug from Juliet and then they'd made Scarlet promise she'd be the baby's official photographer once the child made its appearance.

Monica made a play of running her hands down her body. "Do you think I should get naked with Elton and have Scarlet take our picture? It would be awesome in black and white and would really display Elton's marvelous body art."

"And your own," Juliet said. "Scarlet's very professional, and besides, she's seen you naked enough around the apartment that it would be second nature to her."

"The perils of sharing a place with a dressmaker." Scarlet nodded. She'd lost count of the number of times Monica had called for her to help her model something. She never batted an eye when Scarlet undressed before her or vice versa.

Out of the corner of her eye, Scarlet saw Bryce heading back toward the houses.

"She looks tired today," Juliet said, watching after Bryce with concern. "I don't think she's sleeping."

"Has she told you what happened?" Monica asked Scarlet.

Scarlet shook her head. "No, but then we don't exactly hang out together. We pass in the hallways, but when I've popped in to see if she wants to share lunch, she says she's busy and I don't want to push her." Her gaze followed Bryce. "I think she's pushing herself too much, but who am I to call her on it. I can't mention it to my dad. He's her boss, and she'd likely kill me for bringing it to his attention." Scarlet was worried about Bryce more than she wanted to admit.

"I've only heard bits of what happened," Monica said. "I know it was a very bad car crash and that the others in the car with her all died. As did the driver in the truck that hit them. They said he wiped out a load of cars. Poor guy had a stroke at the wheel. The truck ended up plowing down the road taking out other vehicles like a bowling ball striking a row of pins."

"Bryce was the only survivor?" Scarlet couldn't suppress the shudder that ran through her body at the thought of how close Bryce had come to being just another accident statistic.

"I bet her memories of that night are terrifying," Juliet said.

This gave Scarlet cause for pause. She'd wondered what was causing Bryce to look so haunted. The accident was obviously still very raw and present for her. Scarlet wondered how she could even begin to broach the subject with her, to let her know if she needed someone to talk to, Scarlet was there for her. *Why? Why am I prepared to do that with someone who probably would rather forget what they've lived through than remember it?* She resolved to give it a try anyway. She wanted Bryce to lose that weary look and realize she didn't have to go through everything alone anymore.

❖

The party had been in full swing for hours, but Bryce wasn't enjoying herself. She'd felt sick before she'd left work and now she felt decidedly worse. The room was full of people Gerri worked with, but Bryce couldn't see one familiar face to talk to. She dutifully picked at the food on offer, but even a mouthful of whatever it was perched on a dry crisp bread threatened to make Bryce throw up. She had reluctantly settled for soda to drink in the hopes it would ease her rolling guts. There'd been a flu bug going around, and Bryce had the horrible feeling she had caught it. Her head was hurting from the garish lights that were flashing, and she had to squint against the pain making her sight fuzzy.

"Honey, you're making an awful face. Stop it before other people see and wonder why I go out with you." Gerri slipped her arm through Bryce's and staked her claim.

Bryce started to pull away and saw the flare of anger in Gerri's eyes. "I'm sick. I don't want you catching this." *I'd never hear the end of it.*

"Why do you have to be sick tonight? This was supposed to be a special night for us." Gerri's pout was ugly. Bryce hadn't noticed that before.

"It is a special night for *you*. Your team got the account you've been busting a gut for. I can't help how I feel."

"Well, you're ruining the buzz I've got going," Gerri said petulantly.

"I think I might just go home. I don't want to spoil your party." Bryce saw a woman standing off to their side. She was looking over at Bryce and Gerri but pretending to be nonchalant about it. "I'm sure Amber will be more than willing to fill in for me."

Gerri slipped her arm free. "So now you're going to be jealous too?"

Bryce considered that. She couldn't even work up the energy to be jealous where Gerri's eye wandered anymore. She didn't think she cared enough. Gerri had been a willing partner to their no strings attached arrangement. Somehow, however, Bryce had been pressured into letting Gerri move some of her belongings into her apartment. She wasn't even sure she liked Gerri all that much and had been made amply aware that Gerri liked Bryce on her arm mostly because they made a handsome couple. Bryce's fair coloring and strong physique had complemented Gerri's darker, ultra femme looks. Tonight, Bryce had finally reached her limit of being manipulated by Gerri on what was best for them. What was best for them was always couched in what suited Gerri most.

"I'm leaving," Bryce said tiredly. She was barely able to keep her eyes open against the pain in her head.

"Fine. I won't come over tonight if you're going to be like this." Gerri stormed off, straight into the arms of Amber.

Bryce walked unsteadily to the exit of the club where the party was being held. The heat of the evening hit her as she stepped out into the balmy night air. She all but doubled over as sickness ran through her.

"Hey, you okay?" A man Bryce dimly recognized as one of Gerri's co-workers hovered beside her. Eric someone, she remembered that much.

"I'm not feeling too great," Bryce admitted and managed to stand upright. "I'm going to call a cab and split."

"You're Gerri's partner, aren't you? I thought I recognized you."

Is that what I am, Bryce wondered blearily. "I doubt I am after tonight," she said. "I'm being sick on her precious time. That's a huge black mark against me."

Eric chuckled softly. "Yeah, I hear that. She's a ball breaker. No offense, Bryce, but you can find nicer. Hey, don't you live off Anderson Street? We're heading out that way and can give you a lift." The man leaned in to speak more privately. "This party sucks. There's too much ass kissing going on in there for us. We can't climb high enough on the corporate ladder for those guys to even acknowledge us."

Bryce understood. She'd seen Gerri at work; it wasn't a pretty sight. "I know what you mean." She let herself be steered toward a waiting sports car. The others were already climbing inside.

"I call shotgun for Bryce here. We're dropping her off as we escape this hellhole of sycophants."

Bryce mumbled hello and thank you to the two other men and a woman who introduced themselves while they all piled into the backseat. Bryce got in, fastened her seat belt, and let her head fall back against the headrest.

"You look terrible," Eric told her.

"I feel ten times worse, believe me. Guess that flu bug finally found me." She closed her eyes and felt the car pull away from the curb.

"There's a lot of that sickness going around," Christine said from behind Bryce. "It wiped out most of our team last week. Alan here got it and he looked like death warmed up for days. I hope you feel better soon."

Bryce smiled at her words. The kindness from a stranger soothed her when her so-called girlfriend hadn't shown any at all.

"We'll soon have you home and then you can relax without worrying that you're cramping someone's party style," Eric said.

Bryce was already relaxed, the air conditioning was cool against her fevered brow, her eyes were closed against the streetlights' bright glare, and within seconds, she was fast asleep.

It was the unearthly, thunderous noise that first disturbed Bryce's slumber, but it wasn't until a burning bright light pierced her eyelids that she was forced awake. She opened her eyes in time to see a semi-truck loom large in the windshield mere seconds before it hit the car with an almighty crash. The impact blew out the glass from the car windows. Bryce felt something stab into her forehead and blood began to pour down her face. All she could hear was the horrendous sound of metal being crushed and the terrified screams of the others in the car with her. The car spun as the truck showed no sign of stopping in its path. It plowed right through them, forcing them to slam into the partial divide in the middle of the road that finally flipped the car up and over to rest on its roof.

Furiously blinking through the blood blinding her, Bryce tried to get her bearings. She was trapped upside down in the seat, held in place only by her seat belt. Her shoulder hurt, her ribs were screaming, and she couldn't raise a hand to clear her eyes. She could hear the rumble of the truck as it continued down the street, and she wondered how it managed to still drive after such an impact.

Cautiously, she turned her head to see how everyone else was doing. At first she couldn't comprehend what she saw when she sought out Eric who had been in the driver's seat. That side of the car was totally obliterated, a twisted ruin of destroyed metal covered in blood that revealed only part of Eric's remains in what was left of the seat. Bryce lost the contents of her stomach, throwing up until there was nothing left and she was shaking with the dry heaves. She realized Eric was long gone. Moans came from behind her, but Bryce couldn't turn around from her precarious position to see.

"Hey, are you okay? Christine? Alan? Justin? Hang in there. Someone's got to have seen this and called for help. Someone's coming for us, okay? Someone's coming."

Please God, let someone come.

She strained her ears to hear those behind her. Whimpers and painful gasps could be heard, and Bryce kept on talking, reassuring them someone would help them. She was quiet a moment when she heard the sound of sirens in the distance.

"There are sirens coming. We're going to be rescued." She listened but couldn't hear anything but her own labored breathing. "Hey, no sleeping back there. They'll have us out in no time."

Her words were met by silence. She tried again to turn around, but the seat belt kept her pinned and her body protested at the movement. The pain in her shoulder alone made her want to vomit again so she stayed still.

"Guys?" Bryce could hear the siren's wail. "Someone's coming for us." She peered through the ruined shell of the windshield. "Someone's here. Please let someone be here," she whispered, more to comfort herself. She had the terrible feeling she was the only one in the car who was still breathing.

❖

"Hey, Bryce? *Bryce*?"

Bryce opened her eyes. She stared up into the face of an angel. Vibrant red hair was highlighted by the sun behind her, but there was no halo in sight, just hair resembling a living flame. Bryce slowly came back to wakefulness. A dark angel knelt before her. She was dressed all in black. Old-fashioned intricate lace covered her breasts but let the curves show through. Bryce stared at her dumbly then reached out a hand to the angel's face. The skin was warm to her touch and so soft.

"Did I die?" Bryce asked hesitantly.

"Oh no, sweetie, you are very much alive." The angel's voice hitched with emotion.

Bryce finally recognized Scarlet's voice, and she snapped to full alertness. She blinked to clear her grit-filled eyes until she could see Scarlet beneath the elaborate makeup she had on. Her hazel eyes were emphasized with a skillfully applied black liner, and her lips were a deep blood red. Bryce was mesmerized by her. She really was stunning.

"Scarlet?"

Scarlet smiled with relief and puffed out a breath. "It's okay. I just came in to say good-bye and you were asleep. You didn't exactly look comfortable so I figured I should wake you up. It's time to go home, Bryce."

Bryce ran her hands over her face. "Thank you. I just sat down for a minute to write up my want list for tomorrow and I must have crashed."

"It didn't look like a restful nap."

Bryce grimaced at the understatement. "I was having a bad dream," she admitted, surprising herself.

"Do you get those often?"

"Only when I sleep," Bryce replied dryly. She got to her feet unsteadily and Scarlet hurried to help her. Once standing, Bryce could take in the full effect of Scarlet's transformation out of her work clothes. Bryce was struck dumb. She just hoped to God her mouth hadn't fallen open.

Scarlet ran a hand over her long-skirted dress. "I'm going out tonight right after work so I changed here for quickness. Do you like my dress? Monica made it for me."

"You look…spectacular," Bryce said. The word was woefully inadequate to describe how Scarlet looked. The dress was strikingly romantic; the design cinched the material in at the waist, making Scarlet look elegant and otherworldly. "Beautiful." Bryce swallowed hard. "Not that you don't cut a fine figure in your work clothes either," she added to lessen the heightened sexual tension swirling between them.

"Thank you. It's nice to know I scrub up well." Scarlet grasped her skirt to hold the train up a little. "My contribution to the Goth lifestyle is inspired by the Goth/metal bands, the ones that use symphonic rock to sell their songs."

"Like the music you rock your walls with while you paint?"

"Exactly. Monica loves everything Gothic, but I lean heavily toward the musical side."

"So no vampire fetish for you then?"

"Oh, believe me, Goth is so much more than just a love of Dracula and his ilk." Scarlet smiled at her sweetly. "You'll have to come along to one of our music nights. You might be pleasantly surprised by the types of people it calls to."

Bryce didn't make a comment as she hastily began gathering her gear. She couldn't believe she'd fallen asleep on the job.

"Are you going to stay here much longer?" Scarlet asked, watching her closely.

"No, I had intended to be gone by now, but obviously I fell asleep. I can assure you that was the first time it's happened."

"I'm not in here counting your time, Bryce. I came to see that you were okay. I'm not going to tell my dad I found you asleep. Yes, I'm the boss's daughter, but if you're having a problem you're the one who will have to tell him. I certainly won't. You have my word on that."

Bryce just nodded her thanks. "There's no problem, I must have just relaxed too much and dozed off. It won't happen again."

"Are you existing on no sleep at all? Because, honestly? You never look rested. Didn't the hospital give you anything to help you?"

"They did. It doesn't work," she said shortly.

"Maybe you should go back and tell your doctors that."

"Maybe I should just finish clearing up here so I can go home and you can go show off that dress." The conversation was over for Bryce.

Scarlet didn't move. Bryce could tell that beneath that beautiful surface Scarlet was bristling to argue about this with her.

"If you need me..." Scarlet began.

"I know where you are." Bryce gave her a smile. "Now get out of here. Go start your weekend. I'm fine. I'll let the security guys know I'm the last one out."

"Do you want a lift home?"

Bryce shook her head. "No, thank you. I think a bit of fresh air might clear my head." She shooed Scarlet out ahead of her and gathered up her belongings. "Let's go. I'm sure you have someone waiting on you."

"Just my friends."

"Well, I'll see you on Monday and you can tell me all about it." Bryce hoped she was sounding cheerful enough to distract Scarlet's concerned looks.

Scarlet halted before they were even halfway down the stairs. "Try and get some proper rest this weekend, please. Those shadows under your eyes are worrying me."

Bryce nodded distractedly and shouldered her messenger bag. She hoped Scarlet hadn't seen the flash of pain that made her have to hold her breath. She didn't want to give her anything else to worry over. "Have a good weekend yourself."

She headed down the driveway, waving to the guards who were looking after the houses while they were still being worked on. Bryce was thankful for their presence because it meant she could leave her tools behind and not have to have someone else carry them for her. She didn't want the hassle of having to explain why she wouldn't drive the work van or her own vehicle.

She waved as Scarlet drove past her heading out into the early evening traffic. Bryce took a slow walk toward her bus stop. *God help me, but Scarlet looked so breathtakingly beautiful. I wanted to kiss her so bad when she leaned over me, waking me up*. Bryce all but ground her teeth as this new complication struck home. *She's the boss's daughter, she's just caught me sleeping on the job, and I have a face that resembles a fucking zombie because I don't dare to fall asleep anymore. Because every time*

I do, I'm back in that car with everyone dead and dying around me again. She let out a ragged sigh. *Gerri was right. No one in their right mind would want to put up with who I am now.* She hastened across the road to flag down the oncoming bus to take her home. She jammed her cap on over her forehead. She wasn't in the mood for prying eyes and pitying looks tonight.

Chapter Six

The next morning dawned bright and sunny. Juliet awoke slowly, savoring the lassitude she felt, basking in the knowledge she was working from home today and that Trent was working an evening shift. She turned her head on the pillow to seek out Trent. She was surprised to find the other pillow empty. Juliet lifted her head and spotted an added lump under the bed sheet that signified more than just her belly was under the covers. She listened intently to the soft low voice of her beloved who was obviously in mid flow.

"Link shifted into his wolf form, and Midna leapt onto his back. She spurred him on as they raced toward Hyrule's castle to face Ganondorf."

Juliet's eyebrows rose. She carefully lifted up the sheet to reveal Trent curled up beside her. "What are you doing?"

Trent looked up at her, her sleep-tousled hair falling rakishly across her forehead. "I'm telling the baby a story of heroes and villains and the return of a princess to the Twilight Realm."

"You're telling the baby the story from one of your games." Juliet had recognized the names. "What happened to good old-fashioned fairy tales?"

Trent favored her with an incredulous look. "Fairy tales aren't *real*."

"Of course they aren't," Juliet conceded dryly at Trent's utter seriousness. "So how long have you been telling your tale?"

"Not long, but I can save the finale for next time." Trent started to move back up the bed.

Juliet gasped as she felt the baby kick. "I think the baby wants to hear the rest of the story now." Juliet placed Trent's hand over where the baby could be felt moving.

"That's so cool." Trent shifted under the sheet to place a kiss on Juliet's belly. "Hey, baby. How about you calm down with the calisthenics before you make your mommy dizzy? I'll finish the story for you."

Juliet laughed as the restlessness calmed. "I hope to God you can settle the baby down as easily out of the womb as you can in it."

Trent grinned and smoothed her hand over Juliet's taut skin. "You're up too early, Jule. Why don't you just lay back and rest some more and then I'll make you breakfast in a little while."

Juliet stroked Trent's hair gently, brushing it back from her forehead. "You're too good to me."

"You're worth it." She cupped her hand under Juliet's breast and then down over her stomach. "Every beautiful inch of you."

Juliet languished under Trent's soft caresses. "Finish your story before you wake up my libido." Juliet ran her thumb over Trent's lips and shivered when a warm tongue slipped out to taste her. "The baby wants to hear more about the wolf and his Twilight Princess." She was captivated by the joy in Trent's answering smile. "What?"

"You remembered the game." Trent scrambled up the bed and planted a loud, smacking kiss on Juliet's lips. "You are perfection."

Juliet laughed at her silliness. She lowered the sheet and pulled Trent to her side. "Finish the tale for both of us, please. I want the baby to know what happens to Midna. She was my favorite character in that game."

Trent nodded. "Mine too." She snuggled down and laid a hand protectively on Juliet's bump. "Okay, where was I? Oh yes,

Wolf Link headed toward the castle intent on rescuing Zelda and then undoing Midna's curse so she could be free."

Who needs fairy tales? Juliet held Trent in her arms and felt the baby shift lazily inside her, obviously soothed by the voice of its other mother as she spun tales of elven heroes rescuing princesses. *I'm living one.*

❖

Still mortified at being caught literally napping by Scarlet, Bryce endeavored to stay out of her way as best she could all the following week. She was determined not to be found in the same situation again. She'd fallen asleep briefly on the sofa again the night before. Snatches of dreams had plagued her; always, she found herself back in the crash. But this time she'd had a flame haired angel holding out a hand to rescue her, and that had only added to Bryce's anxiety. The fractious dreams had left her with a bone weary fatigue that had propelled her into going to work early because she had no desire to stay at home.

The houses the Tweedy construction crew was working on were silent at that hour, but Bryce recognized the familiar Honda that belonged to Juliet. Curious as to why she was already on site, Bryce wandered around the back of the house she knew they were working on. Juliet was easy to spot. She was dressed in a bright flowing dress that complemented her blond hair and did little to hide her pregnancy. Juliet was sitting on a little wall, jotting something down in a notepad. She looked up as Bryce drew near.

"I see you're an early bird too," Juliet said with a self-deprecating smile.

"Good morning to you. You're here well before the rest of your crew."

"I'm making up time because later today Trent and I have an appointment at the hospital for a few tests and a tour around the maternity wing." Bryce flinched at the word hospital, and Juliet's look softened. "My being there will no doubt be easier than what you had to put up with while in there I'm sure."

Bryce shrugged, mindful that such a simple gesture could still hurt her so much. "I'll admit, I was glad to be released."

"Well, I have a few hours of being prodded and poked while displaying my big belly to all and sundry. Then I will trail around behind Trent who will be all but taking notes on everything the doctors say." She rolled her eyes skyward.

Bryce chuckled. "She's taking her role seriously, as she should." She sat beside Juliet on the wall.

"I am dreading when they show us the film they have to prepare us with. Natural birth or cesarean. I just know that while all the other parents-to-be will be in shock, Trent will have a million questions. You've no doubt seen her here. Someone that tall, demanding answers, isn't someone you can ignore."

Bryce laughed. "I'd guess not. Scarlet was telling me she'd gotten some nursery ideas for you?" Bryce had never engaged in small talk concerning babies with anyone before, but Juliet's presence was very soothing to Bryce's tired soul. She sensed Juliet was tired too for different reasons, and Bryce felt curiously obliged to keep her company until someone else arrived to keep an eye on her. Not that Bryce would dare to let Juliet realize that was what she was doing for fear of setting raging pregnancy hormones alight.

"Yes, Scarlet came over with her designs for us. We've picked out what we want, and I believe Scarlet may be chasing after you for some help rendering the walls for us."

Bryce nodded. "She's told me what she needs. That would be no problem at all."

"You should come over anyway. Now that you're back in the Tweedy fold, and by default Monica's crew, we should all go out for a meal. After all, we're one big family under the Tweedy umbrella. Though," she said, resting her pad aside, "I've felt we're the long lost cousins seeing as we usually come in on a job after you guys have long left. It's been nice this time to mingle with you all."

"Scarlet says she lives with Monica."

"Yes, I'd moved out to go live with Trent, and Monica was alone for quite some time. Then when Scarlet came back and met Monica through her father, they hit it off immediately. She's a really nice girl." She rubbed a hand over her stomach. "With a figure I envy at the moment."

Bryce didn't quite know what to say. "You'll soon be back in shape once you have a toddler to run around after."

Juliet laughed. "Oh, I'm leaving all the running to Trent. She's got longer legs than me. She will keep up with our child." She cocked her head at the sound of another vehicle crunching the pebbles on the driveway. "That's Monica." Juliet gave Bryce a considering look. "You can go start your work now and stop babysitting me."

Bryce's mouth opened to swiftly refute doing such a thing, but the sharp eyes of Juliet dried up any denials she might have uttered. She grinned sheepishly then spoke with a surprising honestly. "Didn't you think that, just maybe, you were perhaps babysitting *me*?"

Before Juliet could answer, Monica stormed into the garden.

"God damn it, Juliet! I told you not to come in to work early when you could just have had today off for your appointments."

Juliet ignored Monica's exasperated raised voice and kept her focus on Bryce. "If you need me, just follow the voices of the ones telling me off for not being wrapped in cotton wool."

Monica huffed around her. "What if something happened to you while we're not around? Who's going to explain that to Trent because I sure as hell won't." With her hands balled into fists at her side, Monica made for a formidable sight.

Juliet nodded slowly at the sight of her friend's obvious anxiety. "Okay, I'll be more careful. But I wasn't alone today. I had Bryce keeping me company until you arrived to take over the watch."

Monica gave Bryce a relieved smile. "Thank you for keeping an eye on her for us."

"I was merely passing the time of day before I was due to clock in." Bryce got to her feet and reached for her messenger bag. "Good luck with your appointment today. I hope Trent doesn't faint at the first sight of blood."

Juliet snorted softly. "My girl's made of strong stuff. She's been around babies too much, thanks to Elton's family, for her to be fazed by blood or anything else connected to pregnancy. She's more concerned if the hospital has Wi-Fi so she knows which of her handheld gaming consoles to pack while I'm in the early stages of labor. I'm telling you, she's got this all planned out."

Monica snorted. "Yeah, I can just imagine that conversation with the medical staff. Elton asked me the same thing though for when we're sitting in the waiting room."

"Two of a kind," Juliet said. "Bryce, I think it's pizza day today for the landscaping crew. Be sure to grab Scarlet and come down and join them."

Bryce wondered why she'd be issued such an invitation. Her face must have given her away because Juliet instantly explained.

"You're going to plaster my baby's nursery. I think that's deserving of a pizza slice or two. What's your preferred topping?"

"Ham and pineapple," Bryce dutifully answered, knowing when she was beaten. She spared a thought for Trent who probably had long since lost the ability to argue with this woman.

Monica shouted a welcome to Scarlet, and Bryce was embarrassed by how fast her head whipped around. *So much for trying not to see her*. Her breath caught in her chest at the mere sight of her.

"She is very striking, isn't she?" Juliet said softly.

"She's the boss's daughter," Bryce muttered. "I'd be hung from the scaffold by Gregor if I dared go near her."

Juliet just smiled. "Look at her though. Wouldn't she be worth it?"

Self-consciously, and with a nervousness fast becoming a habit, Bryce touched at the scar that marred her face. The edge of the scar was just reachable under the hat she never seemed to take off now. Her time for attracting beautiful women was gone. Her ex had been very explicit in that. Bryce remembered all too well being in the hospital recovering when Gerri had walked in with Amber in tow. Bryce hadn't wanted to deal with Gerri's histrionics so had feigned sleep.

"Oh my God, it's worse than I thought. Look at her face. If I stayed with her now it would only be out of pity and I don't do pity parties very well."

Bryce gripped the bedclothes as the cruel words ripped through her.

"Let's get out of here," Gerri spat out in a whisper. "I need to go get my things from her place and move on. She was a handsome addition on my arm for a while, but I can't be seen with her now. My reputation would suffer. It'd be too much like Beauty and the Beast."

Furious, Bryce had opened her eyes to tell Gerri to get the hell out of her room, but the door was already closing on her swiftly retreating back.

Trapped in her morose thoughts, Bryce jumped when a hand touched her arm. Juliet was looking at her curiously.

"Sorry, I was miles away." Bryce tried to shake herself free from the memories.

"It didn't look like a happy place to be."

For the first time since she'd been released from the hospital, Bryce just wanted to let everything inside her pour out like a tidal wave. The gentle kindness in Juliet's eyes reminded her of the look she'd seen mirrored in Scarlet's eyes when she'd woken her up from the nightmare. *Suck it up, Bryce. You don't need to be seen as anyone's pity case.*

"I'm okay. Just planning ahead for my day." She smiled to couch the blatant lie.

Juliet's eyes never wavered from her, and Bryce easily read in them the moment when Juliet decided to let her get away with it. "Pizza at one o'clock then."

Bryce's reaction was to make an excuse.

"I'd like you there." Juliet stared her down gently.

Unable to do anything but capitulate under that gaze, Bryce nodded and her sympathies for Trent doubled.

"Did someone say pizza?" Scarlet had gravitated to Bryce's side, and Bryce felt her whole body twitch at her proximity. Scarlet favored her with a bright smile. "Hello, stranger."

"One o'clock, come join the gang down here. Bryce has your invitation." Juliet smiled at them both, but the look she gave Bryce made her face scorch.

"Cool," Scarlet said.

"It's a date then." Juliet winked for Bryce alone.

Bryce shot her a steely glare. For a seriously pretty blond, heavily pregnant or not, Juliet Sullivan was dangerous.

"A date?" Scarlet looked down at her work clothes. "Damn, and I'm so overdressed."

Bryce thought she looked great in her black sleeveless T-shirt and well-worn jeans. She tore her eyes away, mumbled her good-byes, and hastened to the sanctuary of her job before either woman could say anything more to mortify her.

❖

The rocking beat of Within Temptation filled the room Scarlet was painting in. She unconsciously swayed to the music while she spread the white paint across the wall with a practiced hand. Enjoying the simple pleasure of doing something she loved, Scarlet began singing out loud. She knew her voice could carry a tune so she wasn't shy about raising it to accompany Sharon Den Adel as she sang about an ice queen wreaking havoc. Over the music, Scarlet could hear the faint noises coming from around the building. Hammering came from downstairs, and there was the faint whine of a drill from the house next door. But from the room next to hers, she couldn't hear a sound. Bryce was working in there, and Scarlet wondered if she'd find her asleep again. She knew Bryce had the darkest shadows under her eyes she'd ever seen and was growing gaunt. Scarlet was determined to make sure Bryce ate her fair share of pizza when they joined Monica's crew for the impromptu picnic. There was something about Bryce that made Scarlet oddly attentive even though she knew Bryce would hate to be fussed over. It was strange. She'd never felt so drawn to someone who posted so many "do not disturb" signs all over themselves.

But Scarlet had never been one for playing it safe.

She finished off her section with a flourish and climbed down from her stepladder. She cleansed her brushes ready for the afternoon's work and tidied up a little. Her stomach rumbled loudly and her mouth watered at the thought of the pizza awaiting her. She gathered up a cold can of soda from her cooler and went to find Bryce.

From the doorway, Scarlet spied Bryce upon her scaffold smoothing plaster across the ceiling. With every sweep of her trowel, Bryce's outstretched arm pulled her T-shirt up to reveal a taut stomach etched with tight muscles. Scarlet couldn't take her eyes away from the well-defined abs that were taunting her with every stroke of Bryce's arm. Her fingers itched to smooth their way across each line to see if Bryce would tense beneath her touch or melt to let her tease further.

"Scarlet?"

By the way Bryce raised her voice, it was obviously not the first time she'd spoken to her.

Scarlet shook herself and knew she was probably blushing a shade of red to rival her hair. She belatedly tore her eyes away from the tantalizing strip of skin still visible because of Bryce's pose. Scarlet dragged her eyes upward and found Bryce staring at her.

"You okay?"

Scarlet nodded. "Are you supposed to be reaching up that high with your shoulder?"

Bryce finished off a corner deftly. "It was my left shoulder I damaged, not my right. I just can't load my board as much as

I used to yet." She climbed down her scaffold with ease and set down her tools. "Did you need me for something?"

Scarlet felt her face flame again at the innocent query. She twisted her hands behind her back to quell the need to lift Bryce's shirt up and explore the skin she'd seen revealed.

"Just wondered if you're ready to eat." She cursed herself for feeling so conscious of everything connected to Bryce. Scarlet was all too aware of her growing attraction with every moment spent in her presence. She watched as Bryce wiped her hands clean and found herself fascinated by the blunt fingertips and short cut nails. Small scars were visible up Bryce's arms, paler now, but etching patterns across her muscles. Scarlet had the urge to touch them, trace them, to acknowledge the damage they told of while celebrating the fact Bryce was still there. Still very much alive. The imperative to run her fingers over the scar etching its cruelty through Bryce's brow set Scarlet in motion, and she stepped forward unconsciously. Startled by her feelings, Scarlet all but jumped back as if scalded when Bryce looked up.

"We'd better go see Juliet if she's still here. She looks to me like a lady you don't keep waiting around when she's summoned you." Bryce snagged a can of soda and ran it across her forehead for the chill.

Scarlet hastily bit back a moan at the innocent act. She tried to act nonchalant but was all churned up inside. Her reaction to Bryce threw her seriously off balance. She watched as Bryce jammed the ever-present cap on to cover up her scar and hide the roughly cut blond hair underneath. Deciding not to question Bryce's actions, Scarlet just nodded and let Bryce lead the way.

"Truth be told, I've worked up quite an appetite this morning. I don't think my sandwiches would have been enough, so pizza is going to feed the beast quite nicely."

Bryce rubbed at her stomach, and Scarlet's body pulsed at the action. It hadn't been done to tantalize, but seeing Bryce touch herself, however innocently, turned Scarlet's body into a raging mass of need.

What is it about this woman that makes me want her so much?

"By the way, thanks for singing to me all morning," Bryce said as they climbed down the stairs and walked through the kitchen.

Scarlet grinned, a little embarrassed. "Sorry. Was I that loud?"

"Not at all." Bryce smiled at her, and Scarlet was captivated by the shy look on her face. "It was a pleasure to hear. Though your choice of music is a little…different from what the guys sing along to."

"It's an acquired taste I admit, but it soothes my soul."

Bryce held the door open for her. "I might have to give them a proper listen to sometime."

Bryce said the words so softly Scarlet barely caught them, but when she opened her mouth to answer, Monica's voice was calling them over to get in quick before the others descended like seagulls. Scarlet wanted so badly to reach out and touch Bryce, but she didn't know if the gesture would be to soothe Bryce or herself.

Chapter Seven

Bright and early the next Saturday morning, Bryce arrived outside the address Juliet had given her. She had to admit, plastering a baby's nursery was a far more productive way of spending her weekend than staring at her own four walls. She cast a curious eye over the house, wondering how much of it would reflect its owners.

Trent opened the door to her knock, and Bryce got to see her close up. The first thing she noticed was that Trent was *really* tall. She had to tilt her head back to look into Trent's eyes. Trent's face was unsmiling, almost moody, but at the sound of Juliet's voice from back inside the house, Bryce watched as Trent's whole demeanor changed. The grin she favored Bryce with was full of a sincere warmth.

"You're Bryce?" Trent held out a hand.

Bryce shook it. "I'm here to get your nursery ready for Scarlet's paint job."

Trent ushered her inside. Juliet wandered out of the kitchen to greet her.

"Trent is so excited with what Scarlet is going to do for the baby's room. I don't know who'll spend the most time in the nursery, the baby or Trent."

Trent just laughed at her. "I've told you I'm more than ready to do above and beyond my fair share of diaper duties."

She snagged an arm around Juliet's shoulders. "After all, you're doing the hard part right now."

"I'd get that promise put in writing," Bryce said with a smile. She'd gotten to spend time with Juliet and already liked her. Seeing her with Trent left Bryce in no doubt Juliet was loved and cared for.

"Oh, I have it on good authority Trent is a wiz at changing diapers and powdering baby butts."

Trent explained. "My friend Elton's family spawns at least one kid every year. You learn fast that, if you have a pair of hands, you're going to end up with a baby at whatever family function you're attending."

"And now you're having your own." Trent's hand touched Juliet's belly. The look they shared made Bryce oddly envious.

"Would you like a drink?" Juliet asked, breaking Bryce from her thoughts.

"I'd love some coffee." *Anything to keep me awake.* "Scarlet said she'd dropped my tools off here for me?"

Trent nodded. "They're in the nursery waiting for you. Let me show you upstairs."

Bryce was surprised by the elaborate lock on an out of place reinforced door she walked past. She gave Trent a curious look. "Are you already making sure the kid never gets out of bed at night?"

Trent just chuckled. "That's my game room. I've got all my consoles and gaming equipment in there. It has to be protected. It's priceless."

"Scarlet mentioned something about you being a gamer."

"Do you play?"

Bryce shook her head at the undisguised hope in Trent's voice. "No. I've never had the time to." She was guided to the nursery. "Wow, this is a nice sized room." She ran a hand over the walls. "This won't take much to render." She tossed Trent a look. "I'll get these walls as smooth as a baby's bottom."

Trent grinned at her. "Thank you for that mental image."

Juliet came in carrying a mug of coffee and a tray with milk and sugar. "I forgot to ask how you take it."

"Baby hormones," Trent said, teasing her. "And you should have called me and I would have come and got this for you."

"You don't have to carry me up the stairs just yet, babe. I can still climb them, albeit a little slowly seeing as I can't see my feet."

The sound of the doorbell rang through the house.

"That's Squirt, my gaming buddy." Trent smacked a kiss on Juliet's forehead and bounded off down the stairs, her feet heavy on each step as she ran down.

Juliet just shook her head. "That will be Kayleigh, my little sister. I swear, get the two of them together and it's hard to tell which one is the thirteen-year-old." She laid the mug and tray on the windowsill. "I'll leave you in peace to go do my chores while my girls play."

Bryce walked around the room, checking all the walls and listening to the sound of excited voices coming from downstairs. Trent's deeper tone mingled with the sound of a young girl's who was apparently talking a mile a minute. Bryce picked up her coffee, laced it liberally with sugar and a dash of milk, and sipped from it while she worked out in her head where to start. The soft sound of music drifted up the stairs, and Bryce felt curiously lost. It wasn't Scarlet's music. Trying to shake off her melancholy, Bryce looked out the bedroom window. She was no gamer, but even she recognized the shape of a Space Invader etched into the pebbles in the garden.

❖

Sometime later, Juliet called her down for lunch so Bryce dutifully downed her tools and headed downstairs. She followed the music coming from the living room and found two high backed gaming chairs set up before the TV. Trent was in one, Kayleigh in the other. On the large TV screen in front of them a

Mario Kart race was in full swing. Kayleigh was urging her kart on, while Trent sat beside her in a more sedate fashion.

"Yes! Yes! I'm gonna win!" Kayleigh crowed as her kart took the lead.

Bryce watched as Trent's kart slowed down. Was Trent deliberately letting Kayleigh win?

At the sound of loud beeping, an agonized howl from Kayleigh soon explained all. "No! Not the blue shell of doom!" On screen, her kart was hit by a large winged blue turtle shell and the kart was blown from the road. Trent's kart picked up speed again and she crossed the finish line first, winning the race.

"Who tossed that shell?" Kayleigh demanded.

"Luigi did," Trent said as her winning Baby Mario started his lap of honor.

"I'm going to run him off the side of Donkey Kong Mountain the next time we play that track."

Juliet came to stand beside Bryce where she was peering into the living room.

"I thought Trent was letting her win," Bryce said in a soft voice.

"Oh heaven forbid, no. Kayleigh would have a fit if someone threw the game just so she won. And Trent is too good a player to let someone else win if she's in the lead."

Bryce could hear Trent give Kayleigh some pointers as to what to do on their next race.

"But she's not above giving her secrets away to those she loves so they can play as well as she does." Juliet's smile was soft as she moved behind the gaming chairs and leaned over. "Time to take a pit stop, you two. Come eat and then you can get back on the tracks and Kayleigh here can chase Luigi down and stomp his sorry ass."

Kayleigh laughed. "Did you get pizza?" She turned around in her chair to lean against its back and give her sister big puppy dog eyes.

Juliet brushed at Kayleigh's hair. "What else would I get you or me at the moment?"

"Yay!" Kayleigh was out of her seat in an instant. "Can I help you set the table? You're not supposed to be doing so much now because of the baby."

Bryce was amused by the look of pained resignation that blazed across Juliet's features. She nodded a hello at Kayleigh as she got caught under her sudden scrutiny. *Oh God, she's got the same soul penetrating look as her sister.* Mercifully, Juliet called her attention away.

"Go grab four plates. You're as bad as Trent trying to keep me from doing too much," Juliet said.

Trent pressed a kiss on Juliet's cheek. "Just making sure my baby mama is happy and healthy." She slipped past Juliet and barely dodged the swat aimed at her rear. "Come have some pizza. We don't want you getting cranky!"

"I'll show you cranky, babe," Juliet said with a smile.

Trent grinned back, her eyes sparkling. "Bring it on, sweetheart." She snagged Juliet around her waist and hugged her. "Bryce, I hope you're hungry. We always have way too much pizza in this house. It's Juliet's number one craving at the moment."

"I could eat a whole pie by myself," Kayleigh called from the kitchen as she clattered plates on the table.

"Isn't that the truth," Juliet muttered. "I swear that kid grows more like you every day." She nudged Trent with her hip. "Especially since she cut her hair short after always wearing it long."

"She's growing up, Jule. She's no longer a little kid. She's a teenager now. Besides, the cut suits her."

Bryce followed them into the kitchen where Kayleigh was expertly cutting the two large pizzas into manageable slices. Bryce surreptitiously checked out the young girl's hair. It was cut short into her neck and teased into soft spikes on the top. Bryce thought she looked like a baby dyke in the making. She wondered how Juliet's parents would handle having two gay daughters in the family.

Bryce felt uncomfortable wearing her cap at the meal table and nervously ran her fingers over the brim. At Juliet's soft nod Bryce removed it but kept it close. She kept her head down to avoid anyone's pitying gaze.

The table was soon busy with everyone finding their seats and feeding their faces. Kayleigh's attention returned to Bryce.

"You're fixing up the baby's room, aren't you?" Kayleigh asked around a mouthful of pizza.

Bryce nodded. She could feel Kayleigh's stare fixed on her face.

"Your scar, does it hurt?"

Bryce blinked in surprise. She wasn't used to someone coming right out and acknowledging the damage done to her face. She willed herself not to reach up and touch the area and draw even more attention to it.

"Not so much now," she said finally.

Kayleigh didn't look away. "It's really neat. It's like you've got Harry's lightning bolt going through your eyebrow."

Bryce frowned. "Harry?"

"Harry Potter," Trent explained, reaching for another slice of pizza.

"Yeah, he's got this wicked scar on his forehead that marked him as the boy that lived. Yours is like that. It's really cool."

Bryce was surprised to realize Kayleigh meant that. For her it was something fascinating, not something that Bryce knew was disfiguring. She'd seen herself in the mirror. She had witnessed firsthand how cruel the scar was as it sliced through her forehead and ended so perilously close to her eye. She'd been lucky she hadn't been blinded.

Lucky. Bryce had grown to hate that word.

Kayleigh leaned toward her with a sweet smile. "I'm glad it doesn't hurt." She settled back in her chair. "Bet you wish it came with magic though because that would be totally awesome!"

At Kayleigh's fanciful exuberance, Bryce felt something shift a little inside her. A weight lifted just a fraction off her soul and let her breathe a tad easier. She ran her finger along the jagged scar. Like Harry, she was marked. She also was one who had lived.

❖

Bryce could hear the soft footsteps of Juliet's measured gait as she climbed the stairs. When she looked at the doorway, Juliet was leaning against the doorjamb watching her progress.

"I'm sorry if Kayleigh made you feel uncomfortable earlier."

Bryce didn't look up from her task. "She didn't. I think she's the first person who has pointed out what happened to my face and hasn't made me feel like a freak."

"I hope that isn't how you see yourself because I can assure you that none of us see you that way at all."

"I've seen this face every morning since the accident. I know it's not pretty. It's a scar that isn't going to go away any time soon. The doctors did as good a job as they could to fix it for me." She shrugged. She regretted it when her shoulder reminded her of the damage done there too. "Guess my good looks have been traded in for the roguish battle scarred look that I now sport."

"That mark doesn't detract from how handsome you are. It just adds an air of mystery. You know women love that. It makes us want to soothe away your pains and discover all your hidden secrets."

"There's no secret to me. I was in a car crash. I walked away."

"I wish I'd have known you then. I'd have visited you in the hospital and driven you crazy fussing over you like my friends are doing to me now that I'm pregnant."

Bryce chuckled, wishing she'd had anyone visit her in the hospital other than the uncomfortable visits from her work mates who had no idea what to say to her. Only Victor Tweedy had been a regular by her bedside and had made her feel cared for. She couldn't help but wonder if his daughter would have done the same had she been back home then. She could easily imagine Scarlet being concerned and then rallying her up and out of the bed to start facing what had happened to her. Bryce wished Scarlet had seen her before the crash, when she'd been handsome and witty and someone the girls had flirted with. Now she was crippled with self-doubts and couldn't even sleep more than two hours a night without waking from terrifying dreams.

Juliet's gentle voice shook her from her musings.

"You're doing a wonderful job." Juliet was studying the room with a smile. "Scarlet will have no trouble painting on these smooth walls. The room will look amazing for when the baby arrives."

"I'm half surprised she hasn't turned up to check that I'm doing the job right." Bryce put the finishing touches to the last wall and carefully climbed back down her stepladder.

"Oh, she's too busy today getting naked with Monica."

Bryce's whole body flinched at Juliet's throwaway comment. She dropped her trowel noisily and grimaced at the sound it made in the empty room. A rush of unexplained jealousy burned through her veins, followed swiftly by an anger she knew she had no right to feel. She quickly picked up her tool and tried to look nonchalant.

"I thought Monica was with her Johnny Depp." She was amazed by how normal her voice appeared.

Juliet laughed. "Monica is as straight as they come, but she does appreciate the female form. And she has a great appreciation for Scarlet's because she is the perfect model for Monica's dressmaking skills. That's what they were doing today once Scarlet finished her shift at the photography studio she works at."

Bryce released a soft "Oh" and felt her stomach muscles slowly unknot themselves.

"I used to be Monica's tailor's dummy, but in my current condition"—she ran her hand over her belly—"it kind of makes it hard to reach the tape measure around my hips. Besides, Scarlet has much more of an aptitude for what Monica creates."

"The Goth thing."

"Well, Monica is Goth. Scarlet's only drawn to the music and fashion so don't expect her to be sporting fangs any time soon."

"She mentioned something about the music to me, and I hear it enough working with her every day."

"Well, this weekend, after Scarlet's shifts they are holed up in the apartment while Monica gets her ready for a concert we're all going to in a few weeks. You'll have to come along to see what all the fuss is about."

As usual, Bryce didn't comment on the invitation. "Do you dress like them?" She found the thought of Juliet in dark colors just didn't sit right.

"Oh God, no. I like the music well enough, but I'll be sporting maternity wear so I'll stand out like a flowery sore thumb. But Trent always dresses for the occasion to support the bands."

Bryce watched Juliet's eyes soften as her thoughts turned inward.

"She looks mighty fine in her long-tailed jacket and wine red shirt." Juliet's voice trailed off and her lips curved with a small, appreciative smile. She shook herself out of where her mind had obviously wandered. "Anyway"—she favored Bryce with a shy grin—"enough of those thoughts. I'll be sure to remind you closer to the time so you can find something suitably black to wear to join us."

"I'll be sure to check my calendar." Bryce tried not to sound dismissive.

"You know I'll just keep bugging you until you give in and do anything I say just to shut me up."

Bryce didn't doubt that for a second. "How does Trent cope with you?"

"I won't give away all my secrets, but I will tell you this. It took all my considerable charms to get that girl out of the gaming room and into my arms. But it was worth every minute. You need something like that to get you back on your feet and enjoying life again."

Bryce felt guilt press down on her shoulders, and she screwed her eyes up against the pain. For a moment, she was back in that nightmare, hanging from her seat belt, wishing for someone to save her and knowing she was all that remained alive in that car.

"Hey, honey, where did you go just now?"

Juliet's voice was soft and her hand was warm against Bryce's cool skin. She felt Juliet squeeze her arm and bring her back to the nursery.

"I'm okay," she said, hoping Juliet wouldn't call her on it this time.

"You will be. I know that." Juliet patted her arm briskly. "Now that you've finished in here, tidy your mess up and get your ass downstairs. Trent's making chili and you are not missing out on that treat."

Desperately trying to get her head back to the here and now, Bryce did as she was bid. "Can you eat chili?"

"Who do you think asked for it?" Juliet gave her a mischievous smile. "And what this woman wants, she gets!" With that, Juliet left Bryce alone.

Scarlet stood unmoving on the small wooden block Monica utilized for her dressmaking. She dared not look down or cause any movement to the fabric that was currently being pinned up just above her ankles. Monica smoothed the fabric down and then looked up from where she was kneeling at Scarlet's feet.

"I think that's done it," she said as she got up and stood back to eye her creation. She frowned critically. "Do you think it needs more cleavage?"

Scarlet looked down. "From my angle there's plenty on show without me having my nipples saying hello too."

Monica nodded and slowly walked around her. "You've got an excellent figure for this. Have you ever thought of being a designer's model?" She helped Scarlet down from her podium.

"Can't say it's ever been high on my list of jobs I thought to try until you made me strip and try that first dress on." Scarlet grinned at Monica's unabashed face. "I've got enough on my plate with working for Dad and doing part-time at the studio. Standing here for you makes for a nice respite from that."

"You know your dad is going to expect you to eventually put down the paintbrush and move into the office to learn the ropes there."

Scarlet groaned. "I'm so not management material. I like to be hands-on with things. It's more fun that way."

Monica began fussing over the fabric draped over Scarlet's shoulder. "Which reminds me, how is Bryce?"

Scarlet's head snapped around. "Hey!" She glared at the innocent look Monica spared her before busying herself again with the dress. "There's been no laying on of hands there."

"You have enough trouble keeping your eyes off her I've noticed."

Scarlet groaned expressively. "Well, can you honestly blame me? She's very easy on the eye."

"She looks like she hasn't slept in months."

"To be honest? I don't think she has," Scarlet admitted.

"Well, she's been through one hell of a trauma. And she hasn't been out of the hospital very long. She's been through a lot, and it's blatant to see by those shadows under her eyes that she's still suffering."

"I know all that. I see it more than anyone when she lets me. I just….I really want to help her if she'd let me."

"So"—Monica edged behind Scarlet's back and began tugging at the dress's neckline—"this undercurrent of flirting you're doing and having lunches together isn't just a pity mission then?"

Scarlet swung around so fast Monica took a step backward. "No! She doesn't need my pity. I just…I just…" Scarlet's voice failed her. *What do I want really from this woman who has burrowed her way so soon into my thoughts and into my heart when I least expected it?* "I'm sorry, Monica. I didn't mean to shout at you."

"Well, I have to say, that's the most passion I've seen from you over another woman since I've known you. And don't forget, I walked in on you trading tongues with the last woman you went out with. You looked bored to tears."

Scarlet felt her cheeks bloom with a blush. "She wasn't exactly knight in shining armor material."

"And Bryce could be?"

"Maybe, if I let her and she wanted to be. I like her a lot, Monica. Even though I know she's *broken* at the moment. I can't help myself. She draws something in me to her."

"Then you need to do something about that attraction if you want it to go further. You're not usually shy in fighting for what you want, Scarlet. You've held your dad off this long so you could pursue your own career with a camera in your hand. Maybe it's time you have it all. The career you truly want and a girlfriend who *is* knight in shining armor material."

"And you think Bryce might be that one? We have only just met." *But she's already becoming important to me. I can't shake that feeling she's meant to be more.*

"Your eyes devour her every time you see her. It's like she's the sexiest thing on the face of the planet and you can't wait to take a bite out of her. I'm just saying, if she's special, then you should see if she fits into your life."

"What if I don't know if this is the right time for that? I'm juggling so many balls in the air already and my dad has plans for me that I'm not sure I can fulfill. Or want to." Scarlet hoped the whine in her voice wasn't too noticeable.

Monica bumped her shoulder. "What if it *feels* like it's the right time?"

Scarlet groaned aloud pitifully. "I've wanted to go visit my grandma all day just for the excuse to go next door and see how

Bryce was doing. Isn't that pathetic?" Scarlet sat down on the block with a thump, not caring about her dress.

"No, it sounds like someone exploring that *like* could maybe become *love*. And that, my friend, is the greatest adventure anyone can partake in."

❖

When Bryce carried her tools down the stairs, she walked through the kitchen and her stomach rumbled at the rich smells coming from the stove. Juliet was at Trent's side, watching her cook.

"Fifteen minutes," Juliet called over her shoulder at Bryce. "No dawdling."

"You're very bossy for a pregnant lady," Bryce muttered.

Trent easily overheard her. "She was bossy before I got her in that way too." She got a swat to her behind for her sass. Trent stole a quick kiss off Juliet in retaliation.

Bryce carried her stuff to the garage where she left it for Scarlet to pick up. Then she joined everyone at the kitchen table. She was grateful for their banter negating her need to think beyond how much she wanted on her plate and instead listened to Kayleigh talk a mile a minute. It was noisy and energetic, but the boisterous family setting oddly calmed the lonely ache in Bryce's chest. For a moment, she wished Scarlet was there, then everything would have been perfect.

Chapter Eight

Scarlet was eager to see Bryce the following Monday morning. She had switched rooms in the one house and was now facing the main road where she could see the bus stop. She wondered how long it would be before Bryce could drive again. Obviously, her injuries made it difficult to be behind the wheel, but Scarlet was a little puzzled as to how she could stretch and wield her plasterer's palette but not sit and drive. She went back to preparing her paint for the day but was soon back at the window checking for Bryce's arrival. She barely held back a whoop of excitement when she saw the bus finally draw up and Bryce step off.

Scarlet hurried from the room and down the stairs, almost colliding with Gregor who asked who had set her ass on fire. Scarlet skidded to a halt in the driveway and ran a hand through her hair making sure it was tidy. She smoothed down her shirt to make sure everything was presentable. Today she was going to be bold and daring. She'd spent the weekend letting her thoughts turn too much toward Bryce. She wanted to get to know her more and hoped Bryce might feel the same way about her. She barely held in her gasp on seeing the more than ever prominent shadows beneath Bryce's pale blue eyes when she drew closer. Scarlet steeled herself to overlook them, knowing full well Bryce wouldn't appreciate the intrusion.

"Hey you. Juliet says you did a fantastic job on the nursery for me."

"It didn't need much work. The walls are all primed now for you to paint gamboling Yoshis on. Whatever Yoshis are. Apparently, they make Trent happy, which makes Juliet happy, so the nursery is a go." Bryce drew to a stop in front of Scarlet. "I'm guessing they showed you my sketch?"

"Kayleigh showed it to me, once she'd wrestled it from Trent. I think there's going to be some fighting over who that nursery actually belongs to."

"Kayleigh's a character."

"She's a strange blend. She's got Juliet's looks but, oddly enough, is very much like Trent. Except for her endless questions." Bryce puffed out her cheeks noisily. "God, she can talk up a storm. She holds more questions than a *Jeopardy* host."

Laughing, Scarlet fell into step beside Bryce as they walked up the driveway. "She's a bundle of teenage energy."

"She worships Trent, that's pretty obvious."

"Trent's pretty easy to fall for. She's got that brooding handsomeness coupled with a fierce loyalty to her friends and loved ones that just draws people in."

Bryce shot her a look. "You're still under her spell then."

"I've grown to love her more since I've gotten to know her from an adult point of view and not the mooning teen who just caught glimpses from Grandma's window. But I'm not *in* love with her. I've moved on from my crush and love her as a friend. Besides, she's Juliet's and for a very sweet natured lady, Juliet is *very* territorial of her girl."

"It must be nice," Bryce said quietly. The look on her face that followed showed she hadn't meant to say that out loud.

"What must?"

Bryce shrugged at her. "To have someone to fight for you. To love you that much that they are yours and yours alone."

"Have you never had that with anyone?"

"No." Bryce shook her head emphatically. "I don't know if I could cope with all that emotion."

Scarlet chuckled. "When the feelings are mutual I'm sure it makes the burden much easier."

"How about you? Have you ever had anyone you've felt that way about?"

"Not yet," she answered simply. She couldn't help but let her eyes linger on Bryce's face, memorizing every sharp angle to her cheekbones and the dimple in her cheek. "But I'm open to the possibility." She dared to take the bull by the horns. "Would you like to go out with me tonight?"

Bryce stopped in her tracks. "Me?"

Scarlet laughed at her surprise. "Yes, you."

"What kind of going out are we talking about? You in need of more plastering?"

"I'm asking you on a date, Bryce." Bryce's eyes widened. She appeared stunned. "I thought maybe dinner, a drink or two, some sparkling conversation."

"Why?" Bryce didn't look at her.

Scarlet was taken aback by the solemn query. The dull light in Bryce's eyes was haunted by dark shadows, and Scarlet desperately wanted to banish them away. She caught Bryce raising a hand under her ever-present cap to run her finger over the scar that marred her forehead. Scarlet recognized the unconscious nervous gesture and her heart ached.

"I'm asking you out because I think you're fascinating and gorgeous and are someone I want to get to know more about." The startled look Bryce shot her at the mention of her looks gave Scarlet a reason to pause. *Doesn't she see that scar doesn't change anything? It doesn't alter the fact she's still an attractive woman at all.* She folded her arms across her chest and gave Bryce a playful scowl. "I'm not without interested suitors, you know. I have it on good authority that the minute I miraculously turn straight Gregor will be the first gentleman caller pounding on my door." She was delighted to see a smile tug at Bryce's lips.

"His wife might have something to say about that."

"Well, she's safe because it's going to be a very long time before I hand in my lesbian card." Emboldened by Bryce's smile, Scarlet reached out to stroke her cheek. Bryce froze at her touch and Scarlet let her hand linger just a little more. "So, what do you say? Will you come out with me?" She trailed a finger down Bryce's neck slowly, feeling the steady pulse that accelerated at her bold move.

Bryce captured her hand and Scarlet thrilled to her touch. Bryce's work-roughened fingers were warm against her own and their strength was obvious.

"I'm not very comfortable out in public."

"Then I'll pick somewhere quiet and intimate. I'd like to spend time with you outside of work. If it becomes too much for you we can always leave." Scarlet squeezed Bryce's hand. "What do you say? Please say yes." Scarlet watched as Bryce wavered for the longest time then finally capitulated.

"If that's what you want."

Her low tone made Scarlet's insides tremble. "So, can I pick you up at seven?"

Bryce shook her head. "Tell me where you want to go and I'll meet you there."

"Bryce, I can come and pick you up. It's no bother."

Bryce hesitated, appearing to be at war with herself. Scarlet waited, eyeing her closely, watching the indecision darken her face. Finally, Bryce spoke.

"I don't ride in cars, Scarlet. I can't yet. I just….*can't*."

Startled by this revelation, Scarlet finally realized why her father had asked for her to drop Bryce's tools over at Trent's house. She had been visiting her grandma anyway and hadn't initially thought anything of it. Her father obviously knew though and was sparing Bryce's feelings. It certainly explained all the buses Bryce traveled to and from work on.

"How about a taxi?" Scarlet asked.

Bryce shook her head. "Still too enclosed." She took a hasty step back and away from Scarlet. "Maybe you should just forget—"

Scarlet reacted quickly and stayed Bryce's hasty departure with a hand on her arm. "The Crimson Dragon on Broadway. I seem to recall there's a bus stop right by it. You're not getting away from me that easily, Bryce Donovan. If I have to get the food hand delivered to your door and bring the chopsticks myself, I will do so."

"Why does this mean so much to you?" Bryce's tone held more than a hint of exasperation.

"Because you're beginning to."

Scarlet had spoken without censure and watched as Bryce's surprise was replaced by the first true smile Scarlet had seen from her. *Oh my God, she's beautiful*. Through the lingering pallor and all too obvious pain left by Bryce's accident, Scarlet could finally see beyond that and was seeing some of the real Bryce beneath. It took all her strength not to reach out and kiss her then and there.

"Your eyes just changed color. What are you thinking?" Bryce asked as she stepped closer, all her attention fixed firmly on Scarlet's face.

"How much I want to kiss you," Scarlet said, her voice breaking as she stared at Bryce's mouth. The smile remained on Bryce's lips.

"You might want to save that for the date. Besides"—Bryce cocked her head toward the men who were starting to file into the buildings—"we don't want to startle our work colleagues or break Gregor's heart."

"They'd enjoy it." Scarlet shrugged, only now noticing that others were milling around them, gathering up their equipment.

"They probably would, but I'd rather they didn't get their jollies from something as special as that first kiss between you and me. I'd rather that was something kept for us alone."

Scarlet swallowed back a moan at the way Bryce's tone had lowered and made the air more intimate between them. She regretted that they were standing on the driveway in plain view of the work site. "Seven o'clock?"

"I'll be there."

❖

The Sullivan-Williams household was hosting a lively get-together that evening. Juliet sat beside Monica as they discussed some work-related issues that had cropped up, and Trent and Elton were seated opposite them with their own agenda.

"Zelda is kinda pretty," Trent said.

"A Ganondorf wouldn't be bullied…well, not too much. Or how about Leon Kennedy instead?"

"Jill Valentine."

"Marcus Fenix."

"There's always Peach."

"And you can't beat Mario."

Juliet half listened as Trent reeled off baby names for a girl while Elton countered with names for a boy. They'd been at it for five long minutes and Juliet had been impressed by their ability to rattle off the most bizarre names of characters from all forms of media. "I've told you both before, there'll be no naming the baby after a character from a game." She shifted uncomfortably on the sofa, trying to get in a better position that eased her aching back.

Elton sighed then brightened. "Baelfire," he announced.

"Ariel."

Monica shook her head at them. "Guys, I'm guessing TV fairy tale characters are off the list too. Besides, everyone knows the Evil Queen in that show is the fairest of them all. Mighty sexy too in her low-cut regal gowns that I am just dying to re-create."

"I just don't want to name my kid anything boring or regular. He or she is going to be amazing just like its mommy so I'm vetoing any old-fashioned name from our grandparents' era. And no fucking reality TV names either."

At Juliet's pointed cough, Trent sighed and reached into her jeans for her wallet. She took out a dollar bill and slipped it into a large jar with the label "Baby's College Fund" stuck on that was set prominently on the coffee table. Between her and Elton, that night alone they'd added twenty dollars due to the "no swearing unnecessarily" rule that was now in play. Trent grinned over at Juliet in contrition. "I'm really liking the current name we're calling the baby though."

Juliet huffed at her. "*We* are not calling the baby anything. That particular name is all your fault, and I am not calling my child *that*!" She ran a hand over her stomach protectively. "I knew you should have stayed at home on the last hospital visit."

Monica looked between Juliet and Trent, waiting for more. "Come on, spill. What's the name? I know for a fact you two haven't gone the cutesy route and haven't been calling the fetus 'peanut' while it's been growing."

Trent never broke her gaze from Juliet. "Newt," she said with a smile.

Juliet grumbled under her breath. "That damned video the nurse showed us has a lot to answer for." She groaned as Trent ahem-ed and pointed to the jar. Juliet deliberately turned away to direct her attention to Monica, ignoring the so-called other adults in the room. "It was to prepare parents-to-be in case of a cesarean birth."

Monica looked puzzled, but Elton guffawed out loud. He began to dramatically writhe in pain, clutching at his chest. He then shoved his hand up his shirt, punching through the gap between buttons, pretending it was an alien complete with gnashing teeth.

"Chest burster!" He and Trent burst into fits of laughter.

Juliet sighed. "That's pretty much what Trent did in class and nearly got us ejected from the screening room." She had to smile as Trent and Elton were now in hysterics at Elton's antics. "So, to Trent, the baby has been Newt ever since."

Monica frowned at Elton's silliness. "Newt's not exactly what I expect to be monogramming into the kid's clothes when he or she goes to kindergarten."

"It'll do for now until we can pick a name we both agree on," Trent said, wiping at her eyes and grinning over at Juliet unrepentantly.

"At least the middle name is sorted. Mom and Dad started a family tradition of always having Grandma's maiden name as a second name. We just need to pick a first name that Trent doesn't think is too normal and I don't think is too outlandish."

"She even said no to Chun-Li," Trent said mournfully.

Hanging his head in commiseration, Elton finally removed his hand from inside his shirt. He picked up his beer bottle instead. "Bummer, dude." He took a long drink. "Hey, how about Thor?"

They both looked over at Juliet who gave them her patented look.

"Guess not," Elton muttered, cowering a little.

"Newt it is then." Trent winked at Juliet who just shook her head at her with an indulgent smile.

❖

Bryce had agonized over what to wear but had finally decided on a pair of dark blue chinos and a sky blue shirt. She had gathered up her wallet on the way out and checked herself in the mirror one last time. She looked thinner than before. The shadows under her eyes still blatantly broadcast the fact she wasn't sleeping. Critically, her eyes swept over the scar before she hid it under the cap. She smiled a little remembering Kayleigh's fascination in its apparent "coolness" to the young girl. A badge of honor. Bryce didn't feel there was much honor being the only survivor in a car she shouldn't have been a passenger in anyway. She brushed aside the thought and fought not to let the morose thoughts spoil the ripple of anticipation that was thrumming through her body. For the first time in a long time, she actually felt alive.

The bus journey was short, which suited Bryce fine because she was eager to get the night started. Scarlet had been very attentive over the lunch break they had shared together and had unashamedly called Bryce out on purposely dodging her the past week. Scarlet had known why too.

"So I found you asleep. Big deal. All I could think of was how sweet you looked and how I wouldn't mind being able to see that look on your face from the comfort of my own bed."

Bryce had been surprised by Scarlet's bluntness and by how totally turned on she had become from Scarlet's admission. Scarlet had just chuckled at her stunned silence.

"I can be terribly forward. You'll have to be prepared for that. I'm not one for sitting back on my heels when I see a good thing. I just have to grab it. Life's too short."

Bryce had the feeling Scarlet was going to be a force to be reckoned with. Before the accident, Bryce would have matched her in confidence and wit. Now, she knew all too well how short life could be, but instead of it propelling her forward to embrace it she found herself wanting to just hide away from it all. She was stepping out of her comfort zone tonight. She was equal parts terrified and hopeful. Maybe now was the time to take a step back into the world she'd known.

CHAPTER NINE

The restaurant Scarlet had chosen was a popular Chinese one. It appeared busy with the evening trade, but the booths were set up to give the occupants an air of intimacy. Bryce walked in and looked around for Scarlet. Her heart felt like it was coming out of her chest. All of a sudden, she was terrified.

Calm down for fuck's sake. Having a heart attack on the first date is not a good way to start the evening.

She saw a flash of familiar red as Scarlet stood up from her booth and waved Bryce over. Bryce nearly swallowed her tongue. Scarlet was stunning in a low-cut emerald green blouse and a long black skirt. Her hair was loose, hanging luxuriously over her shoulders. Bryce was filled with the urge to grab a handful of it and pull her close for a desperate kiss. An ornate hair clasp caught a swath of hair back from Scarlet's face and added a touch of *otherworldly* that Scarlet favored. And wore so well, Bryce thought. She wet her lips, desperately aware that her throat had gone dry over the beauty before her. She brushed past the other patrons and hoped she looked cool and collected, when in reality, all she wanted to do was reach out and ravish Scarlet and taste those deep red lips. *Ravish?* Bryce wondered where that word had come from, but looking at how Scarlet stood out among all the rest, she felt ravishing would only be the start of what she'd like to do to her.

She felt the world stutter in place when Scarlet leaned over and kissed her cheek in welcome.

"I'm glad you're here," she said, easing back down into her seat.

Bryce sat with a less elegant thump. "You look beautiful," she blurted, wondering where all her measured poise and charm had fled to. Scarlet's smile lit a flame inside her chest.

Scarlet leaned conspiratorially over the table, affording Bryce a flash of pale cleavage that made that flame ignite to a scorching heat. "Thank you. I decided to tone down the Goth look for you, just to show you I can dress reasonably normal."

"You didn't have to do that. Don't ever not be yourself. You do look stunning though." She hid her hands under the table and gripped her knees. Anything to stop herself from reaching over the table to grasp on tight to Scarlet's hands to try to anchor herself in this moment. "You must get your looks from your mother because as nice a guy as your dad is, I can't think you got all that pretty from him."

Scarlet's smile widened. "Well, aren't you sweet? My mom was a redhead so I got my coloring from her. The stubborn jaw too, according to Grandma."

"I know you lost her when you were just a kid. I'm sorry about that."

"It was hard, but Dad and Grandma got me through it."

"Your grandma's the old lady who lives next door to Trent and Juliet, right?"

"Yes, and she's very excited that she gets to be an honorary grandma to their child. She's knitting a baby blanket for them as a gift." Scarlet gave Bryce a relieved look. "Took the pressure off me and her not so subtle hinting that she needed a great-grandchild to bounce on her knee. I owe Trent big time for that."

"They're a great couple."

"They're the couple to aspire to," Scarlet said. "To be taken into their circle of friends is great. I love spending time with them and Monica and the rest of Trent's extended family." She leaned forward again. "Though Kayleigh wears me out. That kid is wound tighter than the Energizer Bunny."

"Trent does seem to be the only one to calm her down."

"Kayleigh was pretty much an only child for so long because of Juliet being so much older. Now she's got friends of all ages to play with and she's in her element."

"You'd think she was Trent's sister."

Scarlet laughed. "Juliet has said the same. When Kayleigh made Juliet take her to get her hair cut short, Juliet knew her sister was growing up. But she has said when Kayleigh wants her first tattoo Trent has to deal with the fallout from her parents!"

"Trent has tattoos?"

"She's got a gorgeous one dedicated to Juliet on her arm. And some Space Invaders on the other. Do you have any, Bryce?"

"Hell no. I'm not that fond of needles, but the stint in the hospital cured me of that phobia fast."

"You should get one. They're great reminders of things that have touched our lives."

Bryce grimaced and her hand stopped halfway to her face. "I think I have enough reminders." She lifted her head and saw Scarlet's eyes full of sympathy and something else.

"All the real heroes get scars when they battle," she said simply.

"And Harry Potter."

"Please tell me you didn't get Kayleigh started on that love of hers?"

"Apparently, my scar is cool." Bryce couldn't see it herself, but the acceptance from a stranger was still curiously heartwarming.

Scarlet's gaze never wavered from Bryce's face. "It's more than cool, it's *you*. You can take your cap off, Bryce. I'd like to see those pretty blue eyes of yours tonight."

Anything Bryce could have possibly thought to answer with was interrupted by a waiter hovering to hand them their menus and take their drink order. Bryce noticed that Scarlet paid more attention to her than she did to her ordering. The feeling of acceptance from Scarlet stoked that flame inside all the higher. Once the waiter had left, Bryce took her cap off.

❖

Trent padded into the bedroom intent on a very early night cuddling with a tired Juliet and maybe a quick go on her PS Vita with Killzone Mercenary once Juliet had fallen asleep. She was surprised to find Juliet spread out on her side, naked, and patting Trent's side of the bed invitingly. All thoughts of her game disappeared.

"I thought you were tired." Trent carefully got in beside her. Her hand went to the baby bump, smoothing a path across the tight skin.

"I am, but not that tired. I want you."

Never one to say no to anything Juliet wanted, Trent eased closer. "How do you want me?" she whispered as she stroked Juliet's hair back behind an ear.

"Sitting back against the headboard so I can be sat in your lap. Is that okay?"

Trent loved how considerate Juliet always was of her anxiety of being placed on her back in their lovemaking. The terror of that position had eased considerably with Juliet's patience and love, but Trent appreciated that Juliet still asked. Besides, there was an added bonus now when Juliet took that position. She helped Juliet up to straddle her hips. The weight of Juliet's stomach rested on Trent's flat belly, and she sucked in the gasp she always experienced when Juliet was in this position. Unable to stop herself, Trent ran her hands lovingly around the bump, delighting in the heaviness and the heat pressed against herself. For a moment, it felt like she and Juliet shared the baby between them, the roundness of what they had created fused to Trent's skin too. She loved it; it made her feel closer to the baby and to Juliet.

"Can you feel how much the baby has grown in the last month? My stomach feels huge." Juliet leaned in more, pressing into Trent's grasp.

"It's beautiful. *You're* beautiful. And you're also seriously fucking sexy like this. I could spend all day just looking at you and touching you." Trent leaned forward to kiss Juliet's lips. "You're both amazing. I still can't believe sometimes that you are both mine."

"All yours, especially for the diaper changes." Juliet grinned down at her and tugged Trent back for another kiss, rougher this time, growing in urgency. She growled against Trent's mouth. "But this bump does stop me from just lying properly on you and taking you like I want to."

Trent shivered at the promise laden words. "We can work around that. We always do." She reached up to cup Juliet's face, rubbing her thumbs against cheeks made fuller with pregnancy. "You really are the most beautiful woman I have ever seen." She traced a fingertip across Juliet's smiling lips, lingering to accept the soft kiss given. Trent's eyes drank in the devoted expression that shone from Juliet's eyes. Trent had never dared hope to see such a look meant just for her.

"You're just excited because these got even bigger once my belly did." Juliet took Trent's hands and cupped them under her breasts.

Trent grinned. Juliet had never been small in the breast department, and now she was noticeably larger. Mindful of how sensitive and sore Juliet's breasts could now be, Trent rolled a thumb over a darkened nipple gently. Juliet drew in a shaky breath and Trent stilled, worried she'd caused more pain than pleasure.

"So good," Juliet crooned, encouraging Trent further in her ministrations.

Trent leaned forward and slowly swirled her tongue over and around the hardening nipple, sucking it into her mouth then releasing it with an audible pop. Juliet bucked in her lap, and her excitement smeared across Trent's abdomen. Juliet began rocking in place. Trent desperately wanted to guide her hips into a firmer rhythm but was torn between seeking out the source of the wetness or caressing all of Juliet's body that she could reach.

"You're teasing me," Juliet said, holding Trent's hands together on her chest.

"I can't touch you enough, you're so fucking gorgeous." She squeezed a nipple between her fingertips, watching as it stiffened and reddened. "God, this never grows old."

"Even though I'm unable to lie on my back for long now?"

Trent pulled Juliet as close as she could to reassure her. "You'll be flat on your back soon enough after the baby is born," she whispered wickedly and laughed at Juliet's huff of indignation. "Besides, this bump has definitely made us more creative."

"Oh, honey, you had no problems in that area before you got me pregnant." Juliet shifted again on Trent's lap, rubbing herself harder against Trent's belly. "I need you," she said, lifting up a little so that Trent could slip a hand between their bodies. Trent was greeted by a heated sex that was soaked with Juliet's desire.

"God, you're dripping, Jule." She trailed her fingers across Juliet's labia, gathering up the moisture and spreading it all around her exposed clit. Trent smiled at Juliet's moan as she rubbed around the hardened bud and then gathered more moisture from the source. Juliet's hips jerked at Trent's questing fingers.

"In me now," she ordered, grasping at Trent's shoulders and angling her hips forward.

"In good time," Trent said, spreading kisses all over Juliet's breasts. She smiled against Juliet's heated flesh as Juliet tugged on Trent's hair impatiently.

"No, now. I need you in me. Your tongue is driving me crazy, and if you don't move those fingers where I—" She let out a breathy groan when Trent complied, easing two fingers inside her.

"Who knew pregnant ladies could be so demanding?" Trent teased her. She sucked on a nipple harshly, making Juliet squeal.

"I love it." Trent felt Juliet's walls tighten around her fingers, holding her captive where Juliet needed her the most. Trent's other hand was against Juliet's back, holding her steady as Trent began pumping inside. Trent knew how Juliet's center of balance had changed with the added weight on her front. It was just another excuse to hold her close.

"Can you feel me?" Juliet asked, eyes closed, her head flung back and her long hair cascading down her spine.

Trent could feel everything—the tightening of Juliet's warm walls; the slick, hot wetness that sucked her fingers in deeper; the sweet scent of Juliet's arousal surrounding them and flooding Trent's senses.

Juliet steadied herself by holding on to Trent's breasts. Much smaller than Juliet's, they still served their purpose as Juliet tightened her grip. Her fingers chafed across Trent's nipples and only served to drive Trent to push into Juliet faster, dragging gasps from Juliet's throat.

"Come on, sweetheart, come for me. Let me have you."

Juliet's voice rang out clear as she shouted Trent's name as she came. Trent felt the sweet release of Juliet's passion soak her hand. She rubbed Juliet gently through the spasms until Juliet tugged at her wrist and Trent dutifully pulled out. Juliet fell into her arms, and Trent helped her down onto her side so they could snuggle. Trent ran her hand over Juliet's stomach, painting it with her wetness, signing her name across Juliet's skin.

"I think we rocked the baby to sleep." Trent felt for the telltale signs of the baby swimming around and shifting inside. All was quiet. "Sleep tight, Newt." Trent spoke against Juliet's belly, laying a kiss there before moving back up to plant a longer, more sensuous kiss on Juliet's smiling lips.

"Don't think you can make me come that hard and leave me breathless so that you can call our child that name and think you can get away with it. And you're lucky I let you use 'fuck' still in the bedroom, otherwise you'd be bankrupt and our child would be going to Yale." She ran her hand down Trent's chest and pinched her quickly, making Trent gasp at the swift moment of pain.

"Hey!" she grumbled, but Juliet's hand was already moving on, trailing down Trent's belly and lower still. Juliet shifted more comfortably into Trent's side, moving her hand to slip between Trent's legs. Trent pulled Juliet closer, letting her legs part wider so that Juliet could reach where Trent was ready for her. Juliet traced random patterns over Trent's clit. Shocks of electricity made Trent writhe under her as Juliet nipped at Trent's breast while her index finger rubbed harder with each second. Trent's hold tightened. She knew she didn't need much to be pushed over the edge. She never did in Juliet's care. Her hips left the bed as they pumped erratically under Juliet's handling. Trent loved that Juliet knew how far to go. Trent could do soft and gentle, but sometimes hard and fast was more her want. She muffled a cry in the pillow as she exploded in pleasure. Juliet continued to touch her, helping her ride out the powerful spasms that tore through her. Juliet finally lifted her mouth from Trent's tortured nipple. Trent groaned aloud at the loss of her warm mouth.

"Fuck, you are so good at that." Trent sighed, nuzzling into Juliet's neck and laying a line of kisses along her jaw.

"I miss having you in my mouth," Juliet grumbled, rubbing at Trent's belly fretfully.

"You'll be back on your knees too. I'll make doubly sure of that."

Juliet snorted with laughter. "Don't you mean you'll sit on my face again without fear of hurting the bump?"

"I don't want to hurt either of you. And the fact is you're so much bigger now. I worry about you hurting your back trying to find the perfect position just to get me off." Trent kissed her lovingly. "You're not leaving me feeling unloved. You're still rocking my world."

"It's not the same though."

"No," Trent said. "But the wild 'take me anywhere' sex has only temporarily been put on hold until the baby arrives and we can get back to normal."

"And what if when the baby is here it's never normal again?"

Trent couldn't fail to miss the fear in Juliet's voice. She hooked a finger under Juliet's chin and lifted her head so she could meet her eyes. "Then we create a new normal. It wouldn't pay us to get too set in our ways, would it?" She kissed Juliet's nose gently. "And when we want loud, boisterous, swinging from the rafters sex, we'll call on Uncle Elton to come take the little tyke out for bonding time with a suitable male role model."

"Suitable?" Juliet said, settling comfortably into Trent's side, her head resting on a breast and her ample belly crowding over Trent's length.

"I use the term loosely." Trent ran her hand through Juliet's hair. "I love you. I will do everything to keep you and this baby happy, I promise."

"I love you too, Mama Bear." Juliet hugged Trent to her. She let out a sigh that Trent instantly recognized. She chuckled.

"Your hormones are raging tonight, aren't they?"

Juliet shifted her head a little to nip at Trent's skin in admonishment. "They warned us that there might be a period where the horny hormones would take over." She grabbed Trent's hand and placed it back on her breast.

Trent smiled then kissed her, teasing Juliet's lips open with a persistent tongue. "I'm loving this trimester best of all."

Chapter Ten

The waiter discreetly placed the bill on the table between Bryce and Scarlet. Scarlet snatched it up.

"Hey, I would like to pay," Bryce said, but Scarlet playfully held the bill out of her reach.

"I asked you so I get to pay. You can pay next time and I'll order two desserts."

Bryce brightened at the thought of another night like they had just shared. She'd barely touched any alcohol, but she was lightheaded from the sheer pleasure it was to be in Scarlet's company. She was a joy to listen to, and Bryce had been enthralled by her.

"Bryce?"

Bryce's head whipped around at an all too familiar and very unwelcome voice. Gerri stood just a step away, fixing her jacket to leave. Bryce felt ice water pour through her veins at the sight of her, picture perfect as always.

"You're looking…." Gerri couldn't take her eyes from Bryce's forehead, and a grimace was already slipping onto her lips. She didn't appear to be able to finish her sentence so Bryce took pity on her.

"I look like shit, but thanks for your concern."

Gerri bristled at Bryce's dismissive tone. She turned her attention to Scarlet who was looking at her with great interest. "And you are?"

"Scarlet."

Gerri's face darkened. She narrowed her eyes at Bryce. "I wouldn't have thought you'd have been out in public so soon after your…."

Bryce was less than amused that Gerri still couldn't speak of the accident. "It's been nearly two months, Gerri. Life moves on. Just like you did." Bryce tried not to cringe as the angry words left her lips. She had no chance of moving on when every time she closed her eyes at night she was back in that car surrounded by the dying.

"You still doing manual labor?"

"Yes, I'm still plastering walls," Bryce ground out.

Scarlet stepped in, obviously seeing Bryce's growing discomfort.

"And what do you do, Ms….?"

"Gerri. I'm one of the managing directors at Gregson, Townsend, and Moore. No doubt you've heard of them?"

Scarlet shook her head. "Can't say that I have, to be honest." Her put-down was done with a smile. "Must be impressive though."

Bryce wondered why she'd never noticed until it was too late that all of Gerri's self-esteem was linked to that damned job of hers.

"I'd like to think I'm going places," Gerri boasted, her eyes on Bryce.

"Then don't let us keep you any longer." Scarlet stood, and Bryce was surprised by just how tall Scarlet appeared. She looked around the table and took in the lethal high heels Scarlet wore. She towered over Gerri and deliberately looked down on her from her vantage point.

Gerri's eyes swept over Scarlet from head to toe. She looked back at Bryce with poorly disguised annoyance. "You still have the power to draw the beauties to you. How do you manage that looking like you do now?"

The words cut deep into Bryce's flesh, deeper than the scar ran. Bryce was momentarily left speechless at the cruelty.

"Oh, believe me, it *was* her looks that drew me to her initially." Scarlet stepped closer to Gerri, staring her down. "But for some women, their beauty goes way beyond skin deep. And then there are others"—Scarlet purposely ran her gaze across Gerri's face—"whose beauty is as fake as the accent they employ to perfect their rich and successful façade."

Bryce was surprised that Scarlet had caught that the accent Gerri spoke with was not entirely her own. She had been astonished when Gerri had slipped one time and spoken with more of a Southern drawl than the hard-clipped Boston tone she tried to perfect. It was just another thing she used to further herself in business.

Gerri leveled burning eyes on Bryce. "It looks like you've found a woman more on your level than I ever was."

"No, actually she's way above me, so subsequently miles above you." Bryce shook her head at her. "Just leave, Gerri. I see no point in engaging you in conversation if you can't even be civil in a public place."

"You were better before the accident," Gerri said.

"Yeah, well, I was realizing what a bitch you were well before that night too."

"You seemed happy enough riding on my coattails."

"That's because you were hanging off my arm with a death grip. Get back to Amber. I'm sure she's amply prepared to console you like she was in the hospital room where you made your hateful Beauty and the Beast comment."

Gerri's face displayed her discomfort at being found out for her spiteful nature.

"Yes, I was awake. I heard your comments. I read the letter you left me. You walked away before I was even out of my hospital bed. So walk away again now and count your blessings you don't have to face this every morning over the breakfast table." Bryce deliberately ran her finger the length of her scar and watched as

Gerri winced. "Move on like I'm sure you already have and this *conversation* is just one last twist of the knife in my gut for your petty amusement."

With a huff, Gerri scurried away from the table and left the restaurant, but Bryce didn't watch her leave. Her eyes instead were on Scarlet who only sat back down in her seat after making sure Gerri left. There was a palpable fury blazing in her eyes. Bryce found it only made her more striking.

"Man, what an utter bitch!" Scarlet said. "She's damn lucky the waiter had removed my chopsticks because I would have been tempted to stab her with them."

Bryce laughed shakily. She could feel her whole body trembling after the scene Gerri had just caused. She slipped her cap back on, her bravado for the evening effectively snuffed out.

"How the hell did you hook up with that woman?"

"A blind date set up through a friend of a friend."

"Bryce, honey, you need better friends."

Bryce smiled at Scarlet's exaggerated drawl. She had mimicked Gerri's tone with a cutting precision. "She wasn't so bad before she climbed over a few bodies to get higher up the corporate ladder. After that, she got harder to like. She made me feel like arm candy." Bryce shrugged. "Whatever attracted her to me got well and truly destroyed in the crash." She waved a still shaking hand in the direction of her face.

"Then she's as stupid as she is fake because, scar or no scar, Bryce, you're still a handsome woman."

Bryce snorted at her softly.

"I'm not saying that to be kind, Bryce. It's the truth."

Bryce looked up at Scarlet's sincere tone. "Kayleigh said it was a mark like her favorite magic-wielding hero has. I prefer that to being likened as the Beast to Gerri's Belle."

"You're no beast. Take it from me, Gerri was an utter ass for letting you go, but I'm glad she did."

Bryce looked up again and Scarlet's smile dazzled her.

"It meant I get to be with you, and I've loved tonight."

Snorting, Bryce shook her head. Scarlet held her hands up.

"No, seriously. Great food, wonderful company, a cabaret to end the evening. It's been great." Scarlet leaned across the table. "So much so I'm going to dutifully accompany you to the bus stop now and kiss you good night before you board your ride home."

"Confident, aren't we?" Bryce was amazed by the look on Scarlet's face. It lit up her eyes and made her smile radiant, and it was all directed at Bryce.

"I'm hopeful, very hopeful, where you're concerned." Scarlet retrieved her credit card back from the waiter and gestured for Bryce to lead the way out. Scarlet tucked her arm through Bryce's and crowded close.

"Thank you for tonight." Bryce couldn't remember when she'd had such an enjoyable evening. Certainly never with Gerri. She'd always had a rhyme and reason behind every dinner date.

"I enjoy your company," Scarlet said. "Both in this setting and at work. You're very easy to be around." They drew to a halt at the bus stop. Scarlet leaned forward, slid Bryce's cap up out of the way, and placed a tender kiss on her scar.

Bryce all but leapt out of her skin at the contact.

"The only place I'll expect you to be a Beast is in the bedroom, Bryce Donovan," Scarlet said with a very sinful looking grin.

Before Bryce could utter a word, Scarlet kissed her properly. For a moment, Bryce forgot everything except for the feeling of Scarlet's warm mouth on her own. She tasted of the wine they had just drunk and something that was uniquely Scarlet alone. Bryce released a disgruntled sound when Scarlet pulled back. She hadn't wanted the kiss to end.

"Your bus is coming," Scarlet said regretfully and gave Bryce a hug. "I'll see you at work tomorrow."

Unable to form coherent thoughts, Bryce just nodded and flagged the bus down. She wasn't sure how much she overpaid for her ride in her fumbling for change, but she didn't really care. She took a seat by a window and saw Scarlet still standing there, watching her go. Bryce smiled and mouthed *good night* as the bus pulled away. She caught sight of her reflection in the window and ran a finger along her scar. Lipstick colored her fingertip, left behind by Scarlet's tender kiss. It had been the first time anyone, other than herself and the doctors, had touched her there.

Gerri's cruel words weighed heavy on Bryce's heart. They had tainted some of the pleasure Bryce had felt being back out in public.

The accident had left her emotionally wrecked. Scarlet would come to realize that truth all too soon, Bryce feared. The scars on the outside were nothing compared to the ones she carried inside.

CHAPTER ELEVEN

Trent smiled indulgently as Juliet finished fastening up the buttons on Trent's work shirt and then fussed fixing her tie in place.

"You do know I'm a big girl now and can dress myself?" Trent gently held Juliet's hips and tugged her a little closer. The baby bump kept them apart.

"Maybe I'm just getting some practice in." Juliet smoothed Trent's collar to her satisfaction.

"Sweetheart, I don't think the baby will be wearing a shirt and tie just yet. You're awfully cute. This nesting thing is quite something to watch."

Juliet slapped at Trent's chest playfully. "Hush now. I'm not that bad."

"You have placed fluffy pillows on the sofa in my game room. Don't think I haven't noticed their intrusion."

"I happen to sit on it and I need something comfortable in my condition."

Trent just laughed at her. "Nice try, Jule, but face it. You're nesting in my game room. I'm surprised I haven't found something draped over my gamer chair decorated with ducklings or baby sheep."

"I'm not *that* bad." Juliet hid her face in Trent's shoulder. "I can't help it. It's like my brief craving for fried okra. I can't explain it. It just *is*."

"I'm glad I had the doughnut craving. You can keep the veggies." Trent kissed the top of Juliet's head. "Are you going into work today? You were kind of restless all night."

"I thought I might go get some fresh air."

"Juliet." Trent drew out her name in a warning. "Promise me you won't try to lift, move, or attempt to do too much today. You still have shadows under those beautiful eyes of yours." Trent smoothed her thumb gently across Juliet's cheek.

"I don't have to promise. Monica watches me like a hawk so even if I dared to attempt lifting anything bigger than a flower petal I get yelled at by the Pregnancy Police."

Juliet's pout was so adorable Trent had to kiss it. "You know we just want to keep you and the baby safe. There's no need for someone in your condition to be lifting stuff when you and Monica have non-pregnant people there to do the grunt work. I know I'm hovering, I know I'm probably worrying for nothing, but I also know you can't help yourself. Hence you being out more by Monica's side than here in your office crunching the numbers since you started this business together."

Trent tried to sound exasperated, but she'd been made well aware Juliet wouldn't slow down until she had to. Juliet had come from a high-powered job that demanded all her time and energy. Trying to get her to not put the same work ethic into the landscaping business she and Monica ran was difficult. Trent just needed her not to take any chances, for her sake and the baby's.

"I'll be careful, I promise. I'll just play in the dirt with the plants like I usually do." Juliet looked up. "I'll also try to get details off Scarlet or Bryce about their date last night."

"They had a date? Together?"

"Scarlet is quite enamored with the resident plasterer."

"Bryce seems nice," Trent said. "Kind of quiet for Scarlet who seems…."

"All high heels and loud guitars?"

Trent chuckled at Juliet's very apt description. In some of her heels, Scarlet could even look Trent in the eye.

"Bryce is very quiet, but I'm sensing that's more since her accident. I'm hoping Scarlet can bring her out of herself a little."

"So you're promising me you won't do anything strenuous but instead will spend the day gathering gossip?"

"Nothing new there," Juliet said. "Who knew a landscape firm could be such a hotbed of intrigue?"

"So long as you don't add to it," Trent growled in her ear. "You're both all mine." Her hand lay possessively on Juliet's belly.

Juliet snuggled as best she could in Trent's arms. "Like you ever have to doubt that." She tugged Trent down by her tie. "I'll be careful today like I am every day you go through your damnable list of things I can't do."

"Thank you." Trent's hand moved on top of Juliet's stomach. "Newt, you look after Mommy today, do you hear me? No making her sick, no running around in there too much, and no making her so sleepy she naps in a wheelbarrow."

"If I slept in a wheelbarrow Monica would plant me." Juliet kissed Trent gently then took a bite at her lower lip. "And quit calling the baby Newt!"

Trent bent to lay a loud smacking kiss on Juliet's belly. "Mama loves you, Newt." She accepted the smack on her head with a grin. "Newt was a heroic survivor. Well, she was until they screwed all that up in the next film. Assho—" Trent barely stopped in time from owing another dollar. "Stupid writers," she quickly amended.

"We still need to pick a proper name. We haven't got that long left to decide."

"We'll find something suitable and fitting for whatever we get. You've got your baby name book. Read through it again today, and stay away from large pots and heavy lifting."

Juliet let out a grumble. "I'll kill Monica for squealing on me that one time I tried to move that bag of compost on my own. I have never lived it down since. Chain me to the sofa, why don't you?"

"I would, but you'd charm your way out of it. I have no defenses with you anyway, but I like this." She smoothed Juliet's belly. "I'm defenseless to your every desire."

"And here I was thinking the horny hormones were just mine." Juliet ran her hands over Trent's shirt, cupping her breasts and squeezing just enough to make Trent groan.

"If I get to share the food cravings then I sure as hell am sharing the fun sex ones." Trent kissed Juliet lovingly. Reluctantly, she pulled back. "You're going to make me late for work if you keep squeezing like that." Juliet's pout made her all the more reluctant to leave. She kissed her again, harder. Then again because she couldn't stop. Their breaths grew ragged and their hands began to explore. Trent fumbled in her pocket to pull out her wallet, all without breaking their kiss. She eventually gasped for air and fished out a dollar bill. Juliet graced her with that slow blink that drove Trent wild. She thought it was the sexiest thing she had ever seen. A blink that was just a fraction longer than usual, but when Juliet looked at her again it was either to call her out on whatever shit she had just spouted or it was to deliver a look of pure lust. Trent felt her clit harden at the look Juliet gave her now.

"Say it," Juliet ordered.

"Fuck me. You can put the money in the jar after."

❖

The extraordinary feeling of happiness Scarlet was experiencing made her turn up her music another notch. She knew the other workers were now in the house next door so no one could complain. She enjoyed having the building to herself to play her music loud and dance when the mood took her. She'd laid her paintbrush down momentarily when a particular piece of music came on and had felt the urge to celebrate it. Lost in the song, deaf to all around her but the pulsing beat, Scarlet let the music wash over her as she swung her body sensuously to the rhythm. With her eyes half closed at the emotions she always felt from this particular song, Scarlet didn't see someone standing in the open doorway until it was too late. Her hands flew to her chest over her racing heart.

"Oh my God, Bryce! You nearly gave me a heart attack!"

Bryce was leaning against the doorjamb with a growing smile on her face. "That seems only fair seeing as I nearly had one just from watching you dance like that." She pushed herself off the door and took the few steps closer to Scarlet. "I've never seen anything quite so sexy."

"It looks more impressive when I'm not wearing coveralls." Scarlet tugged at the baggy overalls she was only half wearing. The top half was pulled down and tied around her waist. It revealed a tight white undershirt that clung in all the right places.

Bryce stepped closer still, invading Scarlet's personal space. "You kissed me last night then sent me on my way."

Unable to stop herself, Scarlet shivered at the low timbre Bryce's voice rumbled out at. "I had to leave something as an incentive for you to accept another date request."

"Like you're not incentive enough?"

Scarlet was thrilled by Bryce's appreciative look. "Well, aren't you sweet?" She sidled closer so that their hips bumped. "What brings you over here when I know you're working in a house two doors down?" She ran a finger down Bryce's arm and watched as the muscles twitched.

"I came to say hi and thank you for last night. I had a wonderful evening."

"Enough to do it again?" She smiled when Bryce nodded.

"I'd prefer somewhere less public though, if you wouldn't mind. I'm still feeling a little out of my element around too many people." Her hand fluttered nervously to her forehead before settling on Scarlet's hip. "But the next time it's on me. I'll try for us not to have a repeat performance of the evil ex right after dessert either."

"Good, because I think I'd be tempted to stomp all over her ass if she dared to unleash her vicious tongue in your direction again." Scarlet pressed a kiss on Bryce's smiling lips. "Good morning, by the way." She pulled back but noticed Bryce still had her eyes closed so she kissed her again, slower this time, with a little more pressure and definite need. Bryce's arms slipped around her and pulled her closer as they began languidly exploring each other's mouths.

Scarlet loved the feel of Bryce's lips against her own. She felt a tongue teasing her bottom lip, requesting entrance. Scarlet granted it and moaned as Bryce's agile tongue brushed against her own. Bryce tasted of fresh mint and a hint of her morning coffee. Scarlet couldn't taste her enough. Their breathing was ragged when they finally came up for air.

"I did only come in to say hello," Bryce said, resting her forehead against Scarlet's.

"I love how you say it." Scarlet tugged at Bryce's head, slipping her fingers through her pale hair. "My turn now." Her lips captured Bryce's once again. She then trailed her lips up over flushed cheekbones to deliver a kiss to Bryce's forehead.

"You're making me forget that I should be working and not fraternizing with the painter next door."

"But you fraternize so well." Scarlet whispered her words against Bryce's brow as she peppered soft kisses over the prominent scar. Bryce didn't wear her cap when she worked, and Scarlet could see that Bryce's hair was finally filling in again. She pouted when Bryce finally took a step back. She missed the heat from her.

"I'd better go before you tempt me any further," Bryce said.

"You'd better come back here and have lunch with me." The look Bryce favored her with reassured Scarlet.

"I'll be here."

Scarlet couldn't help but tease her. "Do you want to stay in here and we can maybe make out like teenagers while we share bites of our food?"

Bryce laughed but shook her head. "No. I don't want us to be all about a quick fumble in a half painted room."

"You don't look like the kind of girl who fumbles at anything, Bryce."

"No, but you make it very hard for me to slow down and apply the brakes with the way you make me feel. I figure if we sit outside with the others milling back and forth I'll be less inclined to take a kiss further. At least, not until we're both certain this is what we want."

"And if I said I'm more than certain now?" Scarlet tugged at the waistband of Bryce's black jeans, pulling her closer. Bryce resisted with a deep chuckle that made Scarlet's insides clench with the rush of arousal.

"Then I say let me take you out and we'll see what happens."

Scarlet's fingers slipped inside Bryce's waistband and brushed at soft warm skin. Unable to stop herself, she let her fingers linger and traced a lazy circle idly around Bryce's belly button. Bryce jumped as if electrocuted and let out a whine. Scarlet didn't hesitate in keeping Bryce in place while she felt stomach muscles tremble and twitch.

"Oh fuck, you've got to stop that right now." Bryce's hand trapped Scarlet's beneath her own, inadvertently pressing Scarlet's hand further into her jeans.

"Do you know I sometimes peek in to watch you working? It's just so I can catch you reaching up because your shirts ride up and expose your skin. It makes me want to kiss every inch of your stomach I see revealed." Scarlet stole a kiss from Bryce. With some reluctance, Scarlet withdrew her hand from Bryce's jeans. But not without one last lingering scrape of her fingernails scoring gently across Bryce's quivering flesh.

"Fuck." Bryce's voice shook. She grabbed at Scarlet's arm and stopped her from leaving. "You're going to drive me crazy, aren't you?"

"Only in all the best ways."

CHAPTER TWELVE

The Tweedy Contractors company offices hadn't changed much since Scarlet had been a child. Computers had taken over from the filing cabinets full of the records of completed or future jobs. Scarlet's growth as a child had been measured by what letter of the alphabet on the filing system she had reached. All the company's details were ably run by Alice Judson. She was her dad's long serving office manager. Her delight at seeing Scarlet enter the office trailing after her father had made Scarlet feel five years old again. Her father had disappeared into his office to return a call Alice had told him needed to be dealt with, leaving her and Scarlet alone.

"Well, it's about time you found your way back home, young lady. I was thinking you'd forgotten Missouri existed on the map," Alice said. She took a hold of Scarlet's hands and looked her over. "Haven't you grown into even more of a beauty?"

Scarlet smiled. "I was only gone three years, Alice, and I still came home for the holidays. I haven't changed that much and I saw you at Christmas."

Alice waved her objections away. "Your father has shown me all the photos you sent him. He loves showing them off. You're very talented in that field, young lady. Are you serious about that work?"

Scarlet nodded. "It's more than just a hobby, Alice. I love it. It lets me be creative, and you know that's where my heart lies."

"And yet you're here, helping your father out."

"Once he knew I was losing my job, he started with gentle hints, then the not so subtle coercion. That evolved into the 'I'm not getting any younger' comments. I know he wants me to take over from him, but…"

"But you're not sure if you want it," Alice said.

"I love the manual work. I know it's odd, but I enjoy the slapping of paint on a wall. It's so different from the techniques I employ when I do my portrait paintings. But with my camera work, I can capture a moment and suspend it in time. I don't want those moments lost being shut in this office having to hustle up work for the guys Dad employs. That's a little too much responsibility on these shoulders."

Alice squeezed her arm gently. "You're such a free spirit. Just like your mother was. Victor could never quite keep that girl's feet on the ground."

"I'm grounded, Alice, but I think the earth beneath my feet is a different soil from what Dad wants me to grow roots in."

Alice burst out laughing. "Poetic too. You're way more than just your mother's image."

"What do you think she'd have wanted me to do?"

"She'd have wanted you to live your life your own way. She never got the chance to fulfill her dreams. Life's too short, sweetheart. But your father has had your future planned from the minute he held you in his arms. His business was always meant for you. You're his sole heir."

"I don't know that I can do this. I'd rather just be the painter, plain and simple. I don't want to have to deal with the financial and administrative side of Tweedy Contractors."

"There are courses. You could learn."

Scarlet made a face. "But I'm learning what makes me happy and this"—she gestured around the office—"I don't think this is it."

"Then you'd better find a way to let your father down gently because he's set his heart on you running this business once he retires."

"He's got years yet," Scarlet said. She wanted her own life to live and not take over her father's.

"Then with that thought in mind, you've got ample time to learn if you can fill his shoes or take a brave step forward in your own." Alice patted Scarlet's cheek gently. "You'll make the right choice either way. You are your daddy's girl, after all."

❖

The unrecognized ring tone playing from her pocket distracted Bryce from opening her front door. She removed her phone and stared at the caller ID. She answered it quickly.

"Did you program a new ring tone into my phone without me somehow seeing you do it?" she asked. Scarlet's soft laughter made her smile regardless.

"You left it unattended one lunchtime. It was too much temptation. I wanted you to have something suitable when I called you so I Bluetoothed you my ring tone."

"You are aware I don't know your music?" Bryce keyed her lock and pushed inside. She tossed her keys on the table and settled onto her sofa to talk to Scarlet.

"It's 'Storytime' by Nightwish," Scarlet said.

Bryce was still none the wiser but nodded even though she knew Scarlet couldn't see her. "So, how can I help you other than to confirm your light-fingered appropriation of my phone worked?"

"Should I mention you should lock your phone at all times?"

"I'll take that under advisement," Bryce said drolly.

"I was wondering if you'd care to join me at my apartment for some takeout tonight? I realize you're probably on your way home still."

"I've just literally walked in."

"Oh."

Bryce looked around her empty apartment, so tired of the same four walls staring back at her. "But I can wash up, change out of my work clothes, and come over if that's what you want."

"I do." Scarlet's voice was eager to Bryce's ears. "I live right by an excellent Chinese takeout. I'll order in and we can eat as soon as you arrive."

Bryce wondered at Scarlet's last-minute invitation. "Are you okay?"

"Yeah. I just…would like to see you."

"Does this have anything to do with you skipping out of work early with your dad today? Are you sure you're okay? Oh God, is it him? Is *he* okay?"

"He's fine, I'm fine, don't worry so. I just need a friendly face tonight."

"And you picked me?" Bryce couldn't help the surprise that escaped her voice.

Scarlet chuckled. "You need to realize, Bryce Donovan, yours is the face I want to see most of all."

The sweet burst of joy wasn't something Bryce had felt for some time. It came with a bittersweet pang. Her fingers itched to touch her scar. Maybe if she traced the length enough times she could make it finally disappear, that and the nightmares it brought along with it.

"Give me your address and I'll go find a bus route." She heard Scarlet hesitate. "What?"

"Thank you for doing this."

Bryce couldn't help smiling. "Well, maybe you need to realize that yours is the face I want to see the most too." Scarlet's low moan sent shivers down Bryce's spine. It was deep and rich and disturbingly sensual.

"Hurry."

Bryce was already shucking off her work boots and searching for clean clothes.

❖

Soft, measured footsteps sounded in the hallway outside Trent's game room. She looked up from scrolling along the tiles her PS4's home screen displayed. She caught sight of Juliet as she disappeared into the nursery. Controller in hand, Trent started her game for the evening then selected the online multiplayer mode. Before she picked up her headset, she heard Juliet come into the room behind her. Her hands were occupied with a cup of herbal tea, which was her latest craving, a book, and a patterned blanket draped over her arm.

"Sweetheart, if you're tired you should go rest in bed." Trent had been worried to come home to find Juliet looking pale and worn. She'd started to fuss but had been shot down shortly in a fashion that was so uncharacteristic of Juliet that it had made Trent even more concerned. So Trent had decided a tactical withdrawal from Juliet's line of *ire* was her best call. She had an online match of Call of Duty Advanced Warfare set up with a friend in Texas so Trent was settled in for a night of playing.

A soft kiss was planted on top of Trent's head as Juliet shuffled behind her.

"I'm sorry."

Trent craned her neck to follow Juliet's path. "Jule, you know I'm just worried about—"

"I know," Juliet interrupted, settling herself down heavily on the sofa and fidgeting until she was comfortable. "I overdid it today. I realize that now. I just didn't think I'd get this tired so fast."

Trent looked at her, waiting for more.

"So, I'll start being more mindful of that fact and not push myself beyond what me and the baby can take, Mama Bear."

For once, Trent didn't smile at the nickname Juliet had come up with for her. "How about all these hours you're still working?"

"I'll have a talk with Monica tomorrow. Maybe it's time to limit my exposure in the actual field and start bringing my work home with me."

"You have an office here. It's not far from our bed if you need to nap." Trent couldn't help it; she let out a sigh. "You look tired. Are you sure I can't tuck you into bed?"

"I want to spend time with you tonight. You know I find it oddly relaxing watching you play." Juliet took a sip from her tea. "Your baby is sapping my energy today."

"So Newt is mine when he or she is being fractious?"

"Yes, of course." Juliet settled on the sofa and closed her eyes.

A message came on the TV screen announcing that her gaming partner had just come online and was accepting her gaming invite. Trent picked up her headphones. "Hi, PJ. You ready to blast some Atlas butt?" She listened to her friend's reply. "I will indeed tell Juliet hi from you." Trent looked over at her and smiled. "She's as beautiful as ever and has promised not to snore too loud through our playing if *my* baby keeps making her tired."

Juliet cracked open one eye and favored her with a look.

"No, I don't know how she can possibly sleep through all this noise either. I'm guessing though, with that talent, it means that when the baby cries for its midnight feeds it will be me who'll be hauling her sorry ass out of bed."

"And don't you forget it," Juliet muttered and nestled in deeper into the cushions, draping the blanket over her.

With one last look at Juliet's worn-out features, Trent pulled her attention back to PJ's voice and they started their game. Before too long, Trent was aware that Juliet had fallen asleep amid the shouting and shooting.

Throughout the hours-long gaming, Trent cast furtive looks over at Juliet. She was glad Juliet had sought out her company. That even though she was sleeping, she still wanted to be close to Trent. Trent knew her hovering was driving Juliet crazy, but seeing her exhaustion Trent had felt justified in calling her on it. She'd also sent off a text to Monica advising her that Juliet needed to slow down even more and to tread cautiously around Juliet's fluctuating moods. Trent, however, had been subjected to tempers worse than the one fueled by baby hormones. She'd take whatever Juliet threw at her because Juliet, grumpy or otherwise, never made Trent love her any less. Or feel less loved.

"Stop watching me. You're supposed to be playing your game." Juliet shifted on the sofa and settled back down.

"I can't help it. You're gorgeous," Trent replied then grimaced as another voice chimed in her earpiece. "No. Sorry, PJ. I'm sure you're way cute too, but Juliet has you beat in my eyes. I am too paying attention. See, I just shot that bastard. Goddamnit it, now I have to fork out another fucking dollar. Oh, for Christ's sake, just shoot me now. No, not you. You're supposed to be on my team!" Trent growled as she belatedly shut her mouth before any more swear words could escape. She heard Juliet snicker beside her. Trent spared her a swift glare. "If this child is naughty it so got that trait from you!"

Chapter Thirteen

The apartment Scarlet shared with Monica was nothing like what Bryce had imagined it to look like. Seated next to Scarlet on the sofa, food spread out on the table before them, Bryce could peruse the room at her leisure. It was light and spacious and surprisingly devoid of vampiric paraphernalia. Her eyes were drawn to a painting in progress that stood on an easel. It appeared to be Trent, looking stern faced and focused. Her right hand was outstretched in a pose resembling that of Neo from *The Matrix* halting bullets in mid-air. But instead of bullets, she was controlling a myriad of falling Space Invaders. The stark black, white, and green coloring made the picture look otherworldly. It was also incredibly lifelike.

"That picture is mesmerizing," Bryce said around a mouthful of food.

"Juliet commissioned it without Trent's knowledge. She wanted something for Trent to have in her gaming room seeing as there isn't enough wall space for a mural." Scarlet filled her plate and ate eagerly. "I am so hungry. I can't believe I missed out on lunch today."

"Tell me again why you're wasting your time decorating houses when you have that kind of talent at your disposal? That picture looks like a photograph and it's not even finished yet. It's so lifelike, Scarlet. It's incredible."

"The decorating pays the bills. These paintings are a labor of love. As are the photographs I take at the moment. I have just gotten my foot in the door at a photographic studio here, but it's not full-time like I had before. I need the money I earn from my day job to subsidize what I love doing the most."

"And then there's your dad insisting that you start learning the business." Bryce had heard all about today's hours spent at the office with Victor. "Scarlet, with this kind of talent, contracting is the last thing you should be doing."

"But how do I let my father down gently on that fact? He's made it abundantly clear the business is to be mine and I need to start learning it. He's even talked about clearing a desk in the office for me for when I'm 'ready.' I'm *never* going to be ready."

"You're going to have to fight him all the way, aren't you?" Bryce figured she knew enough about Scarlet that she wasn't going to just let Victor Tweedy steer her into a role she didn't want to fit into. She also knew Victor could be very persuasive to get his own way too.

"Pretty much, but he's my dad and I'm his only child… and you've heard this same argument for the last hour now that even I'm bored with it." Scarlet stuffed her mouth with food deliberately.

Bryce decided to change the subject. "I must have this Goth thing all wrong because you and Monica don't live like I expected you to."

"Monica keeps her coffin strictly in the bedroom with Igor her pet bat."

Bryce wasn't entirely sure she was teasing, but at Scarlet's cocky grin she conceded that maybe she needed to redefine her ideas of what Goth really was.

"Before this night is through, I'm putting some music on and you're going to educate your senses."

"You going to sing to me the whole time too?"

"I just might do that." Scarlet rested her hand on Bryce's leg. "Thank you for just dropping everything tonight and coming over here to listen to me whine and carry on about being the Chosen One in the Tweedy lineage."

"It was my pleasure. I got good food, excellent company, and you got an ear to bend. All I had planned was something reheated and another night staring at the TV." *Though not really seeing it and being frightened to fall asleep again like every single night.* Bryce was thankful for the distraction from her own thoughts. Being with Scarlet made that doubly enjoyable.

Scarlet laid her plate aside and edged closer to Bryce on the sofa. She rested her head on Bryce's shoulder. She traced a faint scar's path along Bryce's arm.

"I have a lot of those." Bryce felt Scarlet's finger run along the patterns left by broken glass and twisted metal.

"They don't frighten me."

Scarlet's warm touch moved across Bryce's skin, electrifying it under each gentle caress.

"And they certainly don't stop me from wanting to climb all over you." Scarlet planted a kiss on Bryce's neck.

Bryce shivered as soft lips found a particularly sensitive spot. Scarlet took advantage of this knowledge and kissed her again in the same place deliberately. The moan that shuddered out of Bryce's chest surprised them both. She twisted so she could taste those lips for herself. The sound that escaped Scarlet only made Bryce deepen the kiss more. She was pressed back into the corner of the sofa cushions as Scarlet eagerly settled herself over Bryce's length. The weight of Scarlet's body pressing down on her made Bryce burn with arousal. Bryce opened her legs and Scarlet eagerly slid herself between them, cradled by Bryce's thighs.

Scarlet speared her fingers through Bryce's hair, tugging at the shorter lengths at the nape of her neck. Her lips clung to Bryce's, her agile tongue tasted and teased until Bryce opened willingly and let her in. Bryce pulled Scarlet closer still, tightening her arms around Scarlet's slight frame.

Scarlet finally drew back a fraction. Her breathing was heavy and her eyes darkened in desire. "I swear I didn't invite you over here just for this."

"How disappointing." Bryce leaned up to plant a kiss on Scarlet's nose. "I'd have caught an earlier bus had I known this was your idea of dessert."

Scarlet chuckled and snuggled herself into Bryce's neck, wrapping her arms around her as best she could. "Tell me I'm not hurting your shoulder or ribs."

"You're on my good shoulder. And my ribs are more than capable of bearing your slight weight." Bryce was glad Scarlet had chosen the position she had. She'd have hated to have shown any weakness. She was tired of being held hostage while her body healed. The slight ache in her chest from Scarlet lying on her was a discomfort she was willing to endure. Having Scarlet in her arms was comfort enough.

"I could happily fall asleep like this," Scarlet mumbled, her breath heating Bryce's neck and her lips moving across her skin. "How about you?"

"I don't sleep anymore," Bryce admitted.

"Why?"

She asked it so softly that Bryce was unable to lie.

"Because when I sleep, the nightmares come and the dead don't stop dying." She heard Scarlet catch her breath and then the arms about her tightened more. After a long moment, Scarlet reached over Bryce's head to retrieve a remote off the side table. Soft instrumental music began playing.

"Then just rest with me while I hold you. I'd do anything in my power to keep those dreams away. Listen to the music and just let me hold you close." Scarlet kissed her. "I'll keep you safe, I promise." She linked her fingers with Bryce's and drew their hands together to rest on Bryce's chest.

Bryce noticed the differences in their hands. Her own were rough and blunt shaped whereas Scarlet's were long and tapered. The hands of an artist. Bryce brought their linked hands up to rest over her heart. She closed her eyes and reveled in the moment. Pressed this close, she could feel Scarlet's full breasts against her own. Scarlet's longer length curled into Bryce's shorter frame made her feel oddly protected. The scent of strawberries and sunshine clung to Scarlet's vibrant hair. Bryce pressed her face closer to breathe her in. The music in the room lulled her and the presence of Scarlet in her arms soothed her. Stripped of her usual coping mechanisms, Bryce slipped into sleep without a qualm.

❖

Bryce struggled against the seat belt suspending her upside down in the car. Pain lanced through her entire body. Blood poured into her eyes, blinding her. She shook her head harshly to try to clear her sight. Behind her she could hear the torturous moans and whimpers coming from the backseat. Desperately, Bryce tried to turn around to see if they were okay. She strained her ears, listening for every sign of life. The driver was already gone, ripped away by the truck that had hit them.

She heard a faint voice calling out. A woman's voice. Calling for *her*.

"Bryce?"

Bryce struggled even more to break free from her bounds. She knew that voice. She could hear Scarlet. *Scarlet* was in the backseat. Fingers fumbling, Bryce tore at the confining belt tying her in place. Agony ricocheted through her as her frantic wrestling jarred her fractured bones and wrenched the air from her lungs.

"*Bryce*?"

She tried so hard to break free from the seat belt. Her fingers grew bloodied as she forcibly tried to rip the belt in two. Her head pounded with an awareness she didn't want to acknowledge. *No one survives in the backseat*. Bryce began to wail, a low, desperate sound as her struggle intensified. She couldn't get free. She couldn't help. She was trapped. And so was Scarlet.

"Scarlet? *Scarlet*!"

❖

Bryce's screaming in the dream brought her abruptly awake to find Scarlet hovering above her, shaking her gently by her good shoulder.

"Scarlet?" Bryce's voice was raspy. For a moment, she wondered if she'd been screaming too. Her throat hurt that much.

"You were dreaming. I had to wake you up." Scarlet ran a comforting hand through the perspiration soaked hair on Bryce's forehead.

At the soft touch accidently touching her scar, Bryce lurched upward, nausea rolling through her gut. She scrambled out from under Scarlet, falling from the sofa to land hard on her knees. On shaky legs, she rushed for the bathroom. She just managed to reach the toilet in time before she threw up the contents of her stomach. Her chest burned with every retch, her ribs aching at the pressure. She was vaguely aware of being followed into the room. Scarlet's hand rubbed soothing patterns over her back as she clung to the toilet bowl.

"I'm okay, I'm okay." Bryce didn't know who she was trying to reassure more, Scarlet or herself. She slipped back and leaned her head against the bathroom wall. With her eyes closed, Bryce heard the sound of water running then felt a soft damp cloth wipe over her sweaty forehead and face. She couldn't help herself; she almost smiled. No one had taken care of her since her enforced stay in the hospital. A cold glass of water was pressed into her hand and Bryce forced herself back up off the cold tiled floor. She rinsed her mouth out and then gulped the remaining water down to ease her sore throat.

"I'm sorry," she said gruffly, only now able to look at Scarlet's worried face as she knelt beside her. "I didn't mean to all but dump you on your ass in my mad dash to get in here."

"I don't care about that. I care about *you*. You were moving around so much you woke me up. You were whispering my name in such a way that it broke my heart. What was happening, Bryce?"

"You were in my nightmare. In the backseat of that damn fucking car. I needed to get you out. But I *couldn't* get to you." Just remembering the dream made bile rise in Bryce's throat, and she pressed a hand to her mouth in reflex. "I don't want to talk about it." She shivered violently. Her teeth began to chatter together as she was hit by the sheer terror her dream had wrought.

"Have you talked to anyone about the accident?" Scarlet hastily draped a large bath towel around Bryce's shoulders to keep her warm.

"I gave the police my witness statement." Bryce wiped her eyes swiftly, but she couldn't stop the tears from falling. *Scarlet had been in the car. No one in the backseat lives.* Desperately, Bryce clutched at Scarlet's leg, needing to know she was there. That she was real. That she was *alive.*

"I don't mean the official stuff. I meant have you talked to someone qualified to help you heal." Scarlet covered Bryce's hand with her own in comfort.

"They offered a psychiatrist. I reneged on going back a second time." Gingerly, Bryce got to her feet and lowered the lid on the toilet. She flushed it then had to sit back down on it. She clung to the sink, horrified to find her strength drained and tears falling unchecked. Her ribs felt bruised and she rubbed at them distractedly, wishing it would all just go away.

"Bryce." Scarlet's tone was scolding even as she rubbed at Bryce's arms trying to warm her up.

"I didn't want to relive it."

"So, you relive it every night instead." Scarlet, taking no argument, helped Bryce up on her feet. Slowly, she led them as far as the kitchen and helped Bryce into a chair at the table.

Scarlet switched the kettle on and began to fuss with mugs and tea bags. Bryce tugged the fluffy towel higher up her neck, all but hiding in it. "Not if I don't sleep."

"You can't continue like that."

"I've managed so far."

"Really? Because I seem to recall finding you asleep at work and then tonight you were out like a light the second I got you on your back."

Despite the seriousness of the situation, Bryce had to smile through her clattering teeth. "So I like cuddling with you and it made me relax too much."

"I'm really concerned. Your lack of sleeping is affecting your life. Look at you, sweetheart, you shouldn't be suffering like this." Scarlet slid a mug of tea on the table. "Drink it. It will settle your stomach."

Bryce distracted herself by sipping the hot liquid and tried not to think about the endearment Scarlet had just spoken. "You want to know about the crash? It won't make any difference. I was in a car crash. I've got the scars to show for it. I was the only one who walked away."

"And how does that make you feel?"

Bryce's head shot up. "Excuse me?"

Scarlet slipped into the chair opposite her. "How does that make you *feel*?"

"I've told you I don't want to get into this." She shook so hard she had to set her mug back down for fear of spilling its contents.

"Well, I know I'm very thankful you survived." Scarlet reached across the table and took Bryce's cold hand. "It frightens me to think how close I came to losing you before I even knew you."

"Three of them were married." Bryce blurted the words out in a rush. She couldn't stop herself. "The people with me in the car. They had wives and a husband and kids. The driver was newly engaged and his fiancé lost him too. I was in a crappy relationship with a woman who came to the hospital only to run when she saw what I looked like. I shouldn't have even been in that car. They were doing me a favor. Yet I got to live and I had no life worth celebrating. The others in that car left families mourning their losses. They didn't deserve that, not when I got to survive."

The grip on Bryce's hand tightened until it was almost painful. "Bryce—" Scarlet started, but Bryce cut her off.

"I need to go home." Embarrassed by the fact she was still crying, Bryce roughly rubbed her face in the towel. She was shaking so much she could barely keep her grip on it.

"It's late." Scarlet pointed to the kitchen clock. It read 10:45 p.m.

"There's a last bus I can catch if I go now. I won't sleep any more tonight, and you don't need me keeping you awake." Bryce finished off her tea and stood up. "Thank you for tonight. I'm only sorry I ruined it."

"You didn't ruin anything and I don't want you to go. You're in no condition to leave." Scarlet stood up as if preparing to bar the door.

"I need to go, Scarlet. You don't need to put up with what I'm going through. I can hardly cope with it myself." Arms suddenly wrapped around her, and Bryce all but crumpled in Scarlet's tight grasp. "Please don't," she gasped, unable to cope with the need to just give in and be comforted.

"I believe you survived for a reason," Scarlet stated fiercely.

"I can't see why."

"Maybe that's because the reason hasn't revealed itself to you yet. I firmly believe everything has a reason for being. You lived because it wasn't your time to die."

Bryce barely managed to keep herself upright. Her knees buckled under the weight of the survivor's guilt that suffocated her very soul. Only Scarlet's arms kept her on her feet.

"Stay here tonight, please. You shouldn't be alone."

"You can't drive me home in the morning, and we have work," Bryce argued weakly. "I won't sleep again tonight, and you need to rest."

"Then just stay here. Watch over me while I sleep and then you can catch the early bus back home in the morning." She cupped Bryce's face in her palms. "I don't want you to leave me. And I don't think you need to be alone with this anymore."

Bryce bit back a gut-wrenching sob. She rested her forehead on Scarlet's shoulder and capitulated. She was too tired to do anything else. "I can't be left anywhere in the dark," she said, mortified by the admission.

"Then I'll leave my bedroom light on. I can sleep through anything. You can read any of the books I have. There's an iPod if you want to advance your music appreciation or you can surf the Internet all night on my tablet." She pressed a soft kiss to Bryce's lips. "I just want you close to me. I can't let you go home like this."

For someone who'd spent so much time alone not coping with the aftermath of what she'd lived through, Bryce finally caved in. She wrapped her arms around Scarlet and just clung to her.

"You're going to be okay, Bryce, I promise you. I'm so thankful you're here with me. I can't imagine my life without you in it."

I can't imagine mine without you either and that's what scares me, Bryce thought.

"I'll camp out on the sofa," she said.

Scarlet tugged her forward by the towel. "Like hell you will. If you're going to stay awake all night you can at least let me cuddle up to you and keep you company while I sleep."

Too exhausted to argue, Bryce let Scarlet lead the way to her bedroom. She complained when Scarlet began removing her shoes but soon surrendered to Scarlet's ministrations. Too drained to move, Bryce listened to the sounds of Scarlet going through her nightly routine in the bathroom. When Scarlet returned, she handed Bryce a pair of sweats and a T-shirt and steered her into the bathroom to clean up. Bryce had to smile at the sight of a new toothbrush laid out with toothpaste already squeezed out neatly on top.

When she returned, the bedroom was brightly lit enough for Bryce to feel safe in. She liked the subtle purple wallpaper and framed landscape photographs Scarlet had hung on her walls. It made a vast contrast to Bryce's apartment where everything was utilitarian. The apartment was nothing more than a place Bryce lived in, not a home.

Scarlet patted the bed, and Bryce slipped in under the covers. Scarlet cuddled into her side. "If you manage to sleep and have more dreams, don't worry. I'm here for you, okay?"

Bryce nodded, knowing she wouldn't dare close her eyes again for fear of returning to that front seat. "Thank you for having me over," she said softly.

Scarlet kissed her cheek. "I promise further invitations to my bed won't always be quite this innocent." Her lips sought out Bryce's. "But for tonight I need you beside me."

I need to be with you too, Bryce realized, pulling Scarlet closer and watching as she snuggled in and closed her eyes.

God, if only it were that easy for me to close my eyes and sleep. Bryce stared down at her, enjoying how Scarlet's soft hair felt against her skin. *But she's here and she's alive. I can watch over her this night and keep her safe...while she keeps me sane.*

Chapter Fourteen

The coffee machine burbled and hissed noisily while Scarlet stood by eager for her first cup of the day. She turned her head at the sound of the front door opening. For a moment, disappointment streaked through her that it wasn't Bryce coming back. Instead it was Monica creeping in, obviously not expecting anyone to be up and awake at six a.m. The look of surprise on her face when she caught sight of Scarlet, arms folded, foot tapping on the floor, made Scarlet chuckle.

"My God, Scarlet!" Monica clutched at her chest dramatically. "Give a girl a heart attack, why don't you! And quit with the disapproving eyes. You look just like my mother used to when she caught me sneaking back in after curfew."

Laughing, Scarlet set to fixing two cups of coffee. "It's not the same. I know exactly where you have been and with whom. You've been with Elton all night, no doubt partaking in all forms of delicious debauchery."

"That pretty much sums up our evening quite nicely." Monica grasped for a mug gratefully and she took a healthy swallow of the scalding hot liquid. "Oh, that is so good. Elton can set the bed sheets alight, but his coffee making skills are sorely lacking."

"That's why you have a live-in lesbian to cater to your 'night after' refreshments." Scarlet sat and took a more leisurely sip of her own drink.

"Seeing as I have just driven my 'walk of shame' home at this ungodly hour, did my eyes, by chance, deceive me? Did I just see Bryce Donovan leaving here as I rolled up?" Monica sat opposite her at the kitchen table and eyed Scarlet over the rim of her mug.

Scarlet nodded. "She left so she could go home and get changed for work."

"Any particular reason why she wouldn't stay in bed with you until a more civilized hour and just have you drive her home?"

"Because she hasn't been able to get into a car since the accident." Scarlet didn't believe she was betraying Bryce's confidence. It was painfully obvious once you realized that Bryce only traveled anywhere in something large with plenty of seating.

"I did wonder. It's got to mess with your mind having people die around you in such a confined space. From what your dad told me about it, they were picking up pieces of the driver off the road. The truck just sliced into their car like a knife through butter."

And Bryce saw it all, Scarlet thought with a sympathetic shudder. She remembered how Bryce had trembled in her arms, how her tears had ripped Scarlet's composure to shreds. Bryce's misery at what she'd lived through, yet couldn't live *with,* had broken Scarlet's heart.

"Sooooo," Monica drawled, "Did you two…?"

"No, we just got to talking and it was too late for Bryce to catch a bus home."

"Convenient. So, what did she do? Sleep on the sofa?"

"No, she didn't." Scarlet shook her head at Monica's not so innocent line of questioning. "I did get her in my bed, and technically we slept together. Well, *I* slept. She apparently read a good part of the book on my bedside table while I'm told I clung to her like a limpet."

"Those dark circles don't lie then. She doesn't sleep much at all now."

"Not really," Scarlet said. "But she did tell me she managed to doze off a few times during the night and got some much needed rest, so I am grateful for that." Scarlet had wanted to hold Bryce tight all night to ward off any more nightmares. Instead, she'd fallen fast asleep cradled in Bryce's arms, lulled by the beat of Bryce's heart under her ear. To know that Bryce had managed some sleep without more bad dreams was a relief.

"She was in bed with you all night, with you dressed in *that*?" Monica waved a hand at Scarlet's short nightshirt. "And you're seriously telling me that she didn't at least once try her luck?"

"She's not like that, Monica." *And after our talk, I wasn't in the mood either. We were both too emotionally drained.*

"Looks like you've found your white knight, Princess."

Scarlet snorted at Monica's fanciful musings. "One night of us *not* tearing up the sheets together does not make her anything of the sort."

"But you'd like her to be?"

Scarlet nodded without hesitation.

"So you really like this woman. It's about time you found a keeper." Monica raised her mug in a toast. "Well, here's to you and Bryce."

Scarlet considered Monica's words while they drank their coffee in silence. *Like? I want to be the one who keeps her nightmares at bay. I want to help her heal, inside and out. After last night holding her in my arms, I fear love is a more accurate description for what I'm feeling.*

"I think I need more coffee," Scarlet muttered, and Monica held up her cup again in agreement.

❖

Bryce deliberately got off her bus a stop earlier to join the line already forming at the local Starbucks. Finally, she reached the counter and was able to place an order for herself and Scarlet.

She also grabbed a couple of pastries for breakfast from the bakery next door.

Feeling oddly lighthearted, Bryce walked the rest of the way to the work site.

Though the early morning was already bright and sunny, Bryce couldn't help but wish she'd resisted the need to leave the sanctuary of Scarlet's bed. Faced with Scarlet's red hair all tousled and her face still soft with sleep, Bryce's decision to leave had been a difficult one. In Scarlet's bed Bryce had found a respite from her self-inflicted insomnia. The small amount of natural sleep she garnered was more than she'd slept in total for months. The insomnia high she usually existed on was tempered by a long forgotten feeling. *Rested.* She felt rested. Buoyed by the extra boost of energy, it put a long missing spring into her steps.

It didn't take long for Bryce to reach the houses. Her chest fluttered with excitement when she spotted Scarlet's car in its usual parking spot. Taking two steps at a time, Bryce followed the recognizable sound that led to Scarlet's location. Music played in a back room, and Scarlet was kneeling at her paint cans preparing for her morning work.

Bryce coughed to attract her attention. "I brought you coffee." She held the cup out and hoped her nervousness wasn't noticeable. She'd cried in front of her, had been seen at her weakest. She was nervous as to how to approach Scarlet in the daylight after what had been seen in the dark.

Scarlet rose and took the proffered cup gratefully. "Good morning again."

Her smile made Bryce's breath release in one long sigh. "Good morning." She held up her bag of doughnuts. "I brought breakfast too seeing as I had to cut our 'morning after' short."

Scarlet took the bag from her, opened it, and grinned. "You can sleep/not sleep in my bed anytime you want if you are going to bring me powdered doughnuts afterward."

"I'll keep that in mind." Bryce leaned in to brush her lips over Scarlet's. "Thank you for last night. Next time I'll try to be less of a basket case on what was just our second date."

"Never apologize, Bryce. I'm just glad I could be there for you. I need to be that necessary."

Her eyes made Bryce's chest tighten with a want she hadn't felt before. "You're more than necessary," she said. Scarlet's eyes darkened a shade, and Bryce was captivated by the emotions she could read in them. In Scarlet's hazel eyes, her deepest feelings were on show, all revealed, naked and unashamed. It was a responsibility Bryce had never expected. This was the boss's daughter, a work colleague, someone she was still just getting to know.

I don't care. I feel like I've been dying little by little every day since the accident. But not when I'm with Scarlet. She makes me not afraid to live. Whether I deserve it or not she makes me feel glad to be alive again. The feeling shook Bryce to her very core.

Scarlet's soft hand cupped Bryce's cheek and drew her out of her introspection.

"How are you feeling this morning?"

"Like I am the biggest fool on the planet for not staying under the covers with you today," Bryce replied honestly.

Scarlet's answering grin was all at once seductive. "I'd have liked that." She set her cup down and used her free hand to tug Bryce closer by her belt buckle. "I liked waking up with you beside me."

"You're quite the snuggler," Bryce said, remembering how Scarlet had wrapped her long limbs around her and clung to her all night.

"I'd gotten you in my arms. I had no intention of letting you go." She tugged Bryce's head down purposefully. Their warm breath mingled and their lips were just a breath away from a kiss.

"Scarlet?"

Victor Tweedy's voice called from somewhere downstairs. It was like a dash of cold water. Bryce stiffened in Scarlet's hold. Scarlet didn't let her grip loosen on Bryce's buckle.

"Don't even think about being caught by the boss," Scarlet said. "I'm all grown up now, and he can't ground me for kissing you."

"I should get going to my job, while I still have one."

"He can't fire you. He needs your skills too much. The fact you want to fuck his daughter and his daughter wants to fuck you is strictly between you and me."

Bryce's simmering arousal skyrocketed at Scarlet's honeyed words. All she wanted to do was slam the door shut and take Scarlet where she stood. "I definitely shouldn't have left your bed this morning if that is what you were thinking." She stole a swift hard kiss from Scarlet's lips. It wasn't enough to satisfy her.

"I think about it a lot." Scarlet's hold on Bryce's buckle got tighter.

At the sound of someone coming up the stairs, Bryce let out a groan. She tried not to fall further into Scarlet's seductive aura. She could read promises in Scarlet's eyes that she knew she would definitely keep. "Work, I have to work," Bryce muttered and pulled further away, finally breaking Scarlet's hold on her.

"Thanks for breakfast." Scarlet pulled a doughnut out and took a healthy bite. Her lips were instantly covered in the soft powdered sugar. It made Bryce sorely tempted to lick and kiss it all off. Bryce backed out of the room before temptation drove her to do the things her imagination was begging her to try. She almost collided with Victor as he reached the landing.

"Morning, Bryce," he said as he walked in on Scarlet. "Hey, you. You have doughnuts? What makes you so special? Have you got one in there for your old man?"

Bryce escaped while she could, hoping that Victor couldn't tell how flustered she was. All these sensations were new to Bryce; she'd spent a long time cut off from feelings while trapped in a loveless relationship. After the crash, everything had revolved around her healing and the nightmarish dreams that even colored her waking hours. Scarlet was flame personified. She burned through Bryce's erected walls of misery, setting her alight with a passion she had never felt before.

Bryce had a feeling that when they finally made love she would be helpless in the conflagration. Scarlet had a way of burning a path through all the shadows that shrouded Bryce. For the first time in a long time, Bryce was seeing the light as something more than that which chased the dark away.

Chapter Fifteen

With a happy sigh to be home early for dinner for a change, Trent pushed open her front door. She was surprised to be met by silence.

"Juliet?" she called out but was met with no response. Trent closed the door behind her, irritation making her frown. "You'd better not have gone to that fucking worksite for something," she grumbled as she toed out of her shoes and walked silently in her socked feet. She poked her head around the door to Juliet's home office. It was empty. She walked through the kitchen into the living room, but again the room was unoccupied. Trent padded upstairs quietly just in case Juliet was sleeping. The door to their bedroom was pulled to so Trent carefully edged it open, expecting to find Juliet resting there. The bed was undisturbed. The nursery was also empty, making Trent reach for her phone. Fear made her fingers fumble over the screen to unlock it.

Where the hell are you?

She checked to see if she had missed any calls, but there were none. She brought up Juliet's phone number and was just about to press the call button when she noticed the door to her game room was ajar. She was concerned primarily because that room was always securely locked. Filled with trepidation at what she was going to see, Trent pushed the door open. Inside she found Juliet fast asleep in her usual position on the sofa. Trent attempted to calm her heart down. She hadn't known what to expect. Juliet had been exhausted all night and had been easy to persuade into staying home for the day to rest. The fact she had given in without any complaining had given Trent cause for concern. She'd lost count of the number of arguments they had had concerning Juliet's need to slow down now.

Trent knelt in front of Juliet and examined her closely. Juliet's breathing was slow and measured with sleep. She didn't look as pale as she had the night previous, and Trent was pleased to see an empty plate and cup on the floor. Not wanting to disturb Juliet, she eased back on her heels to stand. At the last minute, she gently repositioned the blanket that was slipping off Juliet's shoulder.

"Trent?"

Trent shook her head ruefully. Juliet could sleep in the room with guns a-blazing and her shouting out directions, but one blanket shifted back into place and she was instantly awake. She tried not to roll her eyes in amusement.

"You home already?"

"Looks like you've been asleep a while, sweetheart." Trent got back down and brushed at the unruly hair that had fallen over Juliet's brow. "How are you feeling now?"

Juliet rubbed at her eyes. "Much better than I did. But I want to just eat and then spend the night cuddling with you." She tugged at Trent's shirt. "Can we?"

"I'll go order us something in and we'll watch TV in bed. I think I can happily spend the evening just you, me, and Newt chilling out. Scarlet's coming by later, but she can look after herself." She tipped forward under Juliet's gentle tug and planted a tender kiss on her forehead. "Are you going to tell me why you are camped out in my game room? You gave me a heart attack. I thought we were being robbed."

Juliet pouted softly, looking abashed. "I missed you. I looked for something of yours to wear, but I can't fit into anything because of my bump and you being so damn tall and slim." She slapped at Trent's hand that she had reached out for payment at her slip. "I couldn't get comfy sleeping in our bed on my own, not even with me lying on your pillow. So I came in here. This room is all you. I couldn't sleep at first, I'm so used to the sound of you playing and being lulled to sleep by that."

Trent noticed what Juliet had her head resting on. "You're sleeping on my new Atari sweatshirt?"

"It smells like you and I needed you. I was pretty much out like a light after snuggling into it."

Trent had to smile. She'd worry about the creases in her clothing later. She was all for placating Juliet's moods while the pregnancy hormones did their worst. She helped Juliet sit up and then onto her feet.

"Your baby is draining my energy today," Juliet complained half-heartedly.

"If we're having a girl maybe she's a little succubus." Trent studiously ignored the look she could feel directed her way. "And again with it being my kid when it's not being good." She pressed a light kiss to Juliet's hair.

"Your baby made me break and enter into your gaming room because we both missed you desperately."

Her not so innocent look made Trent chuckle. "God help me, I don't stand a chance against two of you."

"We'll try not to gang up on you too much," Juliet promised.

Trent looked down at her snuggled tightly under her arm. "Now why don't I believe that for one minute?"

"Because you know you'll be wrapped around this baby's finger as much as you are wrapped around mine."

Truer words had never been spoken, Trent admitted to herself. "I like the sound of that."

"The baby wants pizza."

Trent groaned. "Really? *Again*? I swear this kid must have some of me in it. Though it can get through more pizza than even I can stomach lately."

"Extra cheese, some olives, and tell them not to hold back on the sauce this time."

"Yes, *Newt*, the only fetus food connoisseur I know." She winced as Juliet poked her in her side. "Extra sauce for Mommy, got it!"

❖

"I saved you a doughnut seeing as I skipped out on our lunch date. Which I apologize for."

At the sound of Scarlet's voice, Bryce lowered her trowel. She was grateful for the excuse to stop for a moment. She rubbed at her shoulder, wincing as the muscles ached from her holding up her hawk for too long.

"Put that down and come take a quick break with me before it's time to go home for the night." Scarlet shook the bag in her hand. "Otherwise I'm eating this last treat and you can go without."

Bryce smiled at Scarlet's tone. "Listen to you. You're already sounding like the boss." She climbed down her stepladder and only when she was at the bottom did she catch Scarlet's disgruntled face. "I was teasing."

Scarlet slumped against the wall. Her pout made her look like a petulant little child. Bryce found it adorable. She tugged Scarlet into her arms and held her close. She ran her hands across Scarlet's tense shoulders, smoothing and soothing her. Scarlet snuggled in closer.

"For the second day running I had to tell Dad I didn't come back to step right into a management position. I told him his pressuring me wasn't going to make me take up the reins any quicker or make me change my mind. And buying me lunch doesn't sweeten the deal any further either."

Bryce kept silent. She let Scarlet vent.

"He's got this grand vision in his head of me just taking everything on now that I'm home. I told him I wasn't ready, would probably never be ready, and that I have dreams of my own I want to follow."

"Your photography."

"Yes. Why can you see that and he can't?" Scarlet shifted in Bryce's arms to look at her.

Even in her low-heeled work boots, Scarlet was still taller than Bryce. Bryce loved how Scarlet curled into her arms. She made Bryce feel ten feet tall how she adjusted to fit so well.

"He's going to end up pushing me away."

Bryce felt a chill run through her frame. *No, not when I've just found you.* "Then you need to explain that to him. Tell him when and only when you are ready will you take over the business. If you ever do at all. Until then you have your own life to lead. He has to realize that."

"I have photographs to take, pictures to paint, plasterers to plunder." Scarlet tipped Bryce's chin up for a kiss. Her tongue slipped past Bryce's lips to deepen it.

Bryce groaned at the torturous teasing Scarlet subjected her to. When Scarlet pulled back for air, Bryce grinned lazily at her.

"Christ, you're good at that," she said, pulling Scarlet back down to take the initiative and kiss the satisfied smug look from Scarlet's beautiful face. She slipped a leg between Scarlet's, felt the surprised gasp that was breathed into her mouth. Scarlet began to rock against Bryce's thigh, riding her in a steady rhythm. In answer to Scarlet's sensuous movements, the warmth Bryce could feel against her jeans caused her own need to flare. Each press of Scarlet's thigh against Bryce's crotch made arousal pool between her legs. The short sting of teeth nipping at her questing tongue made Bryce pull Scarlet tighter on her leg in retaliation. The shudder that ran through Scarlet's body was payment enough. Scarlet's hands drifted beneath Bryce's T-shirt, clutching at her back. She held on tightly as their rocking began to grow desperate. Bryce's hands were stuffed firmly in the back pockets of Scarlet's jeans, cupping her buttocks and holding her in place.

"Hey, Scarlet? You still in here? Have you asked—Oh!" Monica's sudden entrance skidded to a halt as she barged in on them.

Bryce pulled back, her face flaming at being caught. Scarlet wouldn't let her escape her hold, but she did step back with a barely disguised look of frustration coloring her own features.

Monica shook her head at them both. "It's a good thing I wasn't your dad. You'd have been taking over the business sooner than you expected. The way you two were entwined you'd have given him a heart attack on the spot."

Ignoring Monica, Scarlet instead set to gently wiping her lipstick off Bryce's face.

"I came to check if you'd asked Bryce to join us at the concert next weekend. But I see your tongue was too busy down her throat for you to be talking about such mundane matters."

Bryce had to laugh at Monica's teasing bluntness.

"Actually, it was her tongue doing scandalous things to my tonsils," Scarlet retorted. "Thank you for the reminder, Monica." She turned her attention back to Bryce as if they hadn't just been interrupted dry humping in the workplace. "I want you to come to a concert being held at our local club." She again rubbed at Bryce's face with the pad of her thumb. "You can see me in something other than my work attire."

"You forget I've seen you in your party clothes. You looked out of this world."

"You called me an angel," Scarlet said softly.

"You looked like one."

"Okaaay," Monica drawled, breaking in on their moment. "My job here is done. Though I recommend if you two are going to continue with your shenanigans you might want to close the door next time." She backed out of the doorway. "It's a good thing I didn't have Juliet to send on this errand. You two would have sent her into premature labor." She waved at them. "Go get a room. Preferably one that doesn't smell of wet plaster."

Bryce listened to the sound of her footsteps disappearing down the stairs. "Shenanigans?" she asked Scarlet who burst into laughter. "So much for us conducting ourselves in a professional manner."

"You were the one who shoved her leg between mine and started my engine running." Scarlet shifted in her jeans. "God, you left me so wet—"

"Okay," Bryce cut in, all too aware of how uncomfortable her own underwear was becoming. She took a deliberate step back. "Fuck, you are dangerous to be around."

Scarlet stepped forward, deliberately foiling Bryce's movements. "You love the fact I'm dangerous."

Bryce was finding she loved *everything* about Scarlet. However, she held up a warning hand. "No more shenanigans on work time." The pout she received did nothing to calm Bryce's blood down. It just made her want to kiss it right off Scarlet's face. She did exactly that. Leaving Scarlet looking dazed, Bryce stepped well away. "Now give me my doughnut."

Scarlet snorted at her. She deliberately swung her hips as she went to retrieve the bag and held it just out of Bryce's reach. "Haven't you tasted enough sugar, Bryce?" She licked her lips and Bryce felt her stomach clench in reaction.

She took the bag from Scarlet and pulled out a doughnut covered in frosting. "You saved me my favorite one." Bryce took a big bite out of the pastry. She hummed her pleasure at the sweet treat. She hummed even louder when Scarlet's lips latched on to her own and her tongue flicked out to capture any remaining frosting. The doughnut forgotten, Bryce found it all too easy to succumb to Scarlet's kisses.

"So, about this concert…" Scarlet finally drew back and brushed her hand down Bryce's chest. "I know you're not comfortable with social settings, but this is different. It's music and dancing and everyone's eyes are on the stage. You don't have to dress up for the occasion. You can come straight to my place, and we'll just walk to the venue. It's literally just down the block." Her hand slipped to rest over the zipper of Bryce's jeans, and she rubbed a little harder. "Monica is spending that weekend at Elton's so if you'd like to stay over you could. You'd be more than welcome."

Bryce's breath stuttered in her chest as Scarlet pressed harder into her crotch. "If you 'pack' accordingly, I'm sure we could have a fun weekend together."

Bryce got that message loud and clear. Excitement jangled through every nerve. "How did you…?"

Scarlet squeezed Bryce gently. "You have a certain swagger to your walk. I can't help but think you put that to good use when you're wearing the right kind of gear. We'll have all weekend to play if you're open to that."

Bryce was amazed by how well Scarlet could read her. She loved to use a strap-on but very rarely found someone who was willing to let her use it without it becoming a gender issue. To have Scarlet bring it up was more than Bryce could have ever dreamed of. "How about we just skip the concert altogether?"

"I would love to, but I'm taking the publicity shots for the band that evening. Believe me, I'd be more than happy spending that time in your arms while we make some sweet music all our own." She squeezed Bryce again one more time.

Her eyes all but rolling into the back of her head, Bryce let out a pained groan and then a disappointed huff as Scarlet pulled her hand away.

"It's home time, Donovan. Time for you to down tools. If it were up to me, I'd take you home with me now, but I have a nursery to start work on and a standing date with the two mommies-to-be." She gave Bryce a hopeful look. "Do you want to come with me?"

Bryce nearly said yes, anything to stay near Scarlet and the life she radiated. Instead, she shook her head. "I don't want to distract you from your work. We've just proved that we can't be trusted in a small room together. You need to get that nursery sorted, otherwise the baby will be here before you've done your first brushstroke." She pressed a kiss to Scarlet's lips.

"I'll bring breakfast tomorrow," Scarlet said with a resigned sigh.

"I like extra frosting on my treats." She shook her head at the way Scarlet's eyes lit up.

"I'll bear that in mind for next weekend too."

Chapter Sixteen

After being informed that the concert didn't start until late, Bryce had plenty of time that evening to leave work, get home, shower, and change her clothes. She'd chosen a pair of black jeans teamed with a charcoal gray shirt. She'd be the most underdressed there but knew she couldn't compete with what she expected to see. She was nervous about being out of her comfort zone again. Work was fine; everyone knew her and had seen her scar. Her hair was helping to hide some of the damage now that it was growing back. Bryce really didn't want to go out, but she wanted to spend time with Scarlet. So that meant being sociable, no matter how difficult that was.

Bryce had packed a small bag for her stay over at Scarlet's. It consisted of a few T-shirts, clean underwear, toiletries, and a brand new cock and harness she had bought specifically for Scarlet. It had been a long time since Bryce had had the opportunity to use one. She'd lingered sometime over the multitude of toys she'd found online until she felt confident in her choice. Now, making sure it was safely packed away gave Bryce a frisson of excitement that was swiftly turning into need. She needed Scarlet. Bryce hadn't slept properly again since leaving Scarlet's bed. The short naps she'd managed to take in the past week had been dream filled and stressful. She wondered if Scarlet would hold her again and chase the nightmares away.

"Maybe I'll just get lucky and she'll fuck me into unconsciousness," Bryce muttered to herself with a grin. She had the feeling Scarlet wasn't going to be the kind of bed partner to just lie back and take it all.

She honestly couldn't wait.

Bryce left before the images flashing in her head made her have to do something to take the edge off. The steady thrum of arousal warmed her skin as Bryce waited in line for a bus. The journey didn't take long with Bryce's imagination keeping her occupied. Her excitement for the evening added speed to her feet, and she was soon knocking at the apartment door, eager for the weekend to begin.

Monica waved her in. Bryce faltered in her steps when she took in Monica's striking look.

"What?" Monica asked at Bryce's silence.

"You look amazing."

"I forget you've only seen me in my landscape gear." Monica struck a dramatic pose. "This, my dear, is the real me."

Bryce had never seen Monica like this. Her jet-black hair hung straight, framing her face. Her eye makeup was bold, highlighting her eyes. She wore a black leather corset, the panels brought together in place by crisscrossed laces. Her skirt seemed to be made from endless black lace, heavily patterned with roses. It fell to calf length, revealing Monica's heavily buckled boots.

"So? What do you think?" Monica asked, giving her a twirl and making her skirt fan out around her.

Bryce smiled. "I think Elton's an incredibly lucky man. You look fantastic."

"Reevaluating your vision on Goths, Bryce?" Monica asked.

"I'm recognizing beauty however it's packaged."

Monica clapped her hands. "Oh, you're a keeper!" She grasped Bryce's shoulders and spun her around to face the bedrooms. "Wait until you feast your eyes on Scarlet." She turned Bryce back around again. "Keep in mind that she's needed at the concert in an official photographer capacity so no closing that door and not coming out once you lay eyes on her!" With that warning, Monica spun Bryce around again and pushed her toward Scarlet's bedroom.

Bryce knocked tentatively, inexplicably nervous as to what Scarlet was going to look like. She remembered all too well how beautiful Scarlet had looked the first time she'd seen her in her finery. Her very own dark angel, a celestial beauty with flaming red hair. Bryce had wanted to touch her then; now she could. Her second knock was more confident.

"Come in."

Bryce stepped inside and saw Scarlet standing by the bed. Bryce turned back around. "I'm sorry. I thought you were dressed."

Scarlet's laughter made her risk a look over her shoulder.

"I am dressed. I've just got to get my boots on and I'm ready to roll."

Bryce turned around and took Scarlet in from the top of her bright red hair flowing around her shoulders to the tip of her black stocking encased toes. Like Monica, she wore a black corset, her ample cleavage blatantly on display. The black material hugged Scarlet's creamy pale flesh. Bryce looked up to Scarlet's face and found bright red lips curved in a smile at her distracted gaze.

"Do I meet with your approval?"

The corset clung lovingly to the contours of Scarlet's curves. Bryce's gaze dropped lower to where folds of pleated silk fell from Scarlet's hips to fall into a train behind her. The front was what had caused Bryce's consternation. There was no front to the skirt. A small ruffle of silk was the only thing that hid the top of Scarlet's legs. Everything else was unashamedly on show. Black stocking tops flashed a tantalizing strip of Scarlet's pale thigh. Under Bryce's silent perusal, Scarlet got into a pair of thigh-high boots. The sound of the zipper was loud in the room as Scarlet added the final touch to her clothing. Lethal heels added even more inches to Scarlet's height as the shiny black leather hugged her legs like a second skin.

"Bryce?" Scarlet's voice broke Bryce out of her stunned silence.

"You're so beautiful," Bryce said, barely able to take her eyes off her. She stared as Scarlet added ornate silver jewelry around her neck and on her fingers. She sauntered over to Bryce, obviously delighting in the dazed look she was displaying. With nails painted black with stark white tips, Scarlet scored a line down Bryce's chest.

Bryce shivered at the trail left through the fabric of her shirt. Scarlet's perfume intoxicated her. All she could see and hear was Scarlet, and it gave her a peace she hadn't felt in months.

Scarlet groaned from deep inside her chest. "Don't look at me like that with those bedroom eyes of yours." She leaned down and stopped tantalizingly short of completing a kiss. "Take your hat off."

Bryce tossed it aside. She felt Scarlet's breath tickle across her lips. "I want to fuck you while you wear nothing but those boots," she said. She reached out to make patterns on the naked flesh between a stocking and the lace-edged panties hidden by the swaths of silk. She could feel Scarlet tremble at each touch.

"You can fuck me any way you wish." Scarlet leaned in to Bryce and stole a swift kiss. "But you need to stop where your fingers are leading because I need steady hands to operate my camera tonight."

Reluctantly, Bryce removed her hand and instead reached up to pull Scarlet in for another kiss.

"Break it up in there, you two!" Monica called from outside the door. "Time to go!"

Staring into Bryce's eyes, Scarlet grabbed her hand and slipped two of her fingers past the lace covering her sex. Wetness saturated Bryce's fingers. Then just as quickly Scarlet pulled them back out. She held Bryce's hand up to her mouth. Without hesitation, Bryce licked them clean. The taste of Scarlet on her tongue wasn't enough to satisfy her need. Concert be damned, Bryce was sorely tempted to fall to her knees and bury her face between Scarlet's thighs. She was already drunk on the taste of her.

"That's to tide you over until tonight," Scarlet whispered as she teased her tongue across Bryce's lips and then kissed her sweetly. She took a step back and slipped her arm through Bryce's. Scarlet tugged at Bryce's shirt gently. "I like this color on you. You look so handsome tonight."

And you still are that dark angel that brings me forth, blinking into the light.

❖

The music vibrated the floor beneath Bryce's feet. She found herself soaking in the entire experience like a sponge. The music was loud and heavy on guitars. The lead singer could reach a range of notes that impressed Bryce's more cultured ears. She'd been dragged to enough operas with Gerri to gain an appreciation of what was singing and what was screeching. Admittedly, Bryce could only make out some of the words but recognized an obvious passion behind the performance.

Standing in the crowd, it wasn't always possible to see the band, but Bryce was more interested in watching Scarlet. She was still taking action shots but managing to dance in between, something that Bryce found fascinating. The flashing lights easily lit up the bright color of Scarlet's red hair so she was easy to spot as she moved around the floor. Bryce could see Elton and Monica lost in the music. Trent was enjoying the band from Juliet's side.

Bryce noticed Trent wasn't as outwardly expressive as Elton who was dancing beside Monica. Monica obviously knew all the right moves to each song and had a stamina Bryce would have killed for. Juliet was leaning into Trent's side bopping her head to the music and smoothing a hand over her belly. Bryce wondered if the baby was enjoying the music and making itself felt. She admired Trent's long-tailed suit that made her look incredibly handsome. She couldn't help but see why Scarlet still harbored the remnants of her crush on her. There was just something about her. Watching her stand so protectively beside Juliet, keeping the energetic audience away from her, was rather endearing.

Bryce hadn't been paying attention to the music so when the room was plunged into darkness, she froze. Her breath stuck in her chest as the all too familiar feeling of claustrophobia crowded in on her. A bright white strobe light swept over the crowd. For a long, terrible moment, Bryce was back in the passenger seat of that car, waking from the dark and being blinded by the headlights of the truck. Stark terror pinned her to the floor as Bryce prepared herself for the impact she remembered all too clearly. She jerked as if struck when hands cupped her face.

Slowly, carefully, Bryce was drawn back to the reality in the room by Scarlet. She could see Scarlet's mouth moving, could read her own name being spoken over and over. Her hands stroked Bryce's cheeks. The music drowned out Scarlet's voice, but the warmth from her hands slowly reached into her frozen mind. Bryce finally recognized her surroundings and was hauled back in the concert room with a bang as the drums beat out a rhythm. No one was dying; Bryce wasn't in the car. Scarlet was there. Bryce was safe. *Alive*. She swallowed hard and felt another hand resting on her shoulder. Bryce looked behind her and up. Trent stood by, offering her a bottle of water.

For the first time in what seemed like forever, Bryce wasn't embarrassed by what had happened. The flashback had catapulted her back into the passenger seat surrounded by the dead and dying. Scarlet had brought her out of it, back to the here and now. Returned to the music, the dancing, and the obvious signs of life.

Trent twisted the top off the bottle and handed it to her. Bryce drank from it gratefully, savoring the iced water as it slipped down her parched throat.

"Let's step outside," Scarlet said, slipping a hand under Bryce's elbow.

"No, just stay near. I'm back in the room and you need to dance with me."

Scarlet wrapped her arms around Bryce's shoulders and pulled her close. They rocked together to the beat. Their dance was jarringly out of place in the room, but Scarlet didn't seem to mind and Bryce was past caring.

I'm not alone and this dark holds no nightmares.

Bryce tightened her grip around Scarlet's waist and gave herself up to the music, finally recognizing its beauty.

Chapter Seventeen

The walk back to Scarlet's apartment was silent. Scarlet held Bryce's hand tightly in her own. Their shoulders brushed with every step they took. Scarlet was crowded into Bryce's side, needing the comfort and hoping to be giving it in return. She had instinctively sought out Bryce once the damned lights had gone out. Scarlet knew the concert cues and was cursing herself for not staying by Bryce's side. She'd never given it a thought. The fear in Bryce's eyes as the light swept the crowd had torn Scarlet's heart to shreds. Coaxing Bryce back from wherever her terrors had taken her was all Scarlet could think to do. She couldn't stand to think of Bryce living with this constant fear.

Only when Scarlet closed the apartment door did she finally speak.

"Do you want to talk about it?"

She had barely managed to put her camera case down before Bryce was pressed against her. Scarlet could read the intent blazing in Bryce's eyes. Blue had darkened several shades deeper in her desire, and Scarlet's need to talk had vanished. Bryce flung her cap aside. Scarlet threaded her fingers through the soft blond hair, scratching gently at her scalp.

"No. I don't want to think about anything other than how beautiful you look tonight and how much I want to touch you."

At Bryce's kiss, Scarlet groaned loudly into her mouth. She wrapped her arms around Bryce's shoulders to just hold on.

Bryce's warm lips teased Scarlet with soft kisses that grew harder, more demanding. Her tongue slipped between Scarlet's lips, and she welcomed the intrusion, tasting Bryce and wanting more.

Bryce's hands roamed down Scarlet's sides, tracing the shape of Scarlet in her corset. Her fingers slipped under the silk of Scarlet's skirt and brushed at the top of her thighs.

"I've thought of nothing else but you naked, legs wrapped around my hips, wearing these 'come fuck me' boots of yours." Bryce ran a finger along the edge of Scarlet's boot where it met pale skin.

"That can be arranged." Scarlet dipped her head to press kisses all over Bryce's cheeks. She followed along her jawline and then down her neck. She could feel the rapidly beating pulse beneath her lips. Scarlet began to suck at the tender spot. She smiled as Bryce squirmed in her arms.

"Hey! I thought you weren't into vampires," she said, her voice breaking as Scarlet pulled back and ran her tongue over the burning area.

"I'm not. I'm just marking you as mine."

"Do you really need proof? You're the only one able to bring me back out of the darkness when I slip into it."

Scarlet grabbed a handful of her shirt and pulled Bryce into her. "Did you come *prepared*?" She pressed a kiss on the red patch darkening Bryce's neck.

Bryce tilted her head all the more for whatever Scarlet desired to do. "I don't think I was ever prepared for you, darling," she said.

Scarlet smiled against Bryce's skin, loving the sweet name that rolled from Bryce's lips.

"But yes, if you'll let me, I'd like to share something I think we'll both enjoy the pleasure of."

Scarlet pulled Bryce into her bedroom. She dimmed the lights a fraction until Bryce nodded where she was comfortable with them. Then she stood at the bottom of her bed, chewing on a lip.

"Second thoughts?" Bryce asked quietly.

"Hell no," Scarlet assured her. "I'm trying to decide if I want you to take my clothes off or if I should just striptease my way out of them for your titillation."

Bryce grinned. "Decisions, decisions. I'm all for being titillated." She ran a finger down the back of Scarlet's tightly laced corset. "But if you don't mind me fumbling, I'm sure I could at least get you out of this efficiently. As much as I love being teased, right now I'm liable to spontaneously combust just looking at you." She slipped behind Scarlet and began earnestly slipping the laces free from their fastenings.

Scarlet felt hot kisses placed on every bit of skin that Bryce uncovered. She caught the corset before it fell and held it to her. Bryce soon slipped back around and waited for the top to fall.

"Oh my God," Bryce breathed. Scarlet was hard-pressed not to touch herself to alleviate some of the need building just from the way Bryce was looking at her breasts. She shivered under her burning gaze.

"Take off your skirt," Bryce said.

Scarlet easily found the hidden zipper that kept her skirt in place. It pooled to her feet. Clad in just her boots and a pair of scandalous black lace panties, Scarlet warmed at the desirous look that turned Bryce's eyes almost indigo in shade.

Bryce wrestled out of her shirt, obviously trying not to aggravate her still healing body. Judging by her muttered comments, Bryce was frustrated she couldn't just whip the whole thing off her head in one go. Her shirt was flung to the floor haphazardly, and then Bryce zeroed in on her belt. Her trousers were soon dropped to join Scarlet's skirt on the floor.

Scarlet snagged a finger in Bryce's boy shorts. She slipped inside and felt the soft curl of hair that framed Bryce's sex.

"You might want to get your gear, Bryce." Scarlet brushed a tremulous kiss between Bryce's bra-clad breasts. "I need our first time to be fast and furious."

Bryce quickly pulled away and began rummaging in her bag. While her back was turned, Scarlet undid Bryce's bra. Instead of letting it drop, she caught it and squeezed Bryce's breasts through the material. She couldn't miss the shudder that shook Bryce's body or the way she fell back against Scarlet to press her chest deeper into Scarlet's grasp.

"Get on the bed." Bryce looked over her shoulder at her. "Please."

Scarlet did as she was bid. Excitement pulsed through her blood. She knew her panties were already soaked. Slowly, deliberately, Scarlet crawled up the bed, affording Bryce an excellent view of her ass in lace that barely kept her modesty covered. She lay back but rested on her elbows watching Bryce strip completely. She climbed into her harness and slipped the toy into place. Scarlet's eyes were drawn to the cock that Bryce was pushing inside herself and then hooking through the harness.

"I approve of the color." Scarlet smiled at its bright red hue.

Bryce didn't look up as she securely fastened the straps. "It was the only color to choose where you are concerned." She ran her hand over the rounded head of the cock and slid her fist down its length.

Scarlet had to hold back a whimper as she watched Bryce pumping the shaft in her hand. She slipped off her panties and threw them in Bryce's direction. They hit her in the chest. "Come fuck me."

The long, body-stuttering moan surprised Scarlet. It was wrenched from Scarlet's chest as their naked bodies aligned for the first time. Bryce stretched out on top of her; they fit together perfectly. Scarlet devoured Bryce on sight. She was slender with muscles that defined her form. Scarlet could see reminders across her body of what the accident had wrought. She vowed to kiss every scar she found. She started with the easiest and pressed her lips to the prominent mark on Bryce's forehead.

They slipped onto their sides so hands could roam freely. Scarlet cupped and squeezed Bryce's breasts, loving the sensitivity and how dark her nipples grew every time Scarlet pinched them.

Kisses were traded, rough and wet. Scarlet wanted to taste Bryce further and spread soft nibbles and licks around Bryce's breasts. While her tongue flicked at a rigid nipple, her fingers rubbed over the areola and made it even more prominent. Scarlet then sucked it all into her mouth. Bryce bucked against her, pressing Scarlet's head firmly to her chest. Her fingers speared through Scarlet's hair, keeping her in place as Scarlet wrenched gasps from Bryce's lips.

Scarlet kissed a line across Bryce's chest as she switched lazily from one breast to the other. Bryce's hips pumped restlessly against Scarlet's thigh, her breathing erratic.

"You're driving me crazy." Bryce's voice rumbled into her ear. She was all but curled around Scarlet's body while Scarlet took what she wanted from her.

"I'm seeing how far I can tease you until you—"

"What? Snap like a rubber band?" Bryce pushed Scarlet roughly onto her back. "Consider that point reached." She brushed Scarlet's mouth with all too fleeting kisses. Bryce pushed in between Scarlet's legs and pressed down, holding her captive under her. When she finally needed to breathe, Bryce lifted her head from Scarlet's bruised lips.

Scarlet lost herself in Bryce's eyes. She was melting beneath her, high on her musky scent and the way she kissed.

"May I?" Bryce asked softly, nuzzling at Scarlet's cheek.

"You could just take me. I'm desperate for you," Scarlet said, widening her legs to fit Bryce between them just perfectly. She slipped her legs over Bryce's hips, her thigh-length boots rubbing sensuously against Bryce's naked skin. She smiled as Bryce closed her eyes briefly, lost to the sensation.

Bryce reached between them and positioned herself. "Why take when it's more desirable to have what I want freely given?" She nudged the head of the cock between Scarlet's soaked folds. It slipped easily in the copious arousal pooling there.

"I'm yours. Do what you want with me," Scarlet begged, arching her back to try to receive more contact with the toy Bryce was now teasing her with. She could feel the tip touching then retreating from her entrance as Bryce took her time coating the head with Scarlet's arousal. Without warning, Bryce tilted her hips and slid the cock deep into Scarlet in one long stroke.

"Oh my God," Scarlet moaned, feeling Bryce's breasts pressed against her own as she moved above her. Their mingled perspiration glistened on Scarlet's chest. Her boots slid along Bryce's narrow hips as she began to pump inside Scarlet in a maddening rhythm. Scarlet's nails left marks on Bryce's shoulders as she clung to her through every thrust. Shakily, the pleasure building inside of her, Scarlet smiled. "Fuck, you are so good at this."

"I'm out of practice," Bryce replied, lifting up a little to look down their bodies to where they were joined.

"Don't hurt your shoulder," Scarlet said, ever conscious of Bryce's injuries even while Bryce was slowly screwing her out of her mind.

"Fuck my shoulder," Bryce grunted, flexing her hips and sliding further into Scarlet.

"No, fuck me instead." Scarlet pulled Bryce back onto her, loving the feel of Bryce's hard nipples brushing against her own with every thrust. The angle of the cock brushed against Scarlet's hidden rough spot and made her increasingly wetter. She could feel her insides clenching down on each plunge and wasn't sure how much longer she could last.

"You are so beautiful," Bryce whispered as she rested her forehead against Scarlet's and pressed in harder. She flexed her hips, and with each thrust Scarlet's voice rose in pleasure.

"You're going to make me come so hard." Scarlet crossed her heels over Bryce's buttocks, and in her ardor unintentionally dug them into Bryce's ass. Bryce's back bowed, and she pushed the cock deeper still. Her body shook with her exertion, but she never stopped.

Scarlet's eyes didn't move from Bryce's face. Everything else was concentrated on the pleasure mounting between her legs. She could feel Bryce on her, *in* her, and when Bryce shifted her hips just a fraction more, the resulting pressure stole Scarlet's voice. The shaft of the cock was rubbing against her clitoris, and Scarlet knew it wouldn't take much more to make her come. She just hoped the neighbors were out because she had a feeling she was going to be loud.

Bryce began to shake in her own pleasure. A rough keening sound from her made Scarlet dig her heels in more.

"Come with me," Scarlet said as she clutched Bryce closer. She watched as Bryce's skin flushed red as her own arousal peaked. Their eyes locked, and Scarlet's orgasm hit her hard. She *was* loud as she called Bryce's name out in a scream. Her body spasmed as she felt the cock easily slipping through the abundance of moisture inside her. Scarlet had never ejaculated before, but she had a feeling if anyone could make her, Bryce would be the one. She repeated Bryce's name over and over in ecstasy and felt Bryce shudder on top of her as she came. Her frantic writhing atop of Scarlet triggered a second orgasm that rocked through Scarlet and soaked her thighs.

Bryce rested heavily on top of her, but Scarlet didn't care. She luxuriated in it. She clung to Bryce as delicious aftershocks tightened her inner walls around the deeply resting cock.

Scarlet finally loosened her death grip and felt Bryce start to pull out of her as gently as possible.

"Hey, where are you…?" Her head slid back down on the pillow as Bryce replaced the toy with her mouth. She lazily drew her tongue through Scarlet's slick nether lips and lapped at the wetness she found. "Oh God." Scarlet shook anew with every twist of Bryce's tongue at her entrance. "You're going to give me a heart attack," she wailed as she began building up to yet another climax under Bryce's unceasing ministrations.

"You teased me with just a taste earlier." Bryce's reply was muffled against Scarlet's curls that framed the top of her legs. "I had to see if tasting from the source was as sweet as I imagined it to be." She looked up to meet Scarlet's eyes. "It's even sweeter." She dove back in with a grin.

"I'd never done that before, and I'm not known for being shy," Scarlet admitted, pressing her hands down on Bryce's head to nudge her in the direction she needed the most. "Oh fuck, yes….just there. *There*. Oh my God, you'll be the death of me." The minute the words left her lips, Scarlet berated herself for the careless choice of wording.

"No, you reside too much in the light for me to take you into darkness." Bryce slipped her tongue inside Scarlet's sex, teasing her until Scarlet started to spasm again. Only then did Bryce take her clitoris between her teeth and suck hard.

The scream that erupted from Scarlet as she came once more was proof enough of how alive she was in Bryce's hands. She couldn't stop shaking. She whispered Bryce's name and Bryce moved up to cuddle close. Scarlet clutched her to her.

"I'm right here." Bryce smoothed her hand down Scarlet's damp back.

"Promise?" Scarlet knew she sounded needy, but she didn't care. Bryce meant so much to her and she wanted her close.

"I promise. You can close your eyes and rest a while. I'm right here."

"Your turn next," Scarlet said, wishing she could force her muscles to cooperate and move. She'd never been fucked into exhaustion before. It was just one new thing after another making love with Bryce.

"I'll be waiting."

Scarlet felt Bryce undoing the buckles at her hips, shucking the harness off. Next was the soft sound of a zipper being drawn down, and Scarlet's boots were carefully peeled off one at a time.

"I think you speared my ass cheek with those lethal heels."

Scarlet cracked open one eye. Bryce didn't look upset.

"It's okay. I think I liked it." Her shy smile made Scarlet smirk in response. "Sleep, my angel. I'll be right here watching over you tonight."

Scarlet buried her face in the curve of Bryce's neck and breathed in her scent. It soothed her, the warmth and strength of Bryce's arms around her. It felt like home.

❖

Bryce jerked herself awake just before the first scream escaped her. Her chest hitched as her breath came rushing out in harsh, ragged pants. Bryce quickly realized where she was and who she was with. She looked down at Scarlet snuggled tight against her chest. Scarlet's eyelashes were fluttering, as Bryce's jerk back to wakefulness had disturbed her sleep too.

"You okay?" Scarlet lifted her head to capture Bryce's eyes.

"Same old, same old," Bryce grunted, scrubbing at her face.

Scarlet's own hand slid down to rest on Bryce's abs. The soothing patterns she traced there calmed Bryce's erratic breathing down. She shifted restlessly every time Scarlet gently scored her with her nails before returning to the belly rub that was anything but innocent.

"I fell asleep on you." Scarlet pressed soft kisses on Bryce's shoulder then nuzzled her face into Bryce's breast. Her breath was hot over Bryce's hard nipple.

"I wore you out. I was basking in the smugness of that fact when I apparently fell asleep." Her muscles tensed as Scarlet's fingers trailed across her abdomen and slipped down further.

"It's my turn now." Scarlet began to lick lazy circles around Bryce's nipple.

Bryce's whole body twitched as she tried to keep still under Scarlet's maddening touches. She was being driven crazy with every pass of her hot, wet tongue.

"Are you a screamer, Bryce?" Scarlet asked, gently nipping at Bryce's skin before laving her tongue over each stinging bite.

"Not that I've ever been aware of." Bryce was surprised by how much her voice shook when she answered.

"Let's see if I can rectify that." Scarlet smirked up at her from her place on Bryce's chest. "I can think of nothing sweeter than the sound of my name torn from your lips in a cry of pleasure."

Bryce grinned. "You're awfully eloquent in the early hours of the morning for someone who hasn't had much sleep." She writhed under Scarlet's caress. Her hands seemed to be able to touch her everywhere all at once. It was equally distracting and intensely arousing. Bryce gripped at Scarlet's arms to keep herself grounded. Under Scarlet's restless fingers, Bryce felt like she was vibrating out of her skin. She was coming undone with every brush of Scarlet's warm touch. The feeling frightened her. Her hands tightened a fraction more as the all too familiar emotion of worthlessness washed over her. Obviously sensing the change in her, Scarlet lifted her head to look at her.

"Make me forget," Bryce said, burrowing her face into Scarlet's neck so she wouldn't read all that was written on Bryce's face. She screwed her eyes up tight against the tears she could feel threatening to escape.

Scarlet hugged her close. "I'll make you forget everything but me. You'll feel only my hands, my lips, my love."

Bryce pulled her head out from its hiding place to make sure she'd heard right. Scarlet's smile was beautiful to behold and all directed at her.

"Yes, *love*. I could easily fall in love with you, Bryce. I've known that from the very first moment I met you." Her accompanying kiss was passion filled, pushing Bryce back onto the bed.

Bryce let Scarlet take her. She loved the confidence Scarlet exuded, found it sexy and exciting. Gerri had been controlling; everything they did together was planned and scheduled. Scarlet was unpredictable, a little wild and untamed. Bryce was pulled toward her like the proverbial moth drawn to the flame haired fire that Scarlet burned with. For all that she felt she didn't deserve happiness, Scarlet brought that to her.

Scarlet drew back from their kiss but didn't pull away. Her hair fell like a curtain around them, hiding them from the outside world in a drapery of softest silk. She began delivering a series of soft pecks to Bryce's smiling mouth, drawing out the time between each kiss. Bryce growled deep in her throat at her and pulled her down for something less teasing before easing back and capturing Scarlet's attention.

No more hiding. The shadows can't take away every little sliver of light and hope I need to exist.

"I could easily fall for you too," she said, thrilled to witness the joy that suffused Scarlet's face before she was bowled over by the enthusiasm that fueled their next kiss. Finally, when allowed to draw breath, Bryce laughed with joy. It was a genuine, long forgotten sound that Bryce almost didn't recognize coming from herself.

Scarlet's eyes shone with unashamed adoration. "Oh, hello, my love. There you are finally. There's a piece of my Bryce that's been absent for so long," she crooned, scattering kisses over Bryce's eyelids, down her nose, lingering tenderly on her scar. "I've got you. You're safe now," Scarlet whispered repeatedly as she trailed a way down Bryce's body to settle between her thighs.

Just like Scarlet had promised, Bryce forgot everything at the touch of her lips and her tongue. Scarlet spread Bryce's labia apart, her thumbs slicking through the sticky arousal pooled there. She spread the abundant wetness up around Bryce's clit, firmly rubbing over the engorged head. Bryce bucked under every sweet touch. Scarlet's tongue finally entered her, and Bryce grabbed at her head, holding her there.

"Oh God, Scarlet," she whined, her back bowing and lifting her off the bed.

Scarlet drew back for just a second before taking Bryce back in her mouth. "Forget everything but me."

Pleasure blasted through Bryce's every fiber. She felt no pain, no ache from healing scars. She felt only Scarlet. The flashing lights Bryce saw behind her closed eyelids were welcomed, and the only sound she could hear were Scarlet's murmurs of satisfaction as she took Bryce closer to orgasm. Bryce's hips were held by Scarlet's surprisingly strong hands, keeping her in place for Scarlet's ravaging mouth. Firm lips sucked in Bryce's clit at a maddening tempo that forced Bryce to clutch at the sheets, desperate for an anchor.

Bryce's surprised shout at climax filled the silence. She was shaken by the violent aftershocks clenching her stomach muscles and pulsing through her sex. For a long moment, Bryce couldn't remember anything. Instead she just *felt*.

Scarlet slid up Bryce's body and kissed her. Bryce could taste herself on Scarlet's face.

"Neither of us are getting any more sleep tonight, handsome," Scarlet warned her as she began deliberately rubbing herself against Bryce's wetness.

Bryce could feel her arousal sparking back to life with a vengeance with every pass of Scarlet's hard clit brushing against her own. Mindlessly, she lifted her hips to help Scarlet hit the right spot. Bryce grasped Scarlet's breasts in her hands and squeezed gently, loving the feel of full nipples pressing against her palms. She grinned as Scarlet's thrusts grew more erratic when Bryce trapped the hardened nipples between her fingers and squeezed again.

"I've heard sleep is overrated," Bryce said. The dreams wouldn't bother her anymore tonight. Scarlet was going to do her damnedest to chase them all away.

Chapter Eighteen

The weekend afforded Bryce the chance to witness just how talented Scarlet was in her art. Scarlet had been lounging lazily in Bryce's arms, her back snug against Bryce's chest as they were sprawled on the sofa. Bryce had been enjoying their closeness, relaxing after a lovemaking session that had been slow and sensuous. Basking in the warmth of their post-coital cuddling, Bryce had been intrigued when Scarlet whipped out her phone and had taken a candid shot of them both. Bryce had let out a disgruntled "Hey!" when Scarlet shifted from her spot and rushed to gather some paper and pencils. Quickly returning to Bryce's arms, Scarlet settled in and began putting pencil to paper, drawing the picture of them from her phone.

From her vantage point over Scarlet's shoulder, Bryce watched in fascination as pencil lines soon morphed into their very recognizable faces.

"You're very good at that," Bryce said. She was spellbound as time ticked by and Scarlet added color to the page and their features sprang to life. She noted Scarlet didn't shy away from making sure her scar was exactly how it looked. It was a part of her now. Bryce knew she had to accept that. Seeing it added to her face so matter-of-fact on the paper didn't upset Bryce as much as she'd have expected. She was more amazed by how thoroughly Scarlet was documenting the freckles scattered across her cheeks.

Barely daring to breathe and break the spell, Bryce watched Scarlet switch colors, and her flame-colored hair leapt to life on the page. Hours passed in companionable silence while Scarlet worked and Bryce watched on in awe.

"Fuck me, you're astounding." The pride she felt in Scarlet's art suffused her, and she readily accepted the kiss that Scarlet turned around and gifted her with.

"Look at how gorgeous we are together," Scarlet said finally, adding the finishing touches to her picture.

To Bryce it looked exactly like the photograph on the phone. Scarlet had brought them to life just using pencil strokes. What Bryce noticed most of all in both versions of the candid shot was that they looked happy together. When Scarlet held the picture aloft, Bryce couldn't stop herself from hugging her close.

"Have I mentioned how much I adore you?" she asked.

"A few times, but I'm not going to get tired of it so don't ever stop." Scarlet put the picture aside carefully. "I'll frame that later." She twisted in Bryce's arms. "Promise me you won't be disappointed when I choose my art over my dad's business?"

Bryce shook her head. "I'd be more annoyed if you chose house painting over the fantastic things you can do with your photos or paints. You have the most amazing talent, Scarlet. Don't let anyone take you off the path to explore that."

"My last girlfriend told me to quit the doodling and get a proper job," Scarlet admitted with a grimace.

"My last girlfriend told everyone I ran my own business because the fact I worked for your father wasn't good enough for her reputation."

"I still want to slap that bitch," Scarlet growled.

"Maybe one day," Bryce said with a wink.

Scarlet burrowed her head into Bryce's neck. "Can I share something with you?"

"You can tell me anything, everything, darling."

Scarlet got up again and Bryce huffed at her loss. Scarlet laughed at her disgruntled face. She pulled a large album out of a drawer.

"This is my portfolio. One day I want to have my own show. Some of these I'd like up on display." She nudged Bryce's knees and Bryce sat up. Scarlet opened the album, and Bryce got to see Scarlet's photographic work. Landscapes, animals, portraits—Scarlet had a mixture of everything. When Bryce came to the photos of people she recognized, she began to smile. She saw the raw beauty of the intimate, naked shot taken of Trent and a very pregnant Juliet. It showed off their impending parenthood exquisitely.

"Oh my God, that is breathtaking," Bryce said, touched by just how much was revealed in the picture. Not in their nakedness but in their expressions Scarlet had captured. "You can't miss how much they love each other."

"They're what I aspire to," Scarlet said.

"Including children?" She'd never considered that possibility in her future.

"Maybe, one day, if it's something we both want."

Bryce stared at Scarlet. "Wow. Something tells me this weekend has become more than just a passionate romp between the sheets."

"And are you okay with that?"

"It's giving me a lot to consider. Something tells me life with you isn't going to be boring."

"I'll do my best to keep you entertained." Scarlet nudged her with a shoulder playfully.

"And I'll do my best not to let the shadows overwhelm me." Bryce smiled as Scarlet pressed a warm kiss to her forehead.

"I couldn't ask for more."

"Show me the rest of your photos and I'll show you more later."

Scarlet made as if to close the album, but Bryce, laughing, took it off her, and continued turning the pages. She came across a picture of herself. Its inclusion surprised her. Bryce studied herself.

"I look haunted."

Scarlet rested her chin on Bryce's shoulder. "Yes, you do, lover. But look at today." She put her drawing beside the black-and-white photo. "Look how far you've come."

"I still have a long way to go," Bryce said.

"I'll be right beside you," Scarlet promised.

Bryce rested her head against Scarlet's. "I'll do my damnedest to be worthy of your belief in me."

"You won't always have the burden of grief, Bryce. You've got so much happiness to look forward to in your life. I intend to play a large role in that."

Bryce settled into Scarlet's side. "You already do."

For a moment, the shadows lifted off her heart and the crippling pressure shifted from her soul. She closed her eyes, and for the first time in what felt like forever, Bryce faced the future with a little less fear weighing her down.

❖

With the last stroke of paint applied on a very happy Yoshi, Scarlet put down her brush and took a satisfied step back. She did one last check over the whole mural to make sure everything was as it should be. She'd been painting every evening for the past week, and it was now completed.

"Finished." She slipped out of the room in search of where Trent and Juliet were camped out. She followed the noise of heavy gunfire and Juliet's exuberance.

"Blow it up! Blow it up!"

Scarlet stepped into Trent's gaming room and hung back. The TV screen dominated the room, and on it she watched Trent piloting a very large robot armed with massive guns.

Juliet let out a triumphant "Yes!" as an enemy machine was blown to pieces in a raging fireball. She then spotted Scarlet. "Everything okay?" she mouthed.

Scarlet mouthed back "I'm done," and Juliet's face lit up.

"Trent, last mission, sweetheart."

Trent nodded and continued playing. The fight didn't last much longer, and Trent's pilot was soon racing for his evacuation ship, his body cloaked so he couldn't be detected by the enemy camped out to pick off the remaining fighters. As her scores for that round came up on screen, Trent gave a satisfied grunt and then with the press of a button, she exited the game. She laid her controller down and shifted in her seat, looking behind her at Scarlet.

"Is it finished?" she asked.

At Scarlet's nod, Trent was on her feet and helping Juliet up off the sofa.

"What are you playing?" Scarlet asked, looking at the TV screen that displayed a futuristic looking soldier standing ready for action.

"Titanfall," Trent replied, "It's kind of like a Call of Duty with added robots."

"Do you always have a cheering squad when playing it?" Scarlet nodded toward Juliet.

"Not usually, but I think Juliet likes the Titans the best."

Juliet followed them out. "It's addictive viewing, and I'm just grateful not to be asleep. All I seem to do lately is sleep."

"Babies are body draining experiences, or so I'm told," Scarlet said as she ushered them into the nursery and stood back to watch their reactions. Trent didn't disappoint.

"Oh my God. It's freakin' awesome!" She left Juliet's side to go check out the colorful display. She walked around the whole room following the pattern of gamboling Yoshis so she didn't miss a thing. "It's fantastic, absolutely fucking fantastic, and yes, I owe a dollar for that, but it's worth it. I love it, every single piece of it." She reached out but pulled her hand back. "I'll wait until the paint dries before I start touching. Christ, they look so real."

Juliet was just as excited. She oohed and ahhed over the adorable little characters. "It's perfect. Scarlet, you are amazing." She gave her a hug and Scarlet delighted in the press of a very hard baby bump against her.

"Wow, you put off some serious heat with that thing."

"She's one hot mama period," Trent said. She captured Scarlet's face between her hands and planted a gentle kiss on her forehead. "This is just so beautiful. Thank you."

Scarlet knew she was blushing under Trent's hold. "You are both very welcome. Now you just need to finish baking that baby so we can all meet him or her."

"The way I've been feeling this past week, I think it's going to be sooner rather than later." Juliet shifted uncomfortably.

"She's been getting false contractions. Those are so much fun in the middle of the night."

Juliet just grinned at her. "We've been in the car twice and halfway off the drive the last time. Trent is excellent at snatching the baby bag up under one arm and having me under the other."

"It's a good thing I learned to drive now that you can't fit behind the wheel." Trent rubbed Juliet's stomach gently. "No better incentive to get me on the road."

"Well, with all these false alarms we're going to find the quickest route to the hospital before we have to go for real." Juliet patted Trent gently on her chest. "How about you go back to your game while I grill Scarlet here about her lovefest weekend with Bryce?"

Trent spared Scarlet a pitying glance. "She'll have you spilling intimate details in three minutes."

"I might prove impervious to her interrogation techniques."

Trent laughed at her. "You haven't been so far."

Scarlet had to concede to the truth in that. She had spilled her teenage crush on Trent to Juliet within minutes of meeting her.

"I feel so sorry for your child. It'll never get away with anything."

Juliet tucked her arm through Scarlet's. "Come make me a cup of tea and tell me all about your weekend alone with Bryce. This is only Monday; the details should still be fresh in your mind."

"Like I could forget any of it. I kind of told her I was falling head over heels for her."

Trent's voice sounded from her game room. "Ladies and gentlemen! It's a new world record. You never even made it to the top of the stairs."

Scarlet met Juliet's sparkling eyes.

"Even I thought you'd hold out longer than that." Juliet chuckled. "I want details, lots of them. The more salacious the better."

CHAPTER NINETEEN

Scarlet was making the most of a quiet lunch break outside in the company of Bryce and the landscapers. She was scouring the Internet on her phone, checking if any new vacancies had opened at the photography studios she had earmarked on her list. She'd already sent off her résumé to a few. She knew her father was only going to keep applying the pressure the longer she stayed in his employment. She'd started ignoring his daily text messages. He'd soon caught on to this and had gotten his secretary to call her instead. Scarlet was fast reaching the end of her patience.

"Scarlet, I need you to come into the office Friday so I can have you meet some new clients we're taking on."

Scarlet looked up from her lunch as her father headed her way. Bryce, seated next to her, hesitated in taking the next bite from her sandwich. Scarlet tensed as a feeling of dread filled her. *Oh, Dad, please don't do this again now.*

"I have Friday off, Dad. I've just booked it." She was going to a photography exhibition and hoped to pick up some new contacts there.

"That's great, then we can make a day of it."

Scarlet stared at him. "No. I have the day off work as in I will not be working here at the site or with you in your office. I have other plans."

"But I'd like you to sit in on the meetings I have scheduled. They're important."

"No can do," Scarlet said shortly, her annoyance starting to grow. She felt Bryce shift by her side, obviously aware of the storm brewing.

"You have to learn what all this entails one day, so why not Friday? Whatever you have planned can wait, surely?"

"No, it can't. I've told you, Dad, I didn't come back here to learn the running of Tweedy Contractors. Not today, not tomorrow, nor next week. I came back because my last job finished and I wanted to come home." She looked around her. Monica was well within hearing distance and was looking over at Scarlet with concern. "Dad, are you dying?" Scarlet asked baldly.

He blustered. "Not that I'm aware of. What kind of question is that to ask?"

"Then why the sudden need to have me take over your place in your company? If I'd have known you were going to constantly badger me to fill your shoes, I would have seriously thought twice about coming back." He physically flinched at her words.

"Maybe we should discuss this another time," he muttered.

"No." Scarlet had had enough. "You've brought it up every time we've crossed paths and I'm tired of it." She stood, laying her lunch down before she threw it. She was beginning to tremble with anger and an underlying fear. She was standing up against her father, the man who had raised her from the day her mother had died. She loved him. But she couldn't stand being pushed into a role she didn't want to take.

"Tweedy's has always been your company. It's not my dream, Dad. I want to take my photographs and paint portraits and make a name for myself doing what *I'm* good at."

"But this business was always meant to be yours. It was always going to be passed down to you. It's my legacy to you."

"But I don't want it. It's not my dream job. It's not what I've studied for and worked hard to achieve for myself. My photography is. That's *mine*. I've earned that by myself." Scarlet took a shuddering breath. "I've got the day off Friday to try and find a new job doing what I enjoy doing best. My *own* work."

His face fell. "You're leaving me?"

Scarlet shook her head. *There* was the root of his pressing. "No, but I'm leaving your business if an offer comes up. This is what I was working toward when I was away from home, Dad. You didn't keep pressuring me with running your company then."

"I was hoping you'd grow out of it and come home and take your rightful place here," he said sheepishly.

Scarlet's frustration reached its boiling point. "This is not some phase I'm going through. I'm an artist, and a damn good one too."

"I know. I've seen your work. You're fantastic. The best I know."

"Then don't stand in my way to pursue that," Scarlet pleaded. "It's what I need to do. Because it's what I'm going to do, whether you approve or not."

"You're just like your mother. Too artistic for your own good."

Scarlet heard the disappointment in his voice. It broke her heart. "You should have realized then that you never stood a chance. While you let me run wild on the building site, she taught me how to do those paint-by-numbers kits."

"And the rest is all your own God-given talent." He shook his head. "I recognize how good you are. I understand your need to strike out on your own. But this business is yours whether you want it or not because you're all I have. You're my only child. I've built all this for you." He gestured around the yard. "It's always been yours."

"But I don't want any of it. I want to follow my own path, make my own name." Scarlet forced her temper to cool. "I told you when I accepted the job here that it was only until I found something else. Decorating is my fallback job. It pays the bills, but it's not my career."

"You told me you wanted to work by my side. Just you and me."

"I was ten years old when I told you that!" Scarlet couldn't help but raise her voice at him. "We'd just lost Mom. All we had was each other and Grandma. I didn't want to leave my daddy's side. But I had to grow up eventually, Dad. I have to live my own life and you have to let me."

The whole yard was silent. All the workers in earshot were pretending they were going about their jobs and not listening in. Bryce had edged closer to Scarlet. She pressed her knee against Scarlet's leg in a silent show of support.

Scarlet watched her dad as he stared her down. He shoved his hands in his pockets and turned abruptly away.

"Well, it's too late now. I've had the lawyer draft the papers for you. You need to sign them on Friday."

Scarlet reared back like she'd been physically slapped. She willed her voice not to shake when she finally spoke.

"Then I quit."

His shock was plainly visible when he spun back around. "You can't do that!"

"Yes, I can. I'm just another employee here. I'll work my notice and leave. You're not having me sign away my dreams because you're worried you're going to lose me. You won't ever lose me, Dad. I'm your daughter. But you've pushed me far enough away with this constant badgering that I just can't take it any longer."

"But I won't be able to fill your spot for at least a couple of months," he argued weakly, desperate to use any excuse to keep her there.

Scarlet shrugged. "That's your problem, not mine." She gathered up her things and began walking away. She had just one last thing to say. "After all, *you* run the company. *I don't*."

❖

Bryce returned to her apartment that evening to find Scarlet in the kitchen. She followed the unearthly racket Scarlet was making banging the saucepans around. To ensure she had pans left to use, Bryce stilled Scarlet's hands then guided her into the living area. Scarlet wrapped herself around Bryce, clinging to her tightly.

"I quit my job today."

"I know." Bryce ran a hand through Scarlet's hair, hoping to soothe her. "You were very restrained though considering what your dad pulled. Though your leaving as you did meant you missed seeing Monica give him a piece of her mind."

Scarlet groaned into Bryce's shoulder. "Oh God, she didn't did she?"

"Just a little, but at least she didn't stick him with a fork, so that was a blessing."

"She's seen how much he's been expecting of me. He turned up at the apartment a few times out of the blue, just 'dropping by' to talk business. Why won't he hear a word I say when I tell him I don't want the company on my shoulders?"

"Because he'd obviously built so much on the fact you were finally coming back home that he was damned determined to keep you here this time. He missed you, Scarlet."

"He's going to end up pushing me away again. He's smothering me. I have my own life to live."

"He obviously didn't see it like that. Hopefully, he'll come around."

"I'm still going to that show on Friday. I need a studio to take me on full-time. If not, then I need to look further afield."

The implication of those words startled Bryce. "You'd move away again?"

Scarlet nodded against Bryce's neck. "If the right job came up, then yes. I need to do my art. If I can't find anywhere here then I need to start looking where there's an opening."

The consequences of that and what it meant to Bryce stunned her into silence for a moment. Scarlet could be leaving. Not just her job but *her*.

"Have you…" Bryce forced herself not to reveal her fears. "Have you sent your résumé out to many studios that aren't close to home?"

"A few," Scarlet admitted. She lifted her head up to look at Bryce. "I had a horrible feeling this was going to happen when I got back. I was so excited to be coming home that I tried to ignore them. I've sent some résumés out to different cities just to test the waters."

"And if you get offered a job?" Bryce tried not to let the dread in her voice escape.

"Then I'd have to consider it. I've worked too hard to give it all up to sit behind a desk because Dad wants me chained to his side."

Bryce nodded in understanding. "So, what happens now?"

"I work my notice. I've already contacted the photographer I'm currently with and asked for any extra hours they can give me." She rested her forehead against Bryce's. "Have I just burned all my bridges, Bryce? Did I do something really stupid here?"

Bryce's head was still reeling at the thought that Scarlet might be leaving more than just the job behind. "No. You were being backed into a corner. Or more accurately a corner office you didn't want."

Scarlet pulled back. "If I leave…would you come with me?" Bryce's jaw dropped. "Do you really think I could just walk away from you, Bryce?"

"I…" Bryce faltered. She didn't know what she thought. Could she leave? She was in a job where her colleagues could look at her damaged face without flinching. She had a home where she felt reasonably safe so long as she kept the light on. Bryce honestly didn't know how she would cope having to start over in a new environment. Not when she was only just starting to piece her life back together in this familiar one. To be taken out of her comfort zone? The feeling truly terrified her. Her breath began to escape in quick, short pants as the fear rolled over her and started to make her blind to her surroundings.

"Hey, hey. You come back to me, lover." Scarlet's hands ran over Bryce's face.

The familiar touch brought Bryce slowly back to where she stood. She blinked rapidly at the sudden rush of tears that threatened to spill from her eyes.

"I don't know if I can," she whispered. She wrapped herself around Scarlet as the silent sobs wrenched through her body and ripped open her soul.

"It's okay, it's okay," Scarlet said, feathering her fingers through Bryce's hair to calm her.

No, it's not. Because you'll be the loss I won't ever recover from.

Chapter Twenty

Two weeks' notice. Two weeks' notice. Every stroke of paint Scarlet applied to the wall seemed to echo with the mantra. She was equal parts excited and terrified by what she had done. She'd started receiving replies from studios interested in her, so that, at least, was gratifying. It meant she had choices now. Some of the positions were just a few hours' commute away, others were from much farther afield.

Scarlet hated how Bryce's already pale complexion whitened even more on the arrival of each envelope in the mail. She understood Bryce's reluctance to leave. She was still recovering from a trauma, and Scarlet acknowledged that uprooting her would be cruel. Scarlet's logical mind recognized that fact. But her heart wanted Bryce with her. She knew she was falling in love with Bryce. It wasn't a passing infatuation; it was something deeper than Scarlet had ever experienced before. Walking away from her job, walking away from the responsibilities expected of her, was hard enough. Scarlet had never wanted any of that anyway. But leaving Bryce behind? That wasn't something Scarlet wanted to imagine. The pain was a knife plunged into her chest every time she dared even contemplate going alone. The letters arriving were compounding that.

Sooner or later, Scarlet had to make a choice. She didn't want to *not* choose Bryce.

The atmosphere on the site was oddly cautious. Ever since the very public display between Scarlet and her dad, everyone had taken to walking on eggshells around them both. Her dad rarely came on site now, and if he did, he steered clear of Scarlet's location.

I just want to leave, Scarlet thought, then everyone can get back to normal. Business as usual, just without the boss's daughter casting a cloud of discontent over everything.

Alice had been sent in as a go-between to try to talk some sense into Scarlet. Or so her dad had hoped. Instead, Alice had taken Scarlet's side and wished her well. Along with commissioning a portrait of her grandchildren when Scarlet had the time free for a sitting.

Scarlet knew her dad would eventually come around. She remembered him sulking for weeks when she'd initially moved away. He'd finally forgiven her, but it wasn't easy for him to let go. She knew that was because of the loss they had suffered. It still didn't mean he could rule her life now.

Scarlet heard a noise at the open door and looked down from her scaffold. There stood Bryce. *Two weeks' notice.* Scarlet would sorely miss seeing Bryce's face every day. They had taken to spending most of their nights together, in one apartment or the other. Bryce was still plagued by the terrible dreams when she succumbed to sleep. Scarlet wanted to be the only one who drew her out of the nightmares and back into the comfort of her open arms.

"Hey, handsome." She finished up her painting and carefully picked her way down the scaffold. Bryce was ready to meet her at the bottom. She reached for Scarlet's hand to help her step down.

"Juliet's here. I thought you might like to come see her." Bryce pulled Scarlet closer for a lingering kiss. "I'm going to miss being able to sneak to whatever room you're working in and steal a kiss from you."

"I'd better not hear about you substituting Gregor instead." Scarlet grinned at the horrified face Bryce made.

"He'd need to at least shave first." She ran her fingers along Scarlet's cheek. "I prefer less stubble when I'm making out."

"I'll be sure to remember that," Scarlet said, pressing a kiss into Bryce's palm. "I didn't know Juliet was coming today. I thought she was sticking closer to home because her due date is so close."

"I think she was going stir crazy staring at the four walls so she staged a jail break and caught a cab here."

"Trent is going to kill her."

"Trent has no power against those sparkly blue eyes of hers."

"Do I wield that kind of power over you yet?" Scarlet playfully batted her eyelashes at her.

"You know you do and have from the start. Not to mention you bewitched me with your singing."

Scarlet laughed and wrapped her arms around Bryce's neck, hugging her close. "You'll miss my warbling."

"I know."

Her heart clenched at the despondent lilt in Bryce's voice. All Scarlet could do was hold Bryce closer, stealing a few more precious moments in her arms.

❖

The soft silky length of Scarlet's legs, draped over Bryce's shoulders, muffled the sounds of Scarlet's pleasure from Bryce's ears. Bryce's attention was centered on dragging her tongue through Scarlet's arousal. She teased unmercifully as Scarlet shuddered and moaned beneath her. With the tip of her tongue, she licked around Scarlet's now overly sensitive clit. A directing hand in Bryce's hair tightened and pushed her closer still to where Scarlet wanted her attentions. Bryce smiled against the soft flesh she had her face pressed into and deliberately hummed. Scarlet answered with a high-pitched wail as she writhed against Bryce's hold.

"You're driving me crazy." Her hips bucking, Scarlet panted, "Fuck me, please."

Bryce entered Scarlet with her fingers with little preamble. The hoarse scream that ripped from Scarlet's throat made Bryce thankful Monica was sleeping over at Elton's that night. Scarlet's warmth clutched Bryce's fingers tightly, making her work to penetrate her deeper. She knew it wouldn't be much longer before Scarlet would come. She'd been teasing her for much longer than Scarlet could usually take. Bryce sucked Scarlet's clit roughly in a rhythm she knew by heart now. She kneaded at Scarlet's breast in counter point, alternating between flicking her nipple and thumbing the peak. Bryce composed a love theme as her hands played across Scarlet's flushed skin. Scarlet calling her name out as she peaked was all the music Bryce ever needed to hear.

Sated and blissfully boneless, Scarlet let Bryce draw her into her arms to sleep. With a drowsy kiss of thanks, Scarlet was out like a light in seconds. Bryce laid her cheek against Scarlet's hair and breathed her in. Her eyes fell on the envelope lying open on the bedside table. It held a letter offering Scarlet a very prestigious position at a photography studio that would foster her talents and give her the room to explore her creativity. It was a dream job that was perfect for Scarlet.

It was back in Chicago.

Bryce didn't want to hold Scarlet back from pursuing her dreams. She knew Scarlet was so much more than a decorating job would allow her to be. Chicago wasn't home though. It wasn't *here* where Bryce was. Heartsick, Bryce stared blindly around the bedroom. Scarlet always made sure it was bright enough not to trigger Bryce's fear of the dark. She'd grown to feel safe there. If Bryce did manage to fall asleep, only to wake up in the grips of a nightmare, she was comforted by the now familiar sights. She was safe with Scarlet. This apartment felt like home.

Her eyes strayed to the envelope once more. She couldn't shake the feeling of dread that losing Scarlet would bring. Once again, she'd be left hanging in the darkness, with no one there to bring her out of the nightmare.

She placed a soft kiss on Scarlet's forehead. Scarlet deserved a life full of love and light. She didn't deserve the shadows that Bryce had blanketing her world. As she lay forcibly keeping sleep at bay, Bryce cursed her own insecurities and fears for coming between them. Eventually, she drifted off into a restless sleep. As always, she went back to that night, back to being suspended in the wreck of the car, left alone with the dead and dying. When she woke herself screaming, Scarlet was once again drawing her back to the living.

Held in Scarlet's arms, Bryce wanted desperately to confess her feelings for her. All the time that envelope mocked her with its presence. She wouldn't use her love as a means to guilt Scarlet into staying. Maybe it was for the best if Scarlet chose Chicago. She didn't deserve a life of what Bryce had to offer here.

So she clung a little harder to Scarlet, not daring to let go, because this time in her dream, no one had come to her rescue.

Chapter Twenty-one

The atmosphere at Scarlet's impromptu going away party was more somber than a cause for celebration. Her father was still keeping his distance, and most of the workmen didn't know whether being happy for Scarlet was something they should express. Gregor had been uncharacteristically quiet on the subject. Scarlet had a feeling that was due to Juliet having a word with him about the situation not long after it had blown up. The general consensus was they were all sorry to see her go, that the new guy wouldn't be as attractive to be around, and that they wouldn't miss her music playing.

Bryce had been noticeably quiet while they'd tucked into the Subway sandwiches Scarlet had treated them all to as a going-away gift. Scarlet knew Bryce was desperately trying not to influence her choice in what jobs were coming her way. Bryce was supportive, attentive, and honestly interested in what each studio had to offer her. Scarlet hadn't missed the flash of pain that clouded her eyes when the locations were discussed. It tore at her heart to know that Bryce didn't want her to leave but was respectful of whatever she decided to do. She couldn't help but wish her dad had been the same. If he had, she wouldn't have found herself having to make another life-changing decision so soon after moving back home.

Scarlet packed the last of her tools together and wiped off her hands on a rag. She'd finished off the last room for the day. Her two-week period was up; she was done.

"Can I take you home, pretty lady?" Bryce asked from the doorway, her messenger bag over her shoulder and her cap in place ready to face the public.

Scarlet took one last look around the room. "Let's go. I'm done here."

❖

The early evening air was warm on their faces when they stepped out of the house. Bryce had barely taken a few steps before she heard an odd whimpering noise coming from the garden behind the house she'd been working in. She tugged Scarlet to a halt.

"Did you hear something?"

Scarlet listened but shook her head.

The sound appeared again and Bryce headed off to investigate. She easily spotted its source.

"Juliet?" Bryce rushed over to her.

Juliet was sitting on the small fold up chair that was designated for her alone in the work area. She was doubled over, clutching at her belly.

"What are you doing here?" Bryce dropped to her knees beside her. Scarlet took her other side, brushing Juliet's hair back from her face.

"I came to check on some inventory. I can't do that from home, and Monica had already left so I thought I'd just come do it myself." She grimaced. "Probably not the smartest decision I've made today."

"How did you get here? Tell me you didn't drive?" Scarlet asked.

"I got a ride from a neighbor and I was going to call for a taxi to get back." The gasp that escaped her lips was pain filled.

"We need to call an ambulance," Bryce said, scrambling for her phone. Juliet grabbed for her hand to stop her.

"No. I'm not due for another two weeks yet."

"Juliet, I don't think this baby has time to follow your schedule." Bryce winced as Juliet's hold tightened considerably as another pain racked her body. Bryce shot Scarlet a look. "She needs to go now."

Scarlet helped Juliet up from her seat. "Come on, we need to get you out of here."

"You've got to get Trent," Juliet said.

"We will, but I need you in the car so I can get you to the hospital."

"Trent's going to be so upset," Juliet wailed, leaning heavily on Bryce and Scarlet as they guided her to the car. "She learned to drive just for this event."

"She's not going to be upset. She's going to be a happy mama and glad you're both okay." Scarlet pulled out her keys and unlocked the car. "Juliet, I think you're going to have to get in the back. There's more leg room." She helped maneuver Juliet in and then turned to Bryce.

"I need you in with her. She can't be left alone like this."

Time had stood still while Bryce had stopped breathing.

Everyone dies in the backseat.

"Get her out of there," she ground out. "She's not safe in the back."

"Bryce." Scarlet grabbed hold of Bryce's arms and purposely stood in front of her, staring her down. "Juliet is going to be fine, but I need to get her to the hospital as soon as possible. I need you to be with her because she's in pain, she's scared, and we need to just go."

"Everyone dies in the backseat. Get her out, please." A black mist descended, obscuring Bryce's vision. Without warning, she was back in the dark of night, waiting for that telltale sound of a roaring engine. She was waiting for the headlights to come barreling toward them. She braced for the impact as the memory took a hold of her. Instead, she was shaken harshly by Scarlet. Blinking, Bryce stared at her, disoriented and terrified. She could just make out Scarlet's face before her, tense and pleading.

"I can't get in the backseat," Bryce muttered forcefully, her whole body shaking visibly. She felt Scarlet push something into her hand. She stared down at the objects dumbly.

"Then you'll have to drive."

❖

White noise roared through Bryce's head. Dimly, she could see Scarlet's lips moving, but for a brief moment Bryce was deaf to everything but her inner voice.

If I get in the car, everyone dies.

Scarlet's grip tightened on Bryce's face, forcing her to listen.

"Juliet needs us. You have to get us to the hospital. She can't have the baby here, and an ambulance will be too late."

Bryce could hear the sounds of Juliet in distress.

"The guards can't leave their posts. You have to help us." Scarlet caressed her cheeks softly. "I know you're scared. I wouldn't ask this of you any other time, but I need you to do this."

"If I get in the car, something will happen."

"Yes, we'll get Juliet to the hospital in time to have her baby. You can do this." Scarlet kissed her roughly. She brushed away the tears that were streaming down Bryce's cheeks. "Maybe this is it."

"What?" Bryce was shaking as if in a seizure, the weight of the car keys heavy in her palm.

"This is your reason, the reason why you are here. Why you were spared that night. You get to repay it now by saving Juliet and the baby."

Bryce stared at the keys in her hand. "I haven't driven in months."

Scarlet guided her toward the car. "You haven't forgotten how. You can do this. I know you can. No more shadows, Bryce. It's time to help Juliet bring her baby into the light."

Bryce paused at the open car door. She could feel Scarlet's hand on her back urging her forward. Her breath escaped in short, fearful gasps. Bryce eased herself into the driver's seat and felt the nausea rush to her throat, choking her. She hastened to fit the key in the ignition. She could hear Scarlet getting in beside Juliet, calming her down. A cool hand touched the back of Bryce's neck, startling her.

"Don't hyperventilate, Bryce. Take deep breaths, calm and steady," Scarlet said.

Bryce finally got the key in and started the engine. The confined space of the car crowded in on her, crushing the air from her lungs. She opened the window beside her and gulped in a deep breath. She held the steering wheel in a death grip, frozen in place by fear.

Then Scarlet spoke and Bryce breathed again.

"Juliet, give me your phone."

Juliet handed Scarlet her purse. Scarlet began rummaging through it.

"Bryce, get us on the road. We need to go to the nearest hospital. You know the way."

Bryce snorted. She knew it all too damn well. She got the car in motion and edged it forward.

Behind her, Scarlet was flicking through Juliet's phone. "Trent? No, this is Scarlet. We're on our way to the University Hospital's baby unit. No, I don't think this is a false alarm."

Bryce could hear Trent's voice clearly through the phone as she yelled to Elton to "get his ass in gear they were leaving." Bryce had to smile a little. She pulled out into traffic and tried to keep her hands steady as she switched lanes nervously.

"Bryce, you're doing great." Scarlet's hand was on Bryce's shoulder so that Bryce knew she was near.

Scarlet had obviously handed the phone over to Juliet because Bryce could hear her pained voice next.

"Babe, I'm okay, but I think the baby's coming early. These are nothing like the Braxton Hicks contractions. These are much longer." She groaned as another pain hit her. "Oh fuck!"

Bryce was surprised by Juliet's exclamation and snuck a peek in the rearview mirror at her.

"Yes, I'm aware I owe the baby a dollar. That's because my fucking water just broke!" The growl that came from Juliet morphed into a groan of pain. "Where are you? I don't know. Hang on. Bryce, how much longer?"

Bryce's eyes swept the road. "Less than ten minutes," she guessed, flinching as a truck drove past on the other side of her and terrified her. The car swerved a little, and Bryce felt Scarlet's hand tighten on her shoulder.

"Steady, Bryce, you're doing so well."

The labored breathing of Juliet filled the car.

"Is Trent coaching you over the phone?" Scarlet asked incredulously.

Bryce caught sight of Juliet nodding and continued being counted through her breathing, the phone stuck to her ear, but Trent's voice was discernible to all.

"God, you two are too cute for words," Scarlet muttered, propping Juliet against her.

Finally, Bryce let out a loud "We're here!" and swung the car into the emergency area of the hospital. Scarlet jumped out to go get help while Bryce parked as close as she could to the doors for Juliet's sake. Scarlet soon reappeared with nursing staff in tow and Juliet was bundled out of the backseat. But not before she thanked Bryce and apologized for the damage to Scarlet's backseat.

Bryce pulled the car over into a parking space. She all but tumbled out, fell to her knees, and promptly threw up.

That's how Scarlet found her. She knelt beside her and rubbed at Bryce's back compassionately. "Oh, sweetheart, you were fantastic," she said as Bryce retched and heaved.

"I think I'm going to pass out," Bryce whispered, shaking with the realization of what she'd actually done.

Scarlet clutched her to her to make sure she didn't pitch forward to the tarmac. "You did it. You got Juliet here without incident. You drove us, Bryce. You got in the car and got us all here in one piece, safe and sound."

"No one died?" Bryce was lost in the memory seared into her brain.

"Not this time, darling. You saved everyone."

Bryce got to her feet unsteadily once she felt able to move. "Can we go inside and wait?"

Scarlet nodded and held her close. "Let's go get you cleaned up and we'll go find where Juliet has been taken."

A car pulled up beside them with a screech of brakes and Trent shot out at a run.

"Or we could just follow the other mama-to-be," Scarlet amended as Trent disappeared into the building with Elton not far behind her.

Bryce kept close to Scarlet's side, only staying on her feet thanks to Scarlet's grasp on her.

I drove the car. I got us here in one piece, and the sounds of moaning weren't the voices of the dying but instead the kind signaling new life ready to be born.

Bryce smiled to herself as the large, looming shadow that had dogged her for months retreated enough for her to see a most welcome light beckoning at the end of her nightmare-filled tunnel.

Chapter Twenty-two

The waiting room was full of people all there for Trent and Juliet's new arrival. Elton was pacing back and forth. Monica was quietly conversing with Juliet's parents. Kayleigh was unusually quiet, playing on a handheld console. Every few minutes though her head would lift toward the doors whenever someone came through. Everyone was waiting for Trent.

Bryce sat nursing a bottle of water. Scarlet was holding her hand beside her.

"It's been hours," Bryce whispered, checking her watch for the umpteenth time since they'd started their wait.

"Babies take their time. It's a big thing to be born." Scarlet squeezed her hand. "I'm just glad the others at least went home."

All of Trent's colleagues had been waiting with them for the first few hours. Zoe, Rick, Chris, and Eddie had appeared as their shifts had finished. Eddie had turned up with sandwiches made by his mother that he shyly handed out to much teasing and gratitude. They were all due in work the next morning so Elton had sent them home with promises of phone calls the second they learned anything.

Bryce was still shaky after their ordeal but was buoyed by a strange feeling of elation. She'd gotten in a car. It was a huge step forward for her. Though she was trying desperately not to think about how she was going to leave the hospital until the time came. For now, she wanted to stay with Scarlet and wait to hear that Juliet and the baby were all right. Bryce didn't think she could be at peace until she knew they were both okay.

She tuned out the sounds of the hospital until it became just white noise. Bryce's mind was racing with what she had achieved today, albeit none of it by her choosing. But she'd faced a fear and hadn't died. With a shaking hand, she pulled her cap off and ran her fingers through her hair. The scar would never disappear, but it would fade eventually given time. Bryce was tired of caring about it. She'd spent too much time worrying what others might think. If they wanted to stare, so be it. She folded the cap up and stuffed it in her pocket. *No more hiding. Time to face the world with the strength of a survivor.*

Scarlet had her hand resting on Bryce's thigh, grounding her. Bryce placed her own on top of it and Scarlet looked at her.

"Are you okay?"

Bryce nodded. "I'm going to see if I can make an appointment with my doctor next week. Maybe she can suggest a therapist I can go to. I don't think I'd mind talking to someone as long as they don't think medication is the answer to all my problems. I don't need something that will make the dreams intensify or that leaves me like a zombie at work." She could see her decision had surprised Scarlet. "Today has made me realize I'm going to need more help to get through this." She lifted Scarlet's hand to her lips. "Then, perhaps, if I can take this step, I can make a more important one later."

"What one would that be?"

"To be by your side wherever you decide to take a job."

Scarlet flung her arms around Bryce's neck and squeezed her tight. "Oh, sweetheart. You're amazing, do you know that?"

Bryce shifted in her hold to brush at the tears that fell from Scarlet's eyes. "I'd do anything to be with you, Scarlet. I love you so very much. I just want to be with you, wherever that takes me."

Scarlet gasped. Then she kissed Bryce, pulled back to stare at her, then kissed her again just as soundly. "I love you too."

Bryce had never heard anything sound so sweet.

"Excuse me. You two are aware you're in the middle of a hospital waiting room, right?" Monica's voice stopped Scarlet from drawing Bryce closer still. Bryce buried her face in Scarlet's neck. So much for declaring her love at the right moment and in a more romantic setting.

"She loves me," Scarlet announced. Everyone in the room let out a cheer, a quiet one in deference for where they were. She settled back in her chair a little more appropriately, tugging Bryce closer to her. "We'll talk more about this later, away from prying eyes." She shot Monica a meaningful stare.

Elton just waved them on. "Please, continue. I think we're going to be here a while. I'll take whatever entertainment I can get." He looked mournfully over to where Kayleigh sat. "Wish I'd thought to carry my 3DS today. I could have challenged Kayleigh to Super Smash Brothers."

Bryce felt Scarlet's fingers tangling in her hair. She gently rubbed at Bryce's scalp, easing away some of her embarrassment and sending delicious shivers down her spine.

"I like you better without the hat," Scarlet whispered against her temple, pressing a soft kiss there.

"If you keep doing that I won't ever put it back on," Bryce said.

"You've got yourself a deal."

❖

It was another hour later, at 9:50 p.m. when Trent finally came through the doors with the biggest grin on her face Bryce had ever seen.

Everyone shot to their feet.

"Well?" Elton demanded.

"Juliet gave birth to a healthy baby girl half an hour ago," she announced.

Elton pounced on her. He hugged her tightly and lifted her off the ground in his joy. "Hey, Mama!" He let her go after a big kiss and another hug so she could be hugged by her tearful in-laws and a very excited Kayleigh.

"Can I see her?" Kayleigh asked, hanging off Trent's side.

"You can. I'm taking you and your parents back in with me so you get to meet her first and then everyone else can come in. It's a two at a time rule, but we're sneaking you in ninja style, squirt." Trent hugged Kayleigh to her.

Trent received her hug from Monica and Scarlet. Then she came to Bryce.

Bryce looked up at the serious face that regarded her.

"If you hadn't have driven them here, things might not have turned out so good. The baby had somehow turned into the wrong position, which is why Juliet was hurting so much. The doctors needed to get the baby back on track as soon as possible, and you gave them that time." Trent reached out and took Bryce's face gently in her large hands and pressed a kiss to her forehead. "I can't ever thank you enough for getting both of my girls here safely." She released Bryce, and Bryce saw tears glistening in Trent's eyes.

Trent leaned forward slightly, the conversation for them alone. "I've had my own share of nightmares and fears, Bryce. Thank you for forcing yours aside and getting in that car for them." Trent held a hand out. Bryce took it and felt the tremors between them but couldn't say who was shaking the most. "I won't forget what you did. After Uncle Elton and Aunt Monica have seen their new niece, I'll come get you and Scarlet. I know Juliet wants to see you. She's been worrying about you."

Bryce laughed softly, wondering why she wasn't in the least bit surprised. "She had much more important things to be thinking about."

Trent held up her hand. It looked swollen and red. "Well, in between her crushing my hand in a lethal death grip." She shot a look over her shoulder at Elton's loud intake of breath. "Don't worry. I can still game. In between that and the birth and whatever else has been going on, she was worried about you so you need to come see her and put her mind at rest."

Bryce nodded, knowing she was blushing under Trent's undivided attention.

Trent rubbed her hands together excitedly. "Okay, grandparents and Aunty Kayleigh. If you'd care to follow me, you have a gorgeous new family member to wrestle out of her mommy's arms to cuddle." She led them out, Kayleigh dancing excitedly around her like a pup.

Scarlet wrapped her arms around Bryce's waist. "You've just gotten yourself a friend for life. And you know Juliet thinks you're awesome anyway." She squeezed her gently. "Welcome to the gamers, gardeners, and Goths gang, Bryce. You're going to fit right in."

CHAPTER TWENTY-THREE

Trent listened to the tiny grunts and snuffles the baby in her arms was making. Elton had his chin resting on her shoulder as he peered down at the little girl.

"Oh my God, she's beautiful," he breathed, reaching out with a finger to touch her tiny little hand and gasping when his finger was grasped. "Ooooh," he sighed. "Gimme that baby right this second."

Trent settled her in his arms and Elton rocked her gently. Trent just grinned as he sniffed loudly. Elton really was a gentle giant.

Monica sat on the hospital bed next to Juliet who, to Trent's eyes, looked radiant even after all she'd been through.

"Don't you dare start getting broody, Elton Simons," Monica said, narrowing her eyes at him as he made cooing noises at the child in his arms.

"But she's so pretty," Elton said. "And look, she has fuzzy ducky hair."

"She's got Juliet's blond hair at the moment." Trent gently smoothed the decidedly wispy hair down. "And her gorgeous blue eyes, and even her chin. She's a mini-Jule."

Monica already had a hold of the baby and was cuddling into Juliet. "So, really, how are you feeling?"

"Achy, exhausted, and a little freaked by what could have happened. The baby was in the right position up until my water broke. The doctor tried to get her turned around, but she kept flipping back. They nearly had to perform an emergency C-section. Thankfully, they did the delivery with forceps instead. But none of that matters now. I am so happy I can't even begin to explain it. And look at that face." She pointed at Trent who smiled right back at her. "It was worth every excruciating pain to see Trent that happy."

Elton reluctantly released the baby back to Trent. She cuddled her close, kissing her forehead gently and checking and rechecking ten tiny fingers, ten tiny toes. The baby was in a little white onesie, artfully decorated with little yellow ducklings. She yawned and stretched in Trent's hold. Trent couldn't tear her eyes away; she didn't want to miss a second.

"So, I'm guessing that, seeing as you had her naturally, she won't be keeping the name Newt?" Monica hinted not so subtly.

Juliet laughed. "No. No matter how much Trent really hoped she'd get to keep that up."

Trent just cradled the sleeping baby and smiled. She already knew the baby's name. She'd been thrilled when Juliet had agreed to it, and they'd kept it to themselves ever since. She nodded to Juliet to do the revealing.

"Well, you know her middle name had to be Quinn to follow the Sullivan family tradition." Juliet looked at Monica who nodded.

Elton, however, stared directly at Trent with widening eyes. "Dude," he said under his breath. "Oh no, you didn't?" He whipped his head back to listen to Juliet again.

"So we decided on Harley," Juliet said proudly.

Elton and Monica both stared at Trent. Elton in awe, Monica much more suspiciously.

"Juliet, you do know…" Monica began, but Juliet just nodded.

"Yes, I know exactly where Trent got the name from, but it's perfect for our daughter. She's our little Harley Quinn Sullivan-Williams."

Elton bowed his head at Trent. "You are the undisputed master."

Trent held the baby up. Harley blinked sleepily at her mama's voice. "Harley, say hi to your godparents."

Monica squealed at the surprise and hugged Juliet. Elton wrapped his arm around Trent's shoulder and planted a kiss on the top of her head in thanks. He looked down at Harley seriously.

"Harley, just so you know, your mama is probably going to say you can't date any boy or girl until you're thirty. As your newly appointed godparent, I'm here to say you'll be at least sixty and I'm holding power of veto if it's felt they are still not good enough for you." He kissed her chubby cheek sweetly. "FYI."

Juliet chuckled and beckoned Trent over to her. "Monica, go get Scarlet and Bryce in here. Scarlet always has that camera of hers with her. I want some pictures of me with both my girls before I succumb to sleep."

Monica left with a kiss to Juliet's cheek, and Elton followed her with promises they'd pop back in once everyone had left.

Left alone for a while, Trent transferred the baby into Juliet's arms. The baby yawned and squeaked. Trent felt her heart melt.

"Thank you." She brushed her lips over Juliet's temple.

"She's beautiful, isn't she?" Juliet traced Harley's soft cheeks and watched as her little lips pursed.

"She'll need feeding again soon," Trent said. "And that's your gig." She had decided that there was nothing more beautiful than seeing Juliet with Harley snuggled by her breast.

"Hey, Harley. Your mommies love you so much," Juliet said and tucked herself deeper into Trent's side. She rested her head on Trent's chest. "How's your hand, babe?"

"Still game worthy, no thanks to you, Crusher!" Trent said. "Who knew you had such a strong grip."

"All the better to hold on to you with."

"Sweetheart, you've had me in the palm of your hand from the first moment we met."

"And Harley will have you wrapped around each one of her tiny fingers." Juliet nudged a little hand, and Harley closed her fingers around Juliet's.

"Like mother like daughter," Trent said. Her heart was so full of joy and happiness and love she could barely contain it. "Thank you for making my family complete."

"Our own little family." Juliet leaned back in Trent's arms and kissed her tenderly then kissed the baby's head. Harley cooed then opened her eyes to their stares.

Trent felt her heart expand so much she wondered if her chest could hold it in. Little blue eyes searched for her as Trent called her name softly. *God help me, she's every inch her mother's child.*

Juliet chuckled softly. "You are seriously screwed, Mama Bear."

Trent sighed. "Happily."

❖

Three weeks after Harley was born, Elton threw a party to welcome her into the extended family. It promised to be a lively occasion that ran all day. Family and friends were all invited and a barbeque had been promised.

Scarlet finished putting on her earrings and checked herself one last time in the mirror. Casual attire had been the order of the day. Monica's explanation still made Scarlet smile.

"That's because it will all start out normal enough, but you're getting a gathering predominantly of gamers. Sooner or later, someone will break out the Wii remotes and everyone will be playing baseball. There's no point getting your Goth on around geeks."

Scarlet had chosen black jeans with her usual band T-shirt to complement. She was searching for her shoes when Bryce walked by.

"I'll drive us if that's okay?" Bryce said as she finished buttoning up a pale blue shirt over faded blue jeans.

Scarlet didn't hesitate; she simply selected a different pair of shoes. "Great, that means I can go for the higher heels." She caught Bryce's grin as she slipped into the lethal looking spikes. Scarlet had learned not to comment when Bryce worked up the courage to get in a car voluntarily. A great deal of the time, Bryce still bused it to and from places. When she did make the decision, she preferred driving over being a passenger. Scarlet soon realized that as long as she kept up a running commentary while Bryce drove and the car was never left silent, Bryce was managing to cope. It explained the drive to the hospital with Juliet. There had been constant chattering, and Scarlet had never taken her hand off Bryce. It wasn't very often Bryce offered to drive, and after a night fraught with nightmares, she was often set back again but at least she was trying. Scarlet couldn't have been prouder of her.

❖

People took up space in every inch of Elton's home. Most had spilled out into the garden and were congregating around the barbeque pit where Zoe's father had taken roost. When Scarlet and Bryce arrived just after eleven a.m., Scarlet had to squeeze past the loiterers in the hallway already drinking beer. She pushed her way into the living room. Head and shoulders above everyone else, Elton saw her and waved them over to where Juliet sat cradling Harley. Scarlet made a beeline for her. Holding tight to Bryce's hand, she tugged her along with her.

"Hey, you two," Juliet greeted them, accepting kisses with her usual sunny smile.

Scarlet's eyes fell on Harley. "Oh my God, she's already grown more."

Juliet shifted Harley in her arms. Harley blinked at them all and sucked on her thumb.

"She found her thumb today. It's her new favorite thing." Trent came up behind them and hip-checked Elton out of the way. She set a plate of food down beside Juliet. She then gave Scarlet a hopeful look.

Scarlet grinned at her and waved her camera bag. "Like I'd miss documenting this event."

Trent smiled and grabbed a handful of chips from the plate. "Elton, the natives are getting restless. Time to pick your team."

"Told you it would become a game-fest," Monica grumbled from Juliet's side. She was absently playing with Harley's feet and pulling faces at her.

"Let them play," Juliet said. "I'm done being the center of attention. No one will stand a chance once Harley's other grandma is here. Mama Simons dotes on this little girl like she's her own."

"That's because she adopted Trent years ago," Elton said off-handedly. "And thank goodness, because little Harley here has stopped her from looking at me with hopeful eyes for a while."

"Besides, I want to see Bryce play." Juliet favored Bryce with a look, and Scarlet was sure she heard a groan escape under Bryce's breath.

Kayleigh suddenly appeared by Scarlet's side, making her jump. "Yes, Bryce, you're coming on our team. We're starting with Wii Sports." She tugged on Bryce's arm. "It's been proven that playing games helps in the rehabilitation of injuries."

Scarlet looked down at her. Kayleigh's smile was infectious.

"Trent says hospitals and care homes use them on people recovering after operations and stuff." Kayleigh pulled Bryce forward. "Your shoulder counts so you can come play. Come on!" The look she wore made Bryce groan even louder. She glared at Juliet.

"How can I possibly stand a chance when there are two of you with that look?"

Juliet just held Harley up. "Wait until she puts it into practice. Trent's already a goner, and this little one hasn't come into her full powers yet." Juliet laughed as Bryce sighed and let herself be led away by an excited Kayleigh.

Bryce just managed to plant a swift kiss on Scarlet's lips as she was pulled past. Scarlet watched after them and caught sight of her father standing off to the side. She hadn't seen him in weeks. She decided to bite the bullet so she excused herself a minute to go talk to him.

Her father stood in front of the painting of Monica that was hung over the fireplace in Elton's home.

"Hey, Dad." Scarlet had to stop herself from slipping her arm through his and resting her head on his shoulder like she usually would greet him. He didn't take his eyes off the painting.

"You painted this, didn't you?"

"Yes, I did."

"It's captivating. She's so beautiful and you caught it all." He turned to face her. "Just slap me the next time I suggest you take over the business." He gestured back to the painting. "*This* is what you should be doing. It's magnificent. Your mother would have been so proud of you. You've got her talent and more besides."

Warmed by his praise, Scarlet stayed silent for a moment.

He nudged her. "Just so you know, I gave Juliet some paperwork to look over for when she's off maternity leave."

"You bothering a new mom now?"

"No, I'm just getting a foot in the door with a very knowledgeable businesswoman who thinks my company might be a viable asset for her to manage one day. So when the time comes for my daughter to take control of it she'll have someone she trusts to run it in her name. That way, she can continue to forge her own path in life and continue to paint wonderful things like this."

"But you're not handing the business over for a long time yet," Scarlet said, astonished that her dad had agreed with what she and Juliet had been working out between them. Juliet was much more suited to do the job than Scarlet could ever be. Juliet had said that once Harley was in school she'd be interested in taking on more work. Tweedy Construction was *a lot* more work, and Scarlet knew Juliet would be the perfect woman for the role.

"I've missed you," he said softly. "Can you forgive me for trying to hold on to you too tightly?"

Scarlet slipped her hand into his and squeezed. "I already have."

"So, what's happening now? Have you found somewhere to utilize your obvious talents?"

Scarlet smiled at the unhidden pride in his voice. "I have a follow-up interview for a job at the new portrait studio opening here in a month. I met with its boss yesterday and he's very eager to take me on. They want to utilize all my talents so they'll be promoting both my photography *and* my painting. It's going to be perfect for me." Scarlet was so thankful she'd visited the photography exhibition that had been the catalyst for her leaving Tweedy Contractors. The contacts she'd made there had led to her being offered a job all but right on her doorstep.

"And what does Bryce think about all this? Seeing as you two are apparently an item now." He cocked his head over to where Bryce was watching a game being played.

"She wants what makes me happy."

Her dad sighed. "Then she's everything I could wish for you." He looked at Scarlet. "Do I at least get some credit in bringing you two together?"

Scarlet laughed. "I guess so."

"Does that help ease the fact I've been a terrible overbearing father to you since you came back home?" He sounded so disappointed in himself Scarlet couldn't hold the grudge any longer.

"You were being my dad. You just have to realize I'm all grown up now. You can't always hold my hand for me."

"Guess I've passed that job on to Bryce." He let out a pitiful sigh. "I have a horrible feeling I'm going to lose my best plasterer on the job as well one day."

Scarlet smiled in Bryce's direction. She knew her dad couldn't miss the love she felt for Bryce shining out of her eyes. "Whatever we chose, it will be a joint decision and what's best for us both."

"Which leads me to something else."

Scarlet lifted her head to fix him with a stare. "What now?"

"Alice asked me out on a date."

He sounded so shy that Scarlet had to stifle her amusement. Instead, she found it rather endearing. "So she finally gave up waiting for you to make the first move after her being a widow for years?"

"Looks that way. I think it's time to do something for myself."

Scarlet's smile grew. "Yes, it is."

"And seeing as you won't let me worry about you…"

"I don't need you to." She looked over her shoulder to where Bryce was being coached by a very earnest Kayleigh on how exactly to swing the remote. "I've got my own future beckoning and it looks amazing."

"She's healing," he said, watching Bryce's first foray into the world of gaming.

"She's living again, and I'm loving being right beside her as she does."

"You moving in with that girl yet? Settling down, making a future together?"

"I might just do that, Dad. She'd be the one I'd choose to do it all with."

The loud crack of a baseball being hit sounded out in the room, and the cheers for a home run went up. Scarlet's heart warmed to see Bryce enthusiastically congratulated by Kayleigh and the rest of their team. Scarlet gave her a thumbs up when Bryce's eyes sought hers out. The happy gleam to Bryce's face made Scarlet's day.

"I'm going to see if I can get a hold of that baby over there." Her father eased out of Scarlet's hold. "Might be wanting to get some practice in, because you never know, you and Bryce might make me a grandpa one of these days." His grin stopped Scarlet in her tracks. She rolled her eyes in exasperation.

"Daaaad!"

Chapter Twenty-four

Three Months Later

At the first sound of whimpering from the side of the bed, Trent woke up and slid out gingerly from Juliet's spooning hold. She checked that Juliet hadn't been disturbed then hastened to check on Harley in her Moses crib. Harley's face had begun to crease in her distress, little arms waving with annoyance, so Trent scooped her up and carried her from the room.

"Come on, kid. Mommy needs her rest so it's just you and me on the milk run tonight," she whispered, padding downstairs to get the pre-prepared baby milk from the fridge. While waiting for it to warm up, Trent cradled Harley on her shoulder. Fussing, Harley wriggled in her hold.

"Hey, no head butting, Little Miss Impatient. It's nearly ready." Trent prepared the baby bottle and then started back upstairs. She looked inside the nursery that Harley would be sleeping in soon enough, but the rocking chair didn't call to Trent tonight. Instead, she turned around and headed toward her game room. She sat in her chair, settled Harley, and started feeding her. She grinned at how fast Harley began sucking from the bottle. "Wow, you were a hungry girl." She watched as Harley's little fists batted against the bottle. Trent knew all too soon she'd be holding the bottle for herself.

"I know this milk isn't as attractively packaged as when your mommy feeds you, but tonight you've got me." Trent leaned back in her chair and watched her daughter feeding. "You know, if we could just curb the anti-social hours you insist on keeping, you'd be pretty darn perfect."

Trent marveled at just how much Harley had grown in nearly three months. Her hair was growing in but was still the pale blond that Trent adored so much in Juliet. It was also kind of wild and spiky which Trent secretly got a huge kick out of too. Harley smiled now and chuckled and made some very curious noises. She also followed her parents' voices, and that warmed Trent's heart like nothing else did.

"Harley, I always figured I'd be alone. I never figured I'd be lucky enough to find someone as wonderful as your mommy to love me. You're going to adore your mommy. She's awesome. She's rocket scientist smart so you'll never get away with anything, and she's so pretty she makes my heart ache every time I see her. If you grow up half as beautiful as she is then you're going to be locked in your room to keep all the pervy boys or girls away from you." Trent smiled as big blue eyes stared up at her. "You think I'm joking, right? Your mommy doesn't call me Mama Bear for nothing, little cub. No one is going to ever hurt my little girl." Trent nuzzled the fine hair that covered Harley's head. Harley hiccupped. "Try not to guzzle so much, Harley Q. There's still plenty to go if your belly isn't full yet." Trent lost herself in the unwavering gaze staring up at her.

"One day, everything in this room will be yours. Of course, while you're still small and prone to sticky fingers and dribbling, we're going to have to set up some kind of ground rules. We'll work on it until you're able to appreciate how awesome this room is. Of course if, God forbid, you're not destined to be a gamer then that's okay and I promise to stand by whatever alternative non-gaming lifestyle choice you make. You might be into gardening like your mommy, and that's cool too. Just don't track dirt into the house. But if you follow nurture over nature and get hooked on Angry Birds, then this room, my darling girl, every console, every game, every collector's edition will be all yours."

"Just when I think I can't possibly love you any more than I do."

Trent looked up to where Juliet lounged against the doorframe, smiling at her lovingly. She looked beautiful in her sleep-tousled state.

"Why?" Trent asked, following her every movement as Juliet came over to kneel beside the chair. She kissed Trent, then ran a finger over Harley's onesie-covered toes. Harley kicked and pressed her foot back into Juliet's grasp. They'd found she liked her feet held and rubbed.

"For opening your heart to both of us and letting us share your life. Both inside and outside of this marvelous room."

Trent rested her cheek against Juliet's hair. "You're the only one who understands how important this room is to me. Maybe, one day, Harley will too."

"You're wonderful." Juliet's eyes shone up at her.

Trent basked in that look. "You're supposed to be asleep. That's why I got the kid out of our room employing stealth mode."

"I missed you. You know I can't sleep without you beside me."

They both watched as Harley's mouth grew slack around the nipple of the bottle as she'd drank her fill and was slipping back to sleep. Trent eased her up and began rubbing her back gently.

"Burp it out, Harley, otherwise you'll be cranky all night."

Harley burped and released milky bubbles that Juliet hurried to mop up. With a contented smile on her face, Harley's eyes began to droop again.

"Mama, looks like this baby is ready to go back to her crib. I want you back in our bed too," Juliet said.

Trent eased up out of her chair and Harley nestled on her shoulder, a hand clutching at Trent's T-shirt. Trent helped Juliet up and wrapped her free arm around her waist.

"You going to tuck me in too?" Trent said back in their room. She handed Harley over to Juliet and watched her settle the baby back in her crib. A light green Yoshi toy sat nearby, already

Harley's favorite toy. Once she was satisfied Harley was asleep, Juliet turned around.

"I'm going to undress you first and then tuck you in."

Trent swallowed hard at the desire that burned in Juliet's eyes. "You're supposed to be resting. I know you're working from home now, but when Harley keeps you awake at all hours you still need your sleep."

Juliet ignored her and tugged at Trent's T-shirt. "When did you put this on?"

"Just after you fell asleep. If I don't wear something when feeding Harley she gets grabby at the one pair of breasts in the house that can't feed her."

"That's my smart girl." Juliet cupped Trent's breasts in her hands. "But these are all mine." She pushed Trent until she fell back onto their bed. "Now, let me thank you properly for doing the midnight feeds. I just need you to be quiet so as not to wake our daughter up." She followed Trent down on the bed, shoving the T-shirt up roughly, and captured a nipple between her lips.

"Oh fuck," Trent moaned. "I'll try, but thank God our kid's a heavy sleeper once her belly has been satisfied." She shuddered under Juliet's hungry lips.

"Well, she's happy for the rest of the night. Let's see if I can't satisfy you just as much."

❖

Halloween was a big deal in the lives of Scarlet and her friends. It wasn't enough to just have bowls of candy on hand for any trick-or-treater at the door. Instead, parties were organized and costumes were made and no one was left out. Bryce had been roped in very early on and had been told just wearing a mask wasn't going to cut it. Scarlet's parties were a full on cosplay experience. It boggled Bryce's mind.

"You're surrounded by Goths," Scarlet had said at Bryce's surprise. "Halloween is like every holiday rolled into one for us!"

So now Bryce was in Scarlet's bedroom getting changed. Monica had helped her as she had with everyone's costume. Bryce fixed her tie and checked herself over in the mirror. Not for the first time, she was surprised to see herself with brown hair. Scarlet had assured her the dye would wash out quickly and she'd soon be back to normal. Bryce smiled at her reflection.

I like this new normal.

Since she'd been forced back in a car, Bryce had started to regain some of the control she'd lost in her life. Seeing her new therapist was helping tackle the debilitating nightmares. It was a slow, painful process, but Bryce was doing it, all with Scarlet's support.

She and Scarlet were in the stages of working out whether to just pick between their apartments or to go for something new to move in together. Scarlet's new job was showcasing her talents, and she was already looking toward having a small exhibition of her paintings there. Bryce couldn't have been more proud of her.

Scarlet walked into the bedroom and eyed Bryce up and down. "You look perfect."

Bryce stared at Scarlet's own costume. "And I can't believe how beautiful you look blond."

"Blond and armed with a katana, thanks to Elton." Scarlet slid the long sword out from the scabbard fastened to her back and posed. "I dare not ask why he has one of these on hand."

"Do not make me tempted to hang a 'Do not disturb' sign on our front door. Put your sword away, Babydoll."

Scarlet did as she was told. "So, this outfit does it for you?" She wore a short, *very* short, pleated miniskirt teamed with a midriff-bearing top. The costume was complete with a sailor's collar and flap, the perfect Japanese schoolgirl sailor outfit that the film *Sucker Punch* had put its leading character in. Thigh-high socks were complemented with the lowest heeled shoes Bryce had ever seen Scarlet in. Her hair was blond and worn in two pigtails framing her face. To Bryce, Scarlet looked beautiful, innocent, and deadly in an anime fan's dreams come to life.

"I enjoyed the film. Had I known you had the costume in your closet I'd have asked for a private viewing ages ago."

Scarlet chuckled and took a step toward her but was halted by the doorbell sounding. She sighed. "Our guests are here," she said woefully. "You need to get your glasses on. We'll role-play when everyone else has left. Who knows, I may even dance for you." She rocked from side to side seductively.

Bryce's groan was louder than the sound of the doorbell ringing for a second time. She obediently followed Scarlet, noticing that the short skirt was flattering from every angle. She snatched up her glasses to complete her own outfit and began greeting the newcomers.

❖

There was obscure organ music playing in the background. Plastic eyeballs were floating in the punch bowl that held a dubious concoction that Bryce had avoided just on its color alone. She caught sight of Monica sweeping around her old apartment, dressed as the Evil Queen from her favorite TV show. Black leather trousers molded her thighs, a corset cinched in her waist, and a long, patterned cape swirled out behind her. Her hair was pinned up on her head and she wore a lace headdress. Her heels looked as lethal as the dramatic look she was sporting. Bryce thought she looked exactly like the woman she was portraying. And she could tell Monica was loving every minute of people's reactions to her. Apparently, everyone loved a seductive witch tempting them with her forbidden fruit.

Elton, meanwhile, was entertaining everyone with his faux British accent as he pranced around the room as Captain Jack Sparrow. He wore the detailed pirate costume all too well, and his eyeliner was as dramatic as Monica's was.

Another peal of the doorbell welcomed Trent and Juliet. Trent walked in wearing a purple suit with a green vest visible beneath. Her face was painted white with an ugly red slash cutting its path across her mouth, giving her The Joker's trademarked evil smile. Bryce didn't feel so bad about having her hair dyed. Trent's had been colored green. Juliet was in a very curious nurse's outfit. She wore the little nurse's hat on her head, and a white shirt tucked inside a red leather corset. A white miniskirt was worn over two-tone stockings, one red, one blue. She also had white makeup on, but a black eye mask was molded to her face.

Baby Harley was cradled in Trent's arms. Now nearly four months old, she was more alert, always smiling, and quite vocal in her squeals and baby babble. Monica had fashioned her a onesie decorated in black and red diamonds, complete with a soft jester's hat with two horns. Harley kicked and wriggled in Trent's arms as if eager to get the party started.

"Fellow party people, why so serious?" Trent said in a creepy tone of voice that made Bryce shiver. "Harley Quinn is in the house!"

Harley's arms waved as she reveled in the attention that brought. She tugged on Elton's dangling beard and batted at the beads that decorated it. She also wasn't fazed in the least by the Evil Queen who may have been famous for cursing babies but was decidedly soft hearted when it came to this particular child.

"Baby's first Halloween," Scarlet singsonged, ushering the family to a makeshift studio she'd set up where everyone could have their photo taken to remember the night. She picked up her camera and quickly took some shots while Harley was wide-awake and smiling. "You guys look fantastic."

"Your skirt is as short as mine," Juliet said, trying to tug hers down a little more.

"I, for one, am appreciating both of your attentions to detail," Trent said with a sly wink at Bryce. "You're especially rocking the older Quinzel's cleavage, my love."

"You're just lucky I managed to fit into this." Juliet fumbled with her skirt again. "It's a slow process losing the baby weight I gained."

"Sweetheart, you look gorgeous, with or without the psychopathic gleam in your eye left over from baby hormones."

Juliet gave Trent such a withering look that Trent burst out laughing.

"Those baby hormones are still raging, Trent Williams. I'm just one step away from releasing the crazy!"

Trent's laughter set off Harley's giggles, which made everyone smile.

Bryce took it all in. She'd been to many a party, mostly stiff, formal dos where everyone was miserable but too adept at putting on false faces not to let anyone know. Tonight she was surrounded by people in *real* masks, yet everyone was having the best time. For the first time, Bryce couldn't help but wonder if the accident had been an oddly *positive* turning point for her in life. It had pulled her from the miserable existence she was a part of and forced her into another direction entirely. Bryce loved the view now from where she stood. She only wished the people who'd been with her in the car had been there to share in her happiness too. She vowed to appreciate life in order to honor them. The guilt was easing; gratefulness was breaking through. Surviving had been a miracle. Bryce could finally see that.

"Well, look at you," Juliet called softly, bringing Bryce out of her musings. "Kayleigh is going to be hanging off your robes all night when she gets here."

Bryce looked down at her gray school uniform and the red/gray striped tie. Her wizard robes were a handsome finishing touch.

Scarlet joined them both, leaving Trent and Harley holding court with Uncle Elton as the self-appointed jester.

"I took poetic license with the lightning scar." Scarlet traced the jagged bolt that instead of cutting through the middle of Bryce's forehead was edged over Bryce's actual scar.

"Seemed a waste not to use what I already have," Bryce said with a shrug.

Juliet agreed. "It's perfect." Her head whipped up at a particularly loud squeal from behind her. "Please excuse me while I go rescue my daughter from her uncle who is like a high dose of sugar on that kid. There'll be no chance of getting her to sleep tonight if he works her up into a baby frenzy now."

She headed toward Trent who held Harley up and was asking her, "Who's that? Is that Mommy? Doesn't she look sexy in her nurse's uniform?" which got her a playful slap off Juliet and then a swift kiss to follow.

Scarlet snagged Bryce's hand and squeezed it. "How are you doing, Bryce?"

Bryce smiled happily. "I'm doing excellent. I'm hosting a great party. I'm looking quite dashing in my wizard robes, and I'm romancing the prettiest woman in the room who knows some mean tricks with her katana. Life is pretty near perfect."

Scarlet trailed a finger over Bryce's painted scar. "Of course it is. That's because you're a wizard, Harry."

Bryce lifted Scarlet's hand to her lips. "The girl who lived and found love."

"And they lived happily ever after." Scarlet kissed the smile that Bryce couldn't hold back anymore.

Her eyes widened as Scarlet shifted slightly to whisper in her ear. "Tell me you came equipped with your magic wand tonight?"

Bryce frowned at her a moment then snorted when she realized what Scarlet really wanted to know. Laughing, she nodded. "Yes, I did." The sensuous curve of Scarlet's lips did wonders to Bryce's ego. "I promise, once I've made our friends 'disappear' tonight, you and I can go make some magic all of our own."

"And we'll play a little music, perhaps turn the lights down low," Scarlet added.

Bryce just nodded, thankful that her fear of the dark had lessened as the days and weeks rolled by. She reached up and kissed Scarlet with all the love she felt inside.

No more playing in shadow for me. All I need to banish the darkness away is the light I see shining in her eyes when she looks at me. The eyes of my love who knows that I am in pieces but only ever sees me as whole.

The End

About the Author

Lesley Davis lives in the West Midlands of England. She is a die-hard science fiction/fantasy fan in all its forms and an extremely passionate gamer. When her Nintendo 3DS is out of her grasp, Lesley is to be found on her laptop writing.

Her book *Dark Wings Descending*, was a finalist in the Lambda Literary Awards for Best Lesbian Romance 2013

Visit her online at www.lesleydavisauthor.co.uk

Books Available from Bold Strokes Books

Love's Bounty by Yolanda Wallace. Lobster boat captain Jake Myers stopped living the day she cheated death, but meeting greenhorn Shy Silva stirs her back to life. (978-1-62639334-9)

Just Three Words by Melissa Brayden. Sometimes the one you want is the one you least suspect. Accountant Samantha Ennis has her ordered life disrupted when heartbreaker Hunter Blair moves into her trendy Soho loft. (978-1-62639-335-6)

Lay Down the Law by Carsen Taite. Attorney Peyton Davis returns to her Texas roots to take on big oil and the Mexican Mafia, but will her investigation thwart her chance at true love? (978-1-62639-336-3)

Playing in Shadow by Lesley Davis. Survivor's guilt threatens to keep Bryce trapped in her nightmare world unless Scarlet's love can pull her out of the darkness back into the light. (978-1-62639-337-0)

Soul Selecta by Gill McKnight. Soul mates are hell to work with. (978-1-62639-338-7)

The Revelation of Beatrice Darby by Jean Copeland. Adolescence is complicated, but Beatrice Darby is about to discover how impossible it can seem to a lesbian coming of age in conservative 1950s New England. (978-1-62639-339-4)

Twice Lucky by Mardi Alexander. For firefighter Mackenzie James and Dr. Sarah Macarthur, there's suddenly a whole lot more in life to understand, to consider, to risk…someone will need to fight for her life. (978-1-62639-325-7)

Shadow Hunt by L.L. Raand. With young to raise and her Pack under attack, Sylvan, Alpha of the wolf Weres, takes on her greatest challenge when she determines to uncover the faceless enemies known as the Shadow Lords. A Midnight Hunters novel. (978-1-62639-326-4)

Heart of the Game by Rachel Spangler. A baseball writer falls for a single mom, but can she ever love anything as much as she loves the game? (978-1-62639-327-1)

Getting Lost by Michelle Grubb. Twenty-eight days, thirteen European countries, a tour manager fighting attraction, and an accused murderer: Stella and Phoebe's journey of a lifetime begins here. (978-1-62639-328-8)

Prayer of the Handmaiden by Merry Shannon. Celibate priestess Kadrian must defend the kingdom of Ithyria from a dangerous enemy and ultimately choose between her duty to the Goddess and the love of her childhood sweetheart, Erinda. (978-1-62639-329-5)

The Witch of Stalingrad by Justine Saracen. A Soviet "night witch" pilot and American journalist meet on the Eastern Front in WW II and struggle through carnage, conflicting politics, and the deadly Russian winter. (978-1-62639-330-1)

Pedal to the Metal by Jesse J. Thoma. When unreformed thief Dubs Williams is released from prison to help Max Winters bust a car theft ring, Max learns that to catch a thief, get in bed with one. (978-1-62639-239-7)

Dragon Horse War by D. Jackson Leigh. A priestess of peace and a fiery warrior must defeat a vicious uprising that entwines their destinies and ultimately their hearts. (978-1-62639-240-3)

For the Love of Cake by Erin Dutton. When everything is on the line, and one taste can break a heart, will pastry chefs Maya and Shannon take a chance on reality? (978-1-62639-241-0)

Betting on Love by Alyssa Linn Palmer. A quiet country-girl-at-heart and a live-life-to-the-fullest biker take a risk at offering each other their hearts. (978-1-62639-242-7)

The Deadening by Yvonne Heidt. The lines between good and evil, right and wrong, have always been blurry for Shade. When Raven's actions force her to choose, which side will she come out on? (978-1-62639-243-4)

Ordinary Mayhem by Victoria A. Brownworth. Faye Blakemore has been taking photographs since she was ten, but those same photographs threaten to destroy everything she knows and everything she loves. (978-1-62639-315-8)

One Last Thing by Kim Baldwin & Xenia Alexiou. Blood is thicker than pride. The final book in the Elite Operative Series brings together foes, family, and friends to start a new order. (978-1-62639-230-4)

Songs Unfinished by Holly Stratimore. Two aspiring rock stars learn that falling in love while pursuing their dreams can be harmonious—if they can only keep their pasts from throwing them out of tune. (978-1-62639-231-1)

Beyond the Ridge by L.T. Marie. Will a contractor and a horse rancher overcome their family differences and find common ground to build a life together? (978-1-62639-232-8)

Swordfish by Andrea Bramhall. Four women battle the demons from their pasts. Will they learn to let go, or will happiness be forever beyond their grasp? (978-1-62639-233-5)

The Fiend Queen by Barbara Ann Wright. Princess Katya and her consort Starbride must turn evil against evil in order to banish Fiendish power from their kingdom, and only love will pull them back from the brink. (978-1-62639-234-2)

Up the Ante by PJ Trebelhorn. When Jordan Stryker and Ashley Noble meet again fifteen years after a short-lived affair, are either of them prepared to gamble on a chance at love? (978-1-62639-237-3)

Speakeasy by MJ Williamz. When mob leader Helen Byrne sets her sights on the girlfriend of Al Capone's right-hand man, passion and tempers flare on the streets of Chicago. (978-1-62639-238-0)

Venus in Love by Tina Michele. Morgan Blake can't afford any distractions and Ainsley Dencourt can't afford to lose control—but the beauty of life and art usually lies in the unpredictable strokes of the artist's brush. (978-1-62639-220-5)

Rules of Revenge by AJ Quinn. When a lethal operative on a collision course with her past agrees to help a CIA analyst on a critical assignment, the encounter proves explosive in ways neither woman anticipated. (978-1-62639-221-2)

The Romance Vote by Ali Vali. Chili Alexander is a sought-after campaign consultant who isn't prepared when her boss's daughter, Samantha Pellegrin, comes to work at the firm and shakes up Chili's life from the first day. (978-1-62639-222-9)

Advance: Exodus Book One by Gun Brooke. Admiral Dael Caydoc's mission to find a new homeworld for the Oconodian people is hazardous, but working with the infuriating Commander Aniwyn "Spinner" Seclan endangers her heart and soul. (978-1-62639-224-3)

UnCatholic Conduct by Stevie Mikayne. Jil Kidd goes undercover to investigate fraud at St. Marguerite's Catholic School, but life gets complicated when her student is killed—and she begins to fall for her prime target. (978-1-62639-304-2)

Season's Meetings by Amy Dunne. Catherine Birch reluctantly ventures on the festive road trip from hell with beautiful stranger Holly Daniels only to discover the road to true love has its own obstacles to maneuver. (978-1-62639-227-4)

Myth and Magic: Queer Fairy Tales edited by Radclyffe and Stacia Seaman. Myth, magic, and monsters—the stuff of childhood dreams (or nightmares) and adult fantasies. (978-1-62639-225-0)

Nine Nights on the Windy Tree by Martha Miller. Recovering drug addict, Bertha Brannon, is an attorney who is trying to stay clean when a murder sends her back to the bad end of town. (978-1-62639-179-6)

Driving Lessons by Annameekee Hesik. Dive into Abbey Brooks's sophomore year as she attempts to figure out the amazing, but sometimes complicated, life of a you-know-who girl at Gila High School. (978-1-62639-228-1)

Asher's Shot by Elizabeth Wheeler. Asher Price's candid photographs capture the truth, but when his success requires exposing an enemy, Asher discovers his only shot at happiness involves revealing secrets of his own. (978-1-62639-229-8)

Courtship by Carsen Taite. Love and justice—a lethal mix or a perfect match? (978-1-62639-210-6)

Against Doctor's Orders by Radclyffe. Corporate financier Presley Worth wants to shut down Argyle Community Hospital, but Dr. Harper Rivers will fight her every step of the way, if she can also fight their growing attraction. (978-1-62639-211-3)

A Spark of Heavenly Fire by Kathleen Knowles. Kerry and Beth are building their life together, but unexpected circumstances could destroy their happiness. (978-1-62639-212-0)

Never Too Late by Julie Blair. When Dr. Jamie Hammond is forced to hire a new office manager, she's shocked to come face to face with Carla Grant and memories from her past. (978-1-62639-213-7)

Widow by Martha Miller. Judge Bertha Brannon must solve the murder of her lover, a policewoman she thought she'd grow old with. As more bodies pile up, the murderer starts coming for her. (978-1-62639-214-4)

Twisted Echoes by Sheri Lewis Wohl. What's a woman to do when she realizes the voices in her head are real? (978-1-62639-215-1)

Criminal Gold by Ann Aptaker. Through a dangerous night in New York in 1949, Cantor Gold, dapper dyke-about-town, smuggler of fine art, is forced by a crime lord to be his instrument of vengeance. (978-1-62639-216-8)

The Melody of Light by M.L. Rice. After surviving abuse and loss, will Riley Gordon be able to navigate her first year of college and accept true love and family? (978-1-62639-219-9)

Because of You by Julie Cannon. What would you do for the woman you were forced to leave behind? (978-1-62639-199-4)

The Job by Jove Belle. Sera always dreamed that she would one day reunite with Tor. She just didn't think it would involve terrorists, firearms, and hostages. (978-1-62639-200-7)

Making Time by C.J. Harte. Two women going in different directions meet after fifteen years and struggle to reconnect in spite of the past that separated them. (978-1-62639-201-4)

Once The Clouds Have Gone by KE Payne. Overwhelmed by the dark clouds of her past, Tag Grainger is lost until the intriguing and spirited Freddie Metcalfe unexpectedly forces her to reevaluate her life. (978-1-62639-202-1)